# FINDING AUTUMN

Rebecca Grattson

Finding Autumn
A novel from the Seasons of Éire series
By Rebecca Grattson

Copyright 2024 Rebecca Grattson
ISBN: 978-1-0685060-0-0


Self-published and printed by IngramSpark

All illustrations, including book cover design,  Niamh
Conlon.

Thank you for
Celebrating the
magic of
Éire with me!

# Irish mythology

I am Irish. Although, that doesn't exactly mean what I write is completely true to Irish mythology. What I write is based on the love stories I grew up with, the tales of warriors and brave Queens who conquered and defended this little island. This story is part of *my* mythology.

Isn't that the joy of Celtic storytellers, of our ancestors who never wrote their trials and adventures down? They retell their stories over and over again, making slight changes as they do. Their kin and friends share their stories in the same way, changing them with every person they cross.

When you read my story, you may find similarities to other mythologies, particularly with our Goddess Morrigan. In Greek mythology, there is Moirai, who played a very similar role. But why the overlap? We have evidence from the thirteenth century BC of Greek influence on Irish culture at that time, but we should also consider where the Celts themselves came from. Early sources place Celts in Western Europe—perhaps they also came from Greece?

In the end, myths are meant to evolve. They blend, shift, and adapt to new tellers and new audiences. What I have written is simply a continuation of that tradition, where ancient tales meet the present, becoming something new. So, as you read this story, remember: it's not about the accuracy of the myth, but the spirit of storytelling that lives on.

# Dedications

To Amy. Who received this book in the form of voice notes over the years. I will get you an audiobook version one day. But for now, my voice notes will have to do.

To my dyslexic kin. I hope this book inspires you. I hope that inspiration helps you achieve something you once believed you were unable to do. Do not let anyone make you feel less than, just because of who you are. There is a power in our diversity. Like magic, it takes some time to learn how to wield it.

To my family, and anyone else I have to look in the eye; pages 209-216 are not for you!

# Phonetic Glossary

Most pronunciations of Irish places, names and words are presented from the Ulster dialect of the Irish Language.

Letters in lowercase make the letters sound. Letters in uppercase say the letter's name

**Places in Ireland:**

| | | |
|---|---|---|
| Cill O'Laoch | Kill-O-Law-Ugh | Meaning descendants of the lough. The modern town's name is Killyleagh |
| Cuan | Coo-An | Meaning water, or water view. |
| Delamont | Del-a-Mount | Meaning from the mountains, it is a park near Killyleagh |
| Éire | Ear-a | Meaning Ireland. |
| Béal Feírste | Bel   fur-stay | Meaning Belfast, the capital city of Northern Ireland. |
| Donard | Don-ard | Meaning high fort. Donard Mountain is the highest peak in Northern Ireland. |
| Mourne | More-n | A mountain range covering most parts of County Down. |

| | | |
|---|---|---|
| Duiblinn | | Meaning "black pool" where the Poddle Stream met the River Liffey. Diblin is the capital city of the Republic of Ireland |
| Roscair | Ross-key-air | Modern town name is Rostrevor |
| Carlingford | Car-ling-ford | Is Irish name means Bay of the Hag…. |
| Mullach Íde | Mal-a-hide | In English Malahide castle located just outside Dublin. |

**Character names:**

| | | |
|---|---|---|
| Éabha | Eh-va | Meaning sunshine |
| Cian | Key-n | Meaning ascendant |
| Priest Dubhan | Do-van | Meaning black or dark |
| Ní Chaiside | Nick- | (O'Casey) - Meaning "vigilant" or "watchful." |
| Ceira | Key-ear-a | Meaning dark |
| Morrigan | More-E-gone | A Irish Goddess associated with many things, including war, fate, life, death, fertility and prophecy. |
| Chronos | k-ron-os | God of Time. |

| Banbha | Ban-a-ba | The Celtic goddess and Earth Mother |
| Lugh | Low | The God of Justice, sometimes also of sun and light |
| Fomorian | For-more-E-an | Mythical creatures |
| Danu | Dan-U | Danu is actually the Goddess of fertility- this name is used differently in this story |
| Sidhe | She | Mythical creatures |
| Pookas | Poo-ka-s | Mythical creatures |
| Fir Bolg | f-air- bol-ack | Mythical creatures |
| Selkies | Cell-keys | Mythical creatures |
| Failinis | Fain-its | Mythical creatures |

**Irish words and phrases**

| Dia dhuit | D-a-Ditch | God bless you, used as a greeting |
| Míle buíochas | mE-la boy-hass | Many thanks or Thank you |
| Gaeilge | Gail-ick | This is the Ulster pronunciation for what we call our Irish Language |
| Bodhrán | Bod-dr-un | A single-headed, frame drum |
| Mallacht an domhain | Mal-ugh-t an doe-in | Directly translates as "The curse of the world." |

# Chapter One

She was screaming. Screaming as the iron-hot pain hit her but this time it did not ease as before.

"Shh, you need to hush up, we can't have people hearing you," her mother whispered.

"I can't do this ma, it hurts too bad" Erin cried, attempting to roll onto her side to ease some of the pain. Her mother grabbed her shoulder and pushed her back onto the pile of laundry.

"It'll be over soon. But you need to breathe and keep your screaming inside" she warned.

"It's no use, they would have already heard her from the other side of the lough." Her father appeared at the door, crossing his arms over his chest. His frown now leaving a permanent welt between his bushy brows. She pleaded to him with her eyes, crying with the pain and the shame she had brought. Unable to keep it in any longer she released another scream as the agony intensified. The feeling of flesh tearing and red-hot pressure was so intense she feared she would pass out. As it subsided slightly, she propped herself onto her elbows, the laundry no longer providing her with any support. Her mother crouched before her, lifting her skirts and looking between her legs. She was talking to her father, they were angry, not concerned or fearing for their daughter, just angry. She couldn't hear what they were saying over the ringing in her ears and pressure pushing down between her legs.

Some little heads poked out from behind the door, their eyes wide with shock, and faces pale with fear for their sister. Her father slammed the door shut, preventing them from seeing more. Standing by the door, guarding it, arms crossed he demanded, "I am not sure they will believe the bae is ours?"

"I can't think about it. It's too shameful" her mother stood, "They will believe us." She said trying to convince herself.

When their daughter arrived home pregnant some months ago, the family devised a plan. They had found their daughter a husband willing to take on a child. For months they have been spreading the lies across the village and hiding their daughter from the world.

"Ma it hurts! Please make it stop." She screamed louder this time. The fire-hot pain sent shock waves down her spine and across where the baby's head pushed.

Turning back to her daughter, she got back down onto the floor and looked, "Fuck's sake it's too fast. I can't stop it love, we just need to go with it, you need to push." As the pressure turned, blocking her ears, Erin stopped hearing her mother. Everything burned as she squeezed every muscle, screaming and crying as she was being torn apart. Then suddenly it stopped. "Nope love keep going we need to keep going!" her mother urged.

"No, it's done, I am done" She lay back on the laundry sweat dripping down her face. Suddenly the pain returned, along with the screaming.

"That's it now, just push." Her mother urged her. Erin screamed as she pushed, the feeling of tearing flesh intensified as the baby was pulled from her body. "It's done love, it's all done," her mother reassured standing as Erin collapsed back onto the laundry.

Her mother stared down at the baby in her arms. The discomfort making the baby cry. The baby did not look like them. She resembled mortals, yes, but her eyes were bright blue, impossible blue. She has a full head of hair, dark and soft. The baby's eyes twinkled up at her grandmother. *A sign of a witch*, she looked at her husband in shock.

Ignoring her daughter, she pulled a large rag from the pile of laundry, causing Erin to topple onto her back laying on the stone floor. The temperature change was soothing on her back as she closed her eyes, exhausted.

"What's wrong?" her father demanded, moving towards the baby.

"What do you think?!"

"Fuck's sake. She's clearly a witch! They'll notice that!" Turning to his daughter who still lay on the ground, "You stupid girl. Out of all the men, you chose one of those mongrels!?"

"Let me see her," Erin whispered. Her mother held the baby, bringing her down for Erin to see. Immediately the baby stopped crying and sensing her mother near she stilled and calmed. Erin smiled, tears falling from her eyes. "She looks like sunshine," she whispered; memories of her baby's father come flooding back to her. "Her name should be Sunshine." She pressed her nose against the baby's cheek, too weak to reach out with her hand, "Éabha."

Her mother stood taking Éabha with her. Erin closed her eyes, smiling.

"Maybe she will change as she gets older. She's half human." Erin's mother ponders, trying to convince herself. "She does look a lot like Erin."

"Half-human?" her father shouted. "Ma, have you ever seen a half-witch-half- human before?" her mother did not reply, as Éabha began to moan softly from the floor. "No? It does not happen. That bitch went and got herself in trouble with that lot." He glared at his daughter, pale, sweaty and lying on the stone floor. "Now we have to take care of the mess".

Erin could hear her parents shouting and Éabha crying. She wanted to soothe her child and reassure her parents. She had planned to leave and find another place for her and her child to live and grow. She had planned it all. But she could not open her eyes, lift her head, or whisper a single word.

"They'll come to check you know that too, right? They will come and check." Her mother sounded worried, referring to the elders of the village. Juggling the baby into one arm she begins to look around the room. The room was covered in various piles of laundry on the floor. A few large half barrels of water, a washboard and a press taking up most of the space. The walls were lined with jars of dried spices, flowers and leaves, some strange colour fluids, some sparkled and others bubbled.

"We can dull that twinkle and hope she doesn't grow too tall" Erin's mother declared thrusting the baby into her husband's hands. He promptly wrapped the cloth over the baby, turning away from his daughter to follow his wife around the small space. "That's all we can do now and come up with a better plan later."

Pulling blue and dark green leaves from a jar she folded them into the rag, wrapping it around the baby tighter.

"Perhaps because she is a girl with human blood she will not look like a witch?"

"Stupid fucking bitch, how can she make us a target like this, such a fool." Her father muttered.

Her mother and father continue to argue over the heritage of the baby's father, cursing their daughter and rummaging around for more ingredients and rags to cover up the baby. All while their daughter lay on the stone floor. A pool of blood

4

growing around her. Her breaths became fast and few between, eyes closed and head slumped she took her last breath.

# Chapter Two

## Twenty-Eight years later

Cill O'Laoch; in the old language means *Descendants of The Lough*. And so, we worship the lough, her waters, and what she provides us. Of course, we have moved on and no longer believe her to be a single being but more of a spiritual element. Some of the elders in the town remember when we would worship her like the goddesses in the sky. They preach of the dangers of not respecting her, enforce the laws that protect her and disseminate her gifts.

Our town relies heavily on the fishing industry. With markets every day selling fish, crab, lobster. We're not a main port, indeed there are larger ports able to welcome big shipments from around the world. But we welcome many ships with merchants looking to exchange goods or hire crew for their voyages.

Cill O'Laoch sees none of the riches the harbour brings in. The elders quietly take. They call it a tax. To ensure the town is maintained and the lough is kept safe. I am sure most of the money and goods, which go through our harbour, make their way to the capital and into the pocket of the King.

There is always a lot of movement on the waters but at night she becomes still. Her surface reminds me of the rolls of silk fabric sold in the market. They would flow and shimmer as the sellers would unroll them to allow customers to feel. The water of the lough glistens as the moonlight is reflected off her smooth surface.

Our ancestors named the lough, *Cuan*. Her name sounds mystical and haunting. Partly because we are not sure what it can mean. Although most believe her name to refer to Bay or Harbour, some have even translated it to mean Heaven. I do not doubt the lough is perfect, but I would not regard her as heaven. She contains a darkness. Hiding in the depths, amongst the seaweed and resting on the rock bottom. It seeps out when she is being taken advantage of or not being cared for. In truth, the lough is vulnerable and emotional. We need to be mindful of how much we take but also what we give, including love.

My grandparents laugh when I speak of her as if she is alive in that way; as if she can respond, react and relate to me.

I stand on the rocks and watch as the water tries to lick my toes. Beckoning me to step into the cold. With my clothes discarded on the grass, goosebumps decorating my skin, and with a smile, I take a step. Being careful on the slimy rocks, I tread carefully to the water voiding the clusters of seaweed. Soon the seaweed begins to float, and as I get deeper it bobs past lazily. Once I am in far enough, I dive under reaching my arms in front of me and pulling myself through the water. Beneath the glittering surface, starting between the rocks at the bottom, there is a ballet of ethereal seaweed. Swaying gracefully, painting the waters in shades of jade and peridot. As if Cuan herself had woven a tapestry of trees. The long strands delicately sway and twist with the water like dancers in an unseen melody. Reaching towards the light with otherworldly elegance.

As I glide through the underwater world, the tendrils of seaweed gently brush against my skin, offering a tender embrace. Soft and subtle, they wrap around my limbs, as if guiding me through this mystical realm. It feels like I am being guided through a labyrinth, with every touch awakening a sense of connection to the secrets that lie within Cuan herself.

As I flow below her surface I can feel a pulse of recognition, like a hello or a welcome. This is how I know Cuan is so much more than we give her credit for. How I know she can respond to me and how I know I will be safe beneath her surface.

I will never find out how or why, but I have a connection with this lough. Like the Goddess knows me from a different time.

Like tonight and every night, I swim through the forest of seaweed with no clear destination in mind. Closing my eyes, I coast through the water feeling the pulse like a hug around me. It trickles past my ears, smoothing the curls of my hair, and twisting itself around my body. When I am under the water my mind becomes clear. Above the water, I am hunted with thoughts of self-doubt. Underwater I am worthy, above water I am nobody. Unfortunately, I must live above the water.

Time moves differently underwater. It feels slower in the dark green jungle and yet it passes quicker. I break the surface, kicking my legs to stay afloat. Turning from left to right I try to work out where I am and what shore I left from. The moon is directly above me now, telling me I have been under the water for hours not minutes. Floating on my back I admire the moon. My long hair fans out around me as the tide pulls me towards the shore.

My grandmother used to tell a story of a time before the moon, before there was night and day. Diving back down into the darkness of the water, I shake off the eery feeling of the truth behind that story. Yet it cannot be true, because the world was made at the same time as the sun, the moon and the other planets. Stories of the rocks in the sky are just stories.

I wade through the water, avoiding the slimy rocks. The night air is cold, so I quickly grab the nearest bit of clothing to dry myself. The mortals of Éire are reserved compared to the other beings on this island. We remain in the traditional clothing our ancestors and their ancestors wore before. And so, I slide into my now wet petty coat and begin to layer over a smock shirt, a thicker cotton skirt, a blouse, and then a shawl which I fold and wrap around me crossing over at the back and tucking it into my skirt. Finally, another shawl, I drape over my head and let it fall over my shoulders.

Sitting on the damp rock, I start the mission of drying my feet and lacing up my boots. In front of me lies the final element of my outfit. My mother's dagger. It sits in its harness amongst the dark rocks. It's heavy in my hands and cold. The silver metal glows in the darkness of the night. Gold-encrusted symbols decorate the blade, lines twisted and knotted together forming shapes which once held deep meaning on this land. I twist it back and forth so the moonlight catches on the silver blade and sparkles. The handle is small, my hand fits perfectly within it. Unlike other daggers or even swords, this handle is made of a single stone. The green stone is imperfect, with cloudy swirls of greys and green twists around it, with some areas so clear you can see through it. I balanced the dagger by placing my finger behind the cross guard. The gold there and the top of the handle is encrusted in an arrangement of crystals and pebbles. Resembling a rainbow.

Putting the dagger back into the holster I pull my skirts up and tie it to my thigh.

I do not know how my mother came to have this dagger. It is nothing like the treasures of our family or even of our people. I found it one day helping my aunt clear out her bedroom. In a tin box under the bed where my mother slept. She had gathered many personal treasures. Pictures her younger brothers and sisters had drawn her, some money, dried flowers, beads and this dagger. I have kept it on my person ever since. Perhaps I like the feeling of always having part of my mother with me.

I thank the lough for her time and her kindness. Smiling as I often proclaim to not believe in the Gods or Goddesses only to thank them for their gifts to us. A silly little habit I picked up as a child I assume. We used to worship those Gods. The ones that ruled various parts of this earth.

They ruled the earth in a different time, when the world was mainly sand and sea. The sun had only just found himself in the sky and our moon fell in love with him so travelled there too. Soon those gods grew bored of governing mortals. The fae and vampire numbers began to rise, along with the witches. With more beings on the earth being unmanageable they retired to the sky themselves, to their planets. Venus, Mars, Saturn and so on.

Some parts of the world still worship them, these old gods. But in Éire, like many other countries, the mortals, humans, became curious and needed leadership, so they turned to the landscape and worshipped the Earth instead.

It is strange to think that a world that was once ruled by such powerful and mighty Gods and Goddesses would just simply move on.

They gave us a gift once. Although I don't remember the world before this gift, it happened in my lifetime. We call it The *Drenching*. The Gods loved how we cared for the earth and how we worshipped her, so they gifted us with colour. They coloured the earth in vibrant colours bringing life back into the lands.

Our High Priests say the fae and witches want to take ownership of this gift, but we know it was the Gods. Well, I am not entirely sold on that thought. But it's the only reasonable explanation I have been given.

There was a God, perhaps the first God. Or perhaps just the first God we can still remember. With many before him dying off and falling from the storyline. Chronos, his name was. He was created in a time before the sun and moon. Before night and day. Chronos is the God of time. Stories tell of an old man who lives on the souls of children. Of a monster who steals the sun's light every day only for it to escape each morning. Of a warrior who created and then destroyed the most powerful Gods ever known.

He is merely just a children's tale now. Told to scare children into their beds at night, or make them behave or eat their vegetables. If you don't do as you are told then Chronos will come and suck out your soul until there is nothing left. My grandmother used to warn my aunts and uncles as they misbehaved.

I received other warnings, as the God of Time would not want the soul of a witch. My grandparents warned I would be left in a forest far away for the fae to find. The fae of course being very mysterious. According to the stories told of them, they didn't suck the souls of children, they eat their flesh, or once I even heard they skin children and use their flesh as clothing.

What I do know of the fae, from my brief adventures into the forests surrounding our village, is they are strong and silent. They live off the land as we do, but their magic is what keeps the land alive.

I can't say I have seen them, but I have seen evidence of them. In the forest, I have found some strange things, circles of stones with dear horns in the middle, surrounded by burnt ground. Or strips of lace and silk tied to the trees with glittery music floating in the air.

The fae sing songs, we have all heard them. Magic songs to lure people from their homes and into the forest. I do not believe they eat people but use them in their rituals. Or sacrifice them to their Gods.

The fae are not the only mystical beings to be feared. There are their creations, beings, the old gods left behind.

Morrigan or the Phantom Queen. She is one of the last remaining offspring of the old Gods, the forgotten Gods. The only evidence we have that they truly existed. They left her, them, behind to ensure balance throughout the earth. Yet, left ungoverned and alone, she decided chaos is her true friend. Each sister has a power. Not like my power, or the fae's. Their powers are decisions. They decide, who dies, when they die, and who lives- death, fate and life.

A cruel being who holds the power to insight carnage amongst people, vampires, witches, humans or fae. She knows your fate and can manipulate it at her pleasure. She can cut your life with a snap of her fingers.

The Phantom Queen can transform into any figure she wants to, preferring to present as three beautiful women.  Legend says, she went mad when she fell in love with the famous warrior, Cu Chulainn, but he refused her. After a long time of haunting him in battles in various forms, she finally appeared as a crow. Landing on his shoulder in the middle of battle, it is said he simply fell asleep. Bit of a rubbish ending, but now many elders around Éire are suspicious of crows, believing them to be a symbol of death.

Personally, I believe, if you keep your head down and are nice to people, not much harm can come of you.

That's easy for me to say though. I spend most of my days trying not to be noticed. I am not from this village- although I am technically. My father's identity remains a secret which died with my mother. Now, my tall curvy form, with long hair that curls in some places and straight in others, sticks out like a blue goat.

My appearance and my powers kind of scream not human.

It's funny really, how being different in a small village leads most people to believe you are dangerous. I will turn their children into witches, or eat them in a stew, or kidnap their cats! All very laughable, as I hope I am most known for is growing vegetables and bringing a dead cat back to life.

Jumping up with a sigh, I bid a silent goodbye to my lough and head home.

The village is busting at the seams with mortals becoming more anxious to leave now the Vampires have come to rule our lands. For the past hundred years, vampires have maintained strict order across Éire. With King Connor now in power, alongside his brute force of guards. Pushing mortals into the far corners of the island with the lands around Cuan being one of those corners.

I tip-toe through the shadows of the main street, lined with brightly coloured bricked houses. Pausing at the crossroad, I bask in the stillness of the town. Not a single soul is awake at this time. No lights shining through windows, no fires blowing smoke up chimneys.  Just stillness. Our village sits close to the forest of Delamont. Named after the fae settlers who claimed the land long before my people lived here. I am not sure of the history but the land around Lough Cuan was given to human settlers. In exchange, the humans were asked to care for the lough. This is where our worship practices came from, but a long history leads to lots of misinformation. The problem is the Delamont fae, through generations of fighting and change, now hunt of night.

14

Forgetting the promises once made to the humans. I believe they have gone mad through generations of fighting. We hear stories of them hunting each other, but we know they only like one thing. To hunt, kill and eat humans. And they are good at it. Now when the sun begins to drop, we remain indoors and stay still and silent until dawn. We have not had an attack in many years, but I am still cautious of their presence in the shadows.

My mother didn't stay inside at night. She explored the world including the Forest of Delamont. And so, I explore the world at night.

Turning right I head towards home. The houses become more rustic-looking the closer I get to my grandparents. That may be putting it politely. Most houses here are crumbling and the patchwork on the brick, deteriorating mortar or random wood extensions. Making them appear more abandoned rather than purposefully rustic. Our home, however, resembles more of a giant greenhouse than a family home. With my aunts and uncles all successfully married with their own families, my grandfather turned their rooms into glass houses, now working as little nurseries for tiny vegetable plants.

Cill O'Laoch, although most popular for fish, has rich nutritious lands, perfect for growing foods to sustain the village and of course; the kingdom. My grandfather proudly boasts of being the main supplier for the north of Éire. Tomatoes, potatoes, carrots, marrows, onions, leaks, really any kind of root vegetables. For my grandfather, they grow fast. The faster they grow the faster he can sell them and grow more. The people of Cill O'Laoch are a little naïve. Any person with a little common sense would question a man on his growing abilities. Yet somehow, not a soul queried this unusual produce. They simply marvel at it.

My grandparents and I are fully aware they would avoid all our crops if they knew the truth. My grandfather does not have green fingers, he isn't lucky or gifted in any way. The land we own isn't even that great- full of rocks and clay. The large trees of Delamont that border our home, cast shadows over the field resulting in limited sunlight. Horrible growing conditions really.

Sighing, I reach for the garden gate. A trickle of our secret slips out of my hand as I touch the ivy which weaves its way across the low garden wall snaking its way over the pillar and around the gate. Its leaves burst out like wings of yellow and jade green as the vine slithers around its target. The warm sensation tingles in my hands, letting out a little glow before disappearing.

"Sorry," I whisper to the ivy as I push the gate open, ripping its new growth away and letting it fall to the ground. Smiling to myself for talking to plants again, I work my way around the back of the house. Scoping out the windows to ensure everyone is still sleeping. Like the rest of the village, our street and even the forest nearby, is still.

But stillness does not always equal calm.

I left a thin slip of wood in my bedroom window to keep it open, whilst ensuring it looks closed at first glance. As I push the window up and prepare to hoist myself into the room I spy a shadow. It's not large but short and slim. I recognise this form immediately. Preparing myself for what's to come, I hoist myself onto the windowsill.

"Éabha," she growls. I pull myself through the window and land face-first on the floor. "You are putting our lives at risk going out there at night, to the lough as well. Do you really think we aren't fully aware of your night-time antics?!" Is a person able to shout and whisper at the same time? My grandmother is brilliant at that. I pull myself to standing and choose not to respond. My grandmother is unearthly skinny. She always has been, a strange impact from having nine children, I think. Most women go the opposite. But I suppose before I arrived, she worked the fields with my grandfather every day, taking on the same workload as any man. As a result of her low weight, she always feels the cold. She stands in my room wrapped in at least three blankets or throws, a thick pair of wool socks and a scarf wrapped around her hair. For a grandmother, she appears quite young. Her skin has aged from sun exposure, but she still looks decades younger than she should.

"You will end up just like your mother you know!"

"What? Dead?" I retort, a usual response for me in this argument.

"Or worse!" she pushes me to the side reaching for the curtains whilst slamming the window closed. "There are things out there that can sense magic. Your magic!" She jabs a finger to my chest as I pull off my boots tossing them on the floor. "And you are drawing them right to us". My layers of clothing follow leaving me in my damp petty coat. I understand my grandparent's fears, the village is full of terror of what lies outside. My magic is nowhere near as powerful as I believe they feared when I was first born. However, I can feel it inside me, warming and at times trying to claw its way out. It scares me sometimes too.

"Your grandfather and I took you in. Knowing full well where you came from. And this is how you repay us?"

"You're right. I'm sorry. I didn't think". My rehearsed response, I am not sorry.

"Yeah, your mother didn't think either." She storms from my room slamming the door behind her. She is right though, I am ungrateful. I am so thankful to my grandparents, truly as anyone else would have brought me into the woods and left me there for the wolves. But they chose to keep me. No longer relaxed and calm, I climb into bed. Pulling the blankets and duvet up to my chin.

# Chapter Three

Getting out of bed in the morning is a challenge. I lay awake most of the night thinking of everything; thoughts run through my brain constantly and quickly. So quick I cannot process one thought before another pops in. Now in the morning, I lay with the weight of the world pressing against me.

I am startled from my thoughts by a heavy banging on my door, "Girl, wake up we have jobs to do!" My grandfather's voice booms through the wooden door. From the outside, his nickname for me may seem endearing but when he says it, it seems more like he couldn't be bothered to learn my name and so I am just 'Girl'.

Outside the air is clear, the sun shines, with some moisture in the air and clouds coming in from the east, we will get rain today. My grandfather is hunched over some seedlings on the windowsill by the back door. His back cracks as he stands to acknowledge me with nothing more than a disgusted look on his face and a gesture towards the tiny plants around him. "I need these strong enough to be planted today, it's to rain tonight."

My grandmother doesn't look her age, but my grandfather looks his age and then some. He uses his cane to hobble outside. "That's compost for the backfield." He points his cane to a mound of dirt outside, "Then I need all the veg along the back fence and over there by the wall picked. Bring it to the kitchen and then help your grandma clean and package it." He turns to limp back into the house.

"Yes sir." I can feel him turn around to glare at me. Apparently, I get my attitude from my mother, I am reminded of this fact almost daily. With a huff, I hear him go back indoors slamming the door closed behind him.

I decide to start with the compost. Loading a wheelbarrow, I make my way to the backfield, through rows and rows of growing vegetables. Working my way past everything that needs harvesting today I point out any plants that need a bit more help before I pick them. Halfway to the back field I stop by the wall. Everything looks ready to be pulled, although one little area near the end looks to have yellowed slightly since the last time I was here. Crouching down I brush my fingers through the leaves of the carrots. Their tall stems and soft tiny leaves tickle my hands. The yellowing is just the rubbish soil lacking nutrients. Closing my eyes, I allow my magic to seep from me into the soil. I am not selective with my magic, I don't use it sparingly, or only when required. Because the only thing I am good at is making things grow, so I use it all the time. Someday I may wake up and this gift could have vanished, rendering me useless. Until then I make good use of it.

The soil glows gold, pulsing as it drinks in the magic. The warming earth makes my hands tingle. I open my eyes to watch the carrot tops slowly begin to stand tall and turn from yellow to green. *Perfect*, standing I smile down at them like a proud mother.

The fields are packed with produce, my grandfather trying to make as much of the space as possible. Leaving only little narrow walkways to get through. I take a lesser-trodden route back to the house with the forest of Delamont to my side. There are many stories about the surrounding forests in Éire, but Delamont seems to be the tamest. Forests slightly farther out,

Donard or Cairn, we were warned about as children. There are worse things in those forests than the Fae of Delamont.

The wall, crumbling in some places remains tall. The grey stone is now decorated in moss and tiny purple flowers. Sometimes if you stand still, hold your breath and listen you can hear the beasts roaming around the forest floor. Or the creatures swinging from tree to tree. As I stand with a hand on the wall, I hear nothing but stillness. Without meaning to, my hand warms and growth spreads out of my palm. Tiny white flowers spring out and drop down to the ground. But I remain silent, trying to hear for what lurks in the forest, being greeted only with silence.

I am not sure how long I remain standing there whilst the white flowers grow from the wall, clearly expecting to be growing from the ground up and not a wall out, they droop down in sorrow. A snapping branch startles me. I clutch my chest above my heart, hold my breath and focus on the sounds beyond the wall. Unusual sounds. Not scuffling or stomping or creeping. But very confident and sure footsteps.

Closing my eyes I try to focus on the footsteps. Light feet walk towards the wall, pause, and then continue in the opposite direction of the house.

After some time, I let out a sigh, unaware I was holding my breath for that length of time. I have never been by the wall and heard footsteps, so clear and loud. Yes, sometimes you hear some scuffling or digging but never very clear one foot then another. A shiver runs down my spine as I think about who that may have been.

Humans are one of four creatures who walk the lands of the earth. It was not a mortal human walking on that side of the wall, on this side of the village.

A fae, maybe but unlikely in this forest, as the other fae tribes stay clear of the Delamont.

A vampire, again maybe. Vampires tend to live in small groups and stick mainly to the cities where they can find humans willing to give them blood.

A witch is more likely. Witches are one of the oldest creations. They harness the power given to them to change the elements around us. My family believe me to be a witch. I believe they feared I was fae when I was born, but my magic appears similar to the witches who have drifted through our village over the years. I push it all to the back of my mind. Nothing dangerous passes through here only harmless powerless women trying to sell potions and herbal remedies.

Some of the seedlings lined up against the back wall have only just sprouted, others are tall but looking a bit limp. Their little leaves feel too fragile between my muddy fingers. Getting on to my knees I pull a couple of the bigger pots towards me.

Potatoes. Three potato tubers in each pot, each able to produce twelve times their weight and potatoes, easy to grow, easy to store and easy to cook. They are our biggest demand. With my help, we should be able to get nearly 100 potatoes from these pots in a matter of days.

Sitting down on the earth before them, I cross my legs and get to work growing. The ground has been warmed, by the sun, the grass spiking up as I rest my hands on top of it. I can feel my magic wanting to gush out of me. It hammers through my veins down to my fingertips and my toes, begging me to let it out. I ignore its demands, I know what it wants, it wants what I want. Freedom.

Freedom to do as I please, without fear of persecution. Freedom to live without demands, to do as I please, and to meet my own needs. Freedom to be who I am, in the security of my own home. I just want to be left alone. Not in a sad way, but more in an independent, liberated, and peaceful way. My dream is to buy a house with land, near the water, and just live there. Read, cook, relax. Allow the earth to provide for me what she wishes.

Thinking of my dreams brings peace to me, my heart warms and I feel my magic retreat slightly. Retreating in recognition of the bigger picture, just wait and we can be free.

*

The rain has arrived just in time. I sit in the window with my feet up and a blanket around me watching it trickle down the window. Soft grunts come from my grandfather as he lifts some logs from a small pile and throws them on the fire. It sizzles and hisses as the damp wood lands on top of the flames. My grandmother is wrapped up on the sofa, keeping an eye on her husband while she is donning some socks. I feel her eyes jump between me, him and her needlework. They hate it when it rains as much as me because it means I have to stay indoors. Well, I don't have to, but it's cold and wet outside.

Straightening his back with a click, my grandfather flicks his hands on my shoulder as he walks past; "Girl, get the dinner going. I'm going to the barn to check on tomorrow's stock."

With a bang of the door, I pull myself out of my nest on the windowsill and begin to pull random vegetables out to chop for dinner. Lining up three carrots I chop off their green heads and continue to cut them into thin discs. My grandmother has gone still, I can sense her eyes on me.

After some time she announces; "Someone is living in the old Morris house now."

The Morris' passed away over a year ago, and their children had married and moved to the capital. I hear their eldest son is a

23

vampire, although they kept that gossip very tight until they died. Then everyone found out! They tried to sell the family home with no luck, it's been empty for years. People helped themselves to their furniture and even their garden gate, the house had just been left to ruin. "Why would anyone choose to live there?"

"Why would anyone choose to live here?" my grandmother counters.

I move on to mashing some tomatoes into a lumpy sauce, adding odd bits of herbs that catch my eye. I have never been very good at cooking, but I do enjoy experimenting with herbs and spices. Being a port town, we are lucky to have access to various spices from around the world. Although, I am not sure I use them correctly, or what their names are. We all love the warm, sweet and spicy flavours they give. As I cook my grandmother continues, but I don't pay attention. She mentions something about a girl, the house being bought, and something about the windows being replaced.

"She seems strange." My grandmother ponders, clearly wishing I had continued to ask questions so she could share some gossip.

"Strange?" I ask. She hums a yes and she pulls the thread through the toe of a sock. She's making me work for this.

"Strange in what way?" I ask as I roll my eyes.

"Can't put my finger on it but I hear she's got a job in the castle, cleaning." I hear my grandmother setting down her sewing and turning towards me.

"Well, she can't be that weird for Lady Hamilton to give her a job"

"No." My grandmother agrees, getting up to put her equipment away she moves into the kitchen. Placing a pan on the hot stove and turned to find my grandmother coming towards me with leftover chicken bits on a plate. She's still wearing her coat, which reaches down to her ankles. I am sure she is also wearing two pairs of socks.

"That's also strange," she passes me the plate, "There were no jobs going at the castle. Otherwise, I would have marched you up"

I laugh at the thought of it. "Something tells me my dearest aunt would not give me a job"

Yes, Lady Hamilton is my aunt. My grandmother's daughter. Although we shared a room when I was younger, we never really bonded. My aunts and uncles were cautious of me. After their sister, my mother, died, I think they struggled with the loss. And oh yeah, the magic and weird stuff I do puts people off I think.

My aunt went on to marry one of the Hamilton's elder's sons, who refers to himself as a Lord. They live in the Castle on the hill, overlooking the village. And my aunt acts like the queen of the village.

I watch the pot boil, counting in my head. Once satisfied I take it off and steam it with a plate. Whilst everything else cooks, I think about all the other friends I have lost as a result of accidental magic. The tree which grew from nowhere and that dead cat that came back to life. Smiling, I place the large pan on the table. Just as my grandfather comes in, taking the ladle off me, he helps himself to a large portion.

"You'll go up there tomorrow with their delivery," My grandmother informs me taking her place at the table.

"Me? Why?"

"Because I said so." She demands grabbing the ladle, "and I want to know more about the girl."

Rolling my eyes I silently agree.

\*

When I can't go to the lough to swim away my loneliness, I dream of my father. I know nothing about him. Except for one thing, he was not human.

My dreams always start the same, on a battlefield. It's dark, but a green hue settles over everything like a thick mist. Flashes of bright orange and red strikes across the space in front of me. Balls of fire are thrown from all directions. Swords crash together echoing alongside the screams and the cries. My father lays on the dark ground, the mist staying away, creating a frame around him. He's pleading with everyone to stop, crying out for peace, begging his kin to celebrate with him rather than fight him.

He looks like me. As much as a girl can look like her father. He is tall and broad. Wearing armour around his chest and stomach. His arms are huge from training and fighting like a warrior. His forearms are wrapped in a cloth up to his elbows. My eyes are drawn to the rope bracelet on his left wrist. A small dark blue piece of sea glass hangs from the plated rope. Every night I try to get a better look at his bracelet but I cannot seem to get close enough.

He screams in agony as a ball of orange light strikes him on his side. He quickly turns and cuts down the culprit with his sword. Magic runs out of his fingers, like pink veins. He shouts pleading with those around him to stop. When they don't, he blasts a ball of energy in their direction. The shock makes the trees shake and the earth quiver. People jump from the trees above me landing in a crouch before running towards him, swords or fireballs at hand. Some have glowing hands, sending more blasts across the area.

He blocks a blow from behind only to turn to find a sword pressed against his chest. Slowly, painfully slowly, his kin pushes the sword through his chest, splitting his ribs, slicing through his heart and reappearing on his back. My father's face pales, and his eyes weep as he turns to look at someone high up in the tree. I am sure he cries out or moans in some way, but I cannot hear over an intense scream from the tree above me. *No,* a woman shrieks.

I try to get to him, to bring him back or to hold him. I used to try to save him with my magic, try to push the life back into him and make him breathe. But I know it does not help. I never manage to get to him. My feet are stuck firm to the earth, I am stuck and helpless amongst the carnage.

The battlefield fades into the mist as my father's body lies there. The light dims to a grey-green shadow. The trees disappear into the shadows. I step forward, as the magic releases my feet, towards the body of the man I do not know. I know what happens next, but I am not in control of my steps anymore. Finally, after fighting with myself and my own body, feeling unable to move or control my actions, I am standing above him. Once I pulled the sword from him. Heard the squelch of his heart and lungs as I disturbed their rest. Felt the blood drip down the blade and ooze out of the hole in his chest. Those sensations still haunt me today. Giving me a sickening feeling in my stomach when the images appear in my mind randomly.

I now know there is no point trying to help him. I stand, without the ability to close my eyes, turn away or run into the shadows of this haunted forest. I stand over him and watch as he reaches up and pulls the sword from his chest. A movement which should be impossible, a dead man pulling a long sword from his own chest as he lays bleeding out on the forest floor. But my father is made of magic.

He sits and turns to me. Those blue eyes once filled with passion and life are now muted and dead. His ash blonde hair falls around his face as he frowns at me, eyes glaring unblinking. And I prepare for the next part of my nightmare.

Just as he pounces with an animalistic growl, the magic holding me still, releases and I run. It doesn't matter what direction I run in; the ending will always be the same. As he grabs me by my neck and turns me to face him. He lifts me up by my hair and pins me against a tree. His nose is just a breath from mine, as he pulls me up by my hair until we are eye to eye. Sometimes I feel like I am looking at a mirror as his blue eyes bore into mine and his damp hair falls wildly around his face.

"Give me back my magic," he spits. His hands glow golden, and a sharp piece of slate appears between his fingers. Pushing a knee into my stomach to hold me still, he brings the sharp stone to my neck and pushes. I don't know if I scream aloud, no one has ever complained, but here, in this dreamland the pain is agonising and I scream so loud I fear the banshee may mistake it for her call.

"You stole it from me," He growls pushing the stone further into my neck. I can feel the blood trickle out of me, running over his hand and down my chest.

I cry; *please, no, I didn't take anything, please let me go, please.* The words come to me but I am beyond any ability to speak.

I know it is useless as every night he becomes so frustrated he kills me. And tonight is the same as every other night. He screams in rage as he pulls my hair, forcing my neck to become unbearably straight and my head to hit the tree behind me. I can feel hair strands snapping away from my scalp. He retracts the blade only to lift it up past my right ear and down through my throat at an angle.

Then I wake. Grasping at my throat like I have been suffocating this whole time. I can still feel the memory of the

28

blood trickling over my fingers and down my arms. I rub my neck frantically and check for blood using the moon as my only source of light. Nothing, and yet it still feels so real.

My bedroom lays still. Outside the moon casts a white glow over the garden. Shadows jump from one vegetable to the next. I imagine it to be foxes or rabbits, out looking for their dinner. I study them to avoid the overwhelming fear I hold of the other half of myself. The half that my father thinks I stole from him.

# Chapter Four

"Sit still will you," My grandmother pulls a brush through my tangled hair. The repetitive movements become more irritating with each tug at my scalp. My body instinctively tenses moving away from her.

"Gram that hurts," I plead, trying to avoid another tug.

"I need to tie it up." She begins to pull my hair together like a bunch of flowers, "Did you know, Mrs McCoy stopped me last week." Snapping a band in place, she pulls some strands to tighten it. I think I know where she is going with Mrs McCoy, so I don't move, "She mentioned seeing you with what she thought was a dead bird."

"Oh." I try to wiggle free, only to be pulled back by my new ponytail. She pulls my head back until my ear is at her lips, her breath is a warm warning.

"Please just remember you cannot be seen to be using your magic, if the elders or the King find out what you are we will be dead."

"Mrs McCoy sees things. Remember she thought a Pooka was living under her bed?" I smile up at her, in the hope she'll let this one slide. Like all the other times she had to ignore some of the strange rumours about me.

"This village is full of busybodies, if they hear something that could be true, they will believe it." She lets me go with a slight push.

I stand, turning to look at her with my hands on my hips. "And you my darling," my grandmother reaches out to pull a hair behind my ear, "Are odd, so they will believe it."

The shock of being called odd to my face wore off a long time ago.

"Just you remember girl." She leans in close pointing the hairbrush at me. "We kept you this long out of necessity. We should have tried harder to marry you off. But remember who you owe your life to. Eh?" I stare at the ground, as shame creeps its way up my spine, making itself comfortable around my neck.

My grandmother is right; I need to be more careful. No one can find out what I am. Although infrequent, I remember times when people like me were executed, sometimes by fire, beheading or other times hanging. I've spent my life hiding from everyone outside of the family for fear I too would be handed over and killed.

I feel a little like a dressed-up pig as she wraps a shawl around my shoulders clipping it in place with a plain lined pin. Making me look smart to give a good impression. Whilst also hoping I return with gossip.

Hamilton castle is small compared to the paintings of ones I have seen which decorate the mountains and coastlines of Éire. The grey brick gatehouse forms the opening of its walled perimeter, with stumpy sandstone towers at each corner connecting the chunky battlements which protect the castle itself. The lime-washed towers of the castle peak out above its defending walls, growing taller as you make your way towards it. Along the pebble dirt road lined with bricked houses of Cill O'Laoch slightly richer residents. They line the street like Lady Hamilton's adoring fanfare.

I hate visiting the castle. Not because the staff are not nice, or because it's up a hill. It's because of my aunt. She is the

32

closest to me in age and a constant reminder of how less I am compared to her. Although she rarely visits her parents, my grandparents and I hardly see her on the odd occasion I do deliver here. The last time I was invited to the castle was for her wedding. I dread the thought of spending time with her. And so, I drag my feet through the square.

The square is the true heart of the village. Usually, a hive of people bustling around from stall to stall. At this time in the morning traders and sellers are just setting up. Some have built permanent storefronts into the old houses, of which the front only remains. The crumbling buildings at times are held together with timber or patches of concrete. The backs of the homes, or what remains of them are in far worse condition. However, still good enough for some families to reside.

Some buildings have boarded up windows others have just left them abandoned creating urban habitats for animals. The only buildings that are not in disrepair are the elder's meeting space and the hospital. The hospital is my favourite building, it is a sandstone building that sits tall above the others. Although the windows on the upper floors either have bars or are boarded up, they seem to shine in the rising sun. Several steps lead up to the large oak front door and way above it is a clock tower. The only clock we have in the village. It's been broken for twenty-eight years. My grandparents say it stopped the day I was born, but I have since learned that many parents say that to their children born around the same time. No one has bothered to try to fix it.

To the north and east of the village just outside of the market area are archways, leading out of the village and into the forest beyond. They used to be guarded with large gates which closed at night. I don't know why they stopped using them. Money is most likely, but not through lack of need. Everyone is very suspicious of anyone 'travelling through' or new traders who we have not met before, or who isn't linked to another person in the village.

I pull my basket of food closer to my chest and push on up the hill towards the castle.

The sun was just peeking out between the buildings behind me as more venders venture out into the square to set up for the day. Rows of wooden stalls and carts appear from under the tarps that keep them safe during the night. Soon merchants will appear through the archways in the hope of buying, selling or trading their goods

The Gate House casts a dark shadow over me, blocking out all sunlight. I always feel uneasy near the castle, or perhaps it is the lack of sunlight. I am also nervous of how observant the guards are. Rumours spread about me every so often, I can't have a guard seeing something strange, that even I cannot explain, and tell everyone.

A guard pokes his head out from a hidden doorway, looking me up and down he gestures with a nod of his head to the left, "Goods and servants enter round the back."

Of course they do, I think to myself. Why would the beautiful Lady Hamilton and her charming husband want to see the likes of servants and lay people from the front window of their shining castle. I smile a thank you and turn to walk down the side of the castle, along the shadow of the battlements, which personally, seem a little ostentatious. Cill O'Laoch has not seen battle or war in hundreds of years.

The sun shines on the other side of the castle, casting me in a shadow once again. My magic begins to hum inside me-bursting to get out and fearing what lurks in the shadows as usual. Or perhaps she wants to bathe in the light the sun provides, finding the darkness uncomfortable and cold.

The service entry is at the very back corner. Another guard opens the gate for me, barely registering who I am. It slams shut behind me. The heavy basket of vegetables starts to get heavier as I make my way towards the kitchens, which I know are behind the coal shed and around their herb garden.

The kitchen is a flurry of activity. Light streams through the door which is propped open with a barrel of stale-smelling wine or ale. The temperature change hits me in the face, right away making my temples sweat. Pots are steaming or boiling over on the stove, two people are at the butcher block in the middle hacking away at what used to be a dear, others are cutting up fruits, a large woman is kneading dough, flour is flying everywhere, and everyone is shouting. Shouting instructions, curse words or simply laughing at others' stories. Staff in uniform run around trying to prepare for breakfast. Silver trays and bowls are being passed around with little care. Ceramic plates and cups are tossed between them, narrowly avoiding the chefs who are now sawing with hack knives to cut through the deer's leg bones. Sweat trickles down my back from watching the chaos fold out in the heat of the steam.

I just need to drop off the delivery and leave. I can tell my grandma the new girl wasn't here.

"Ah, Éabha, we were expecting your grandfather," I look round and find the women kneading the dough staring at me, hands on hips and face covered in flour. "Not to worry just leave that load there, the money is in the tin by the door." Placing the baskets on the ground by the smelly barrel of wine, I grab the tin on the shelf just above. Counting out the paper notes and some coins and fold them away neatly into my purse.

"You weren't expecting to see the lady today where you Éabha?" a woman dressed in a grey dress suddenly appears striding towards me, her white starched apron sways as she moves. She runs her hands down her front smoothing out some invisible wrinkles on her apron.

"What? No, I just..." I spin to address her, edging slightly closer to the door. She walks around me as if inspecting me, my appearance or my unusually tidy hair.

"Just that we don't usually see you on this delivery."

"Oh well I..." I step back as she steps closer.

"Your grandfather usually comes, later on, and stays for tea." She steps slightly closer again.

"I know, it's just that he... well I... " *Let me leave please!*

"Will he still be coming?" She demands, her hands on her hips.

"He probably will be yes..." *I have no idea.*

"If he doesn't, can you tell him we have a banquet planned and he needs to talk to the Lady about the menu." I am cornered now, my back hits the trim of the back door, as she closes in on me.

"Yes, I..." I try to take a subtle sideways step out of the kitchen.

"Don't know why she likes to oversee the menu, when she's not the one cooking," another woman says, they all snicker but continue to chop, throw or kneed.

"Oh, shhh you! Sure, what else will she have to do to pass the time?" The woman covered in flour tosses some in her direction as if to emphasise her point. Laughter fills the kitchen.

"I'll just ..." gesturing to the outside with my thumb I side-step my captor and begin to leave, again.

"She could be helping Éabha in the gardens," They laugh again. Harder this time.

"What are they laughing about?" a voice comes behind me making me jump.

"You're Éabha?" The voice behind me asks. I didn't have time to register her before. Behind me stands a young girl, in a neat brown dress and white apron. Her uniform seems crisper than her colleague's so I can assume she's new. Her skin is white like she has never been outside, with hazel eyes and golden blonde hair, which she's twisted up into a bun. She looks new, she looks different. She looks like the type of girl my grandmother would want to know all about.

"You're Ceira?" I ask in response, and she smiles making her cheek brighten and her eyes sparkle slightly.

"The joys of a small village, everyone knows the newcomer" She laughs, it sounds like music.

"Yes, and everyone knows the weirdo," I inform trying to laugh along with her. Her face falls and I suddenly realise what that sounded like, "Oh no, I didn't mean you," I feel my face pinkening as embarrassment claws its way up from my chest. "I mean me. I am the weirdo."

She laughs, with a slight singsong rhythm to it. "Well as a blow-in, who may or may not be weird, I don't know many people."

"I could show you around if you like?" *Fuck, what did I just say?*

"Would you mind?"

"No, when do you finish?" *Ok, we are doing this.*

"Just after dinner service."

"I will come by and walk you home. Give you the grand tour on our way back." I plaster a fake smile on my face, in a bid to look inviting.

"Perfect." She smiled walking into the kitchen. Wait, she smiled, a genuine smile. She wants to spend time with me?

I am still smiling as I walk through the square. I catch people looking at me, usually I am not in the square this late in the morning. Usually, I am not this happy. But today I do not feel the need to hide from the village, I don't feel like covering my face with my cloak or wrapping myself in layers, so they do not recognise me as the strange girl of the town.

*

Ceira spoke in an accent I didn't recognise. Her words are soft and almost feel warm. The more comfortable she became chatting, the shorter her words became, like she was rounding off the edges. Whereas I sounded sharp and spiky in comparison.

She was as tall as me. Thankfully, usually, I tower over people. But many of my family are tall, for humans. My grandfather is the same height as me, but I am tall for a woman, which I am reminded of regularly.

Ceira's blonde hair lightened in the sunshine, I notice, as we walk side by side towards the market square. She has taken it down, placing hairpins on the sleeve of her work dress and allowing the soft curls to swing naturally over her shoulders.

I have never given a tour of Cill O'Laoch before. I planned it all day, deciding to cover only the important parts; the market square, tavern, hospital and the water. Ceira did not seem interested at all in my tour. But she smiled and 'hmmed' and 'ohhed' appropriately. She asked questions too, like what I did for work and where my favourite spots are. Walking back up to the village from the water I simply pointed out the hospital and tavern. The tavern is more interesting than the latter. Its old brick has been painted a muddy red to match the colour of the Hamilton family crest. A wooden sign hangs above the door with a picture of a sailboat, seen better days.

"Do you drink? I know some places are funny about ladies drinking in taverns." Ceira gestured towards the pub.

"Oh, I don't know actually, never been in."

"Shall we?" she asks.

"Erm…" I hesitate as she moves towards the door. The tavern is full of people. Loud, rowdy and drunk people. People I usually only see at the temple when we are all well-behaved. Anxiety trickles down my spine as I feel my magic tingle on my fingertips.

It's hot, loud, and dimly lit inside. Sawdust covers the floor soaking up the spilt ale, but our feet stick to the areas missed. There is a thick smell of smoke, the lingering taste in the air of fishermen. However, I could overlook this, as there is also the cosy smell of a wood crackling fire. No heads turn as we enter; the room doesn't go silent. I don't even think anyone notices us- me.

Ceira instructs me to find a seat. As she moves towards the bar. Looking around it is hard to identify a space that isn't already occupied. Moving away from the fire to the cooler end of the tavern I spy an empty table. People notice me now. I note a few sideways glances as I shuffle between people. Sitting down with a sigh, I note a few smiles as people catch my eye. Perhaps I am more accepted amongst the drinkers of the town.

Ceira slams two large glasses of amber-coloured liquid in front of me, which throff over, spilling slightly on the table. "This place is great," she beams.

A few beats of a drum signal quiet across the pub and everyone turns towards the sound. A lone man sits on a stool near the fire on the other side of the tavern. With his a bodhrán drum in hand, he looks around his peers. Another man pulls up a stool beside him with a fiddle, then another, then one young boy with a whistle stands up, propping himself on the windowsill by the main door, he whistles confirming his attendance. When they start to play the air around us becomes alive. The lilting tunes dance playfully above the steady hum of the bodhrán.

This song is a call to celebrate and dance. I turn to find Ceira being pulled out of her seat and whirled into a makeshift dance floor. I awkwardly clap along to the song. They sing about the rocky road to Duiblinn, or a girl they fell in love with in Gaillimhe, or maybe it was Dori. Whatever it was and whoever they fell in love with, I can feel the connection as I happily watch my new friend dance the night away.

# Chapter Five

Two thousand, six hundred and thirty-one steps. That's how many steps it takes from our front door to the temple's door. I count every single one, every Sunday. It helps me ignore the stares from others as I walk past. I tread lightly through the cobblestones, grass paths and dirt tracks, that take us through the village and along the side of the lough towards the temple by the village wall.

My appearance sets me apart. My dark hair cascades down my back, coiling at the ends, whilst most style their hair straight. And my eyes have a slightly brighter tint to them than others. I am a twin of my mother; I am told often. Who looked like my grandmother. The only difference; was the curl of my hair and my blue eyes.

As we walk towards the temple, whispers dance around me like shadows. I have kept my powers hidden from everyone outside the family, except for a few minor incidents when I was too young to understand the consequences. These coupled with my slightly peculiar appearance makes people suspicious of me. I don't blame them. I think it's a natural reaction, we must keep ourselves safe from danger.

The crowd grows as we walk along the lough's wall. The salty air relaxes every muscle in my back, one at a time. I didn't realise I was so tense before. As I relax and hold my head higher to allow the wind to catch my hair, I catch bits of conversation.

*Do you remember what she did to that cat? You would think she would have left to live in the woods by now. Do you think it was her mother or father who was the witch?*

My head starts to drop, training my eyes on my feet again, my grandmother steps in. My heart swells. I am not sure if she reacts to maintain her own appearance or because she understands how these comments affect me.

"Lovely morning, Shannon. And how is Paddy? We saw him leaving last night before your husband's boat got in," my grandmother joyfully shouts.

"Oh Micheal, good to see you out again. I hear that fae turned your wee man purple!" she smiles to another.

Rounding the corner the temple comes into view. Its shadow creeps towards us as the building grows bigger with each careful step I take. Eventually, the chill of the shadow covers us as the temple towers down with a discerning stare. The structure is old, with some obvious repair jobs over the years, creating a patchwork of various stonework. The front and only remaining tower used to act as a lookout. Now falling into disrepair, it is not safe to climb the stairs to reach the top anymore.

"Twenty-four more steps," I mutter to myself as we start to climb the small slope to the main door. The wooden doors were gifted to the temple by an artist in a village on the other side of the lough. The glossy stained wood is adorned with carvings depicting ancient rituals and mythical creatures, but primarily features our Goddess of the lake in various poses and dresses. It creaks open offering a welcome to the faithful. But for me, it only offers a refuge tainted by the scepticism of others crowding themselves inside.

The temple is meant to be a place for solace and communion. For me, it feels like a cage of judgement. We once used to rejoice about the world around us, of everything the lough has given us, of the safety of our village and those we trade with. It has now slowly turned into a place of lectures and warnings.

As I enter, I feel the space quiet and conversation cease (although I may have imagined it), replaced by an awkward stillness broken only by the echoes of our footsteps towards the next empty pew. Bowing my head and lacing my fingers together, I begin to give thanks to the Goddess of the lough.

"Welcome," the high priest announces from the front. My head remains bowed whilst others all recite a welcome back to him.

The high priest stands in his white robes, decorated with gold embroidery around the cuffs and hemlines. While his congregation sit in various shades of brown and green. Except for my aunt and her husband, who communicate their wealth by sitting apart from everyone in vibrant colours. All the priests wear white. I don't know how they keep them so clean when we can just about manage to keep a beige-coloured shirt clean. I guess that's what money buys.

That and ignorance of the struggles of those whom they claim to care for.

Long before me, the priests provided refuge for those in need. They worked with starving families and encouraged trade in the village. Now they remain in their temple preaching and shaming us.

"Let us begin by giving a silent thanks for our mother's lough, for all she provides. And to the earth for all that she offers to us." The priest calls from his throne-like chair.

In unison everyone slides from their wooden pews onto their knees, bowing their heads in prayer. This is the only stage of our service that is actually worthwhile. I love the lough and I am grateful to her and the earth. Eternally grateful for the peace they give me and the warmth they offer me when I need it. So, I pray for their forgiveness of who I am and thank them for the protection they seem to have granted me.

I am the first to slip back into my seat, something I know the high priest, Dubhan, notices as he observes us from his throne in front of the altar. To his side, three other elders sit with their heads bowed, also giving thanks. Their white robes are decorated with blue embroidery around the cuffs, setting them apart from Dubhan.

Behind them is a plastered wall painted a tranquil blue. Nothing decorates the wall, perhaps it is making a point about simplicity and our modern lifestyles. Although this seems a little deep for the priests of the temple to have thought of. The altar is a work of art. The most expensive thing in the village, I believe. A white stone block with veins of grey and silver. Its front is decorated by gold emblems of twisted knots and swirls. Much like those which decorate the blade of my mother's dagger.

Priest Dubhan stands. Clearing his throat, he summons everyone's attention. "Brothers and sisters," His voice bounces off the cold stone walls. "We gather in the light of the Divine to rejoice in the blessings bestowed upon us." He raises his hands allowing his long sleeves to fall open around him.

"Are we not fortunate to live in such a beautiful and harmonious village? Where the sun's rays kiss Éire with warmth fuelling the fields and our mother lough." *I fuel the fields with magic*. The thought makes me smirk, which I quickly drop as I catch my grandmother's side-eye.

"Let us cherish the bonds of community that bind us together, and not dwell on the shadows that may lurk in the corners of hearts, for ours should only be guided by unwavering faith." *Oh, those shadows might be me.*

"We should not be blinded by our own contentment." His anger becomes almost tangible. "Unseen and insidious forces are at work. That seeks to disrupt the delicate balance of our existence. A force which could lead us off the path of righteousness with tempting promises of power, knowledge and love." He leaves a long pause, not too long but long enough for the priests at the front, and some of the congregation, to turn and look at me.

"There have been whispers, I am sure you have heard. Murmurs of strange occurrences that defy explanation." *Ok, I will take that one.*

"Miracles not of divine origin!" *Miracle is a bit much.*

"But born from the dark recess of these lands." *This is the part when he starts to spread fear. Is a good miracle a positive thing? Are giving or healing not a good thing?*

"Such temptations are but illusions. Veils that obscure the true radiance of the divine. Let us not be swayed by the magic, the false promises and the greed. Or we could be led down a path of despair and rumination." *Beware of the dark-haired one, who feeds the village and brings the sunshine.* I laugh again, whilst also trying to maintain a straight sombre face.

"I do not speak of those who remain hidden in the forests. Those Witches," He spits, "And fae who smell like lilacs and lavender. No, I speak of those among us." I am not sure he could make it any more obvious.

"Stay vigilant for the light of faith shall guide us through the darkest of times, illuminating the path to salvation and every last life in Éire." *In summary; can we stop speaking to Éabha we don't trust her she's too different.* He sits, as another priest takes the stage.

I spend the rest of the service on my knees praying.

*

Loneliness is strange. I had come to find comfort in it. Security even. But loneliness was killing me. Slowly. I realised.

It created an ache in my chest, which I had once gotten used to. A normal ache of the body, I told myself. The ache rattled around the void inside me. It would scream sometimes; "Fill me!" It was easier when I listened to it. More peaceful. If I ignored this ringing in my ears, this constant tug in my brain, it slowed me down. Bringing me to bed, to darkness I didn't want to see.

So, I fed the ache. With anything and everything. It dulled it slightly.

Dulled it until Ceira came into my life.

I realise now what I had been missing. A connection to another person. An understanding I would always have someone there to take away the loneliness I used to find comfort in.

It's been weeks since Ceira arrived, and we have spent all our free time together. She has made other friends, from work and around. They greet her with kindness and include her in their socialising. But she spends her time with me.

Sometimes I meet her after work, other times she will appear in the garden with a smile on her face and an idea. She likes to explore, although sometimes I think she's hunting. We explore the forests bordering the village, not venturing too far in.

Ceira has some, unusual, ideas about the creatures who reside in the forests. She talks of the fae the most.

"The fae think they're better than everyone else, looking down on mortals as if we're mere playthings for their amusement," she explained to me once as she climbed over the wall into the forest.

"Everyone knows the fae love to steal human children, replacing them with their own changelings," she stated as we walked past a group of small children, wobbling on their feet, as they rush after their mothers in the market.

"fae lack genuine emotions. They might mimic human feelings, but it's all an act to manipulate us," she told me as I made my deliveries to the elders. The statement made me smile as I looked into the emotionless eyes of the elder Ceiran as he took his parcel of potatoes for the week.

Ceira believes one day the fae will rise up and try to overturn the power the vampires currently hold. She talks about needing to be prepared, how we have all become complacent, and reliant on the king's guards for protection. This led Ceira to bring me to her garden.

She had cleared it of everything, no greenery, or nice sitting place, just a blank space. In the middle is a clearly defined dirt circle, marking the area where she walks the most. Along the back wall of her house, is a small row of weapons, wood swords, spears and round wood shields. Like the ones children play with, but larger and heavier looking.

"Erm, lovely," I say as she goes to get her sword.

"This is where I train," I can feel her rolling her eyes at me as she turns swinging her sword back and forth in one hand, she looks comfortable and confident with the weight of it.

We don't speak as she moves into her ring. With her sword held firmly in her hand, she begins a series of fluid movements. Striking out with the sword and bringing it back to block an invisible attack. Again and again, she rehearses this routine. Turning with grace or spinning round in a low stand every third strike. Her eyes are focused, like she can see an invisible opponent before her.

Soon her movements speed up, as she includes a range of thrusts together with aggressive grunts. Each one appears precise and controlled. I could see her face reddening in heat, sweat beads running down her forehead, and her breaths quickening. But she remains undeterred, her focus unwavering.

Ceira is well trained, professionally trained, as no guard at the castle could attack and defend as she could.

I applaud her as she comes to a stop. She takes her time to allow her breathing to return to normal before turning to me with a slight curtsey and a smile.

"Why thank you," she fans herself with her hand, "You're too kind."

"Where did you learn that?" I take her play sword from her and marvel at its weight

"Erm, my parents I guess?" she moves over to a bucket, cupping some water and tossing it over her face. I don't know much about Ceira. She doesn't talk about where she came from, her family or what brought her here. The times I have tried to bring it up, she quickly changes the subject. So, I have learnt not to press her. Allow her to keep her secrets as I keep mine.

"Do you wanna learn?" she asks lifting another sword and leading me into the centre of the ring.

"First, let's see your stance," Ceira instructs, positioning herself with her feet slightly apart, knees bent but only a little and her back straight. I try to mirror her exactly, wanting to impress her.

Smiling she places her hands on my shoulders pushing me back, straightening my back even more. Lightly, she kicks my feet out a bit wider, "Good, now bend your knees slightly," Ciara guided, circling me, "It will help with your balance, but also with power." Nodding I try to keep my eyes focused, just as hers were, absorbing every detail and instruction she gives.

She rounds me as I stay frozen in position.

"Watch closely," she instructs as she pushes her sword forward and back again, ending in the same stance.

I try to mimic these movements, tentative at first. The weight of the sword is difficult to hold up and straight. She nods with encouragement, and I try it again. Over and over, I strike out with the sword. Switching hands when Ceira instructs.

"Relax your shoulders, Éabha. Let the sword become an extension of your arm."

Slowly she introduces blocking, holding my arm she demonstrated the perfect position. Over and over, I mirrored her offence and defence. Until sweat began to blur my vision and I could no longer hold the sword straight.

Dropping the sword I collapsed to the ground, my breathing heavy as I looked up at the cloud-filled sky.

"You're better than I thought," Ceira says getting onto the ground beside me. We stay there as the clouds glide past, until our breathing returns to normal.

"Come on," Ceira stood, turning she reaches out her hand. Taking it, I let her pull me to my feet, she grunts at my weight.

"You're supposed to be strong!" I laugh.

Ceira tidies away her weapons, turning to go inside her house. "There's music later, you wanna come?"

"Yeah sure," Ceira goes to meet her work friends regularly in the evening before dusk. But this is the first time she has included me. "I'll go and get changed."

"No, come on, you can borrow something here."

*

49

My borrowed dressed in uncomfortable and tight. It's thin as well. Ceira didn't want me to wear or bring my shawl. Cold bumps decorate my arms as we walk side by side towards the pub.

"Ugh," Ceira spits, as we pass the last of the merchants packing up for the day. A lady packs her bag, filled with tiny glass jars and bunches of leaves or flowers. "Witches are nothing but filthy parasites." Ceira declares within earshot of the old lady. "They suck the life out of everything good, leaving nothing but rot and ruin in their wake. If I ever met one, I'd show her exactly where her place is- in the dirt, beneath my feet." She glares at the women, who look on in shock and fear as we pass.

Ceira's words cut through the air, sharp and careless. I feel my stomach twist as the insult lands, a deep unease settling in my chest. She doesn't know, she can't know but hearing her speak like that makes it clear; I'll have to hide this part of myself from her. My throat tightens, and I bite back the urge to defend witches, to defend the witch we pass. Instead, I nod along, forcing a smile, all the while feeling a growing distance between us.

In the tavern, Ceira's friends try hard to hide their displeasure at seeing me with her.

"Oh, Éabha, it's nice to see you. We don't usually see you out... in public," one says, smiling through gritted teeth. Their eyes flicker over me, lingering on the borrowed dress that doesn't quite fit right. Ceira pretends not to notice, but I can tell it stings by the way she fusses over the way it sits on my shoulders.

Throughout the afternoon, we listen to the music session. Some of the group sing along, others dance, all in good spirits. I try to lose myself in the noise, to focus on the melodies instead of the sharp glances and whispered jabs.

Before the sun begins to set, the tavern fills with more people, and the air grows thick with heat and ale. I do my best to ignore the comments her friends make, sticking mostly to the sidelines, trying not to embarrass Ceira.

But it's hard. Despite the warm feeling of kinship, I feel when I'm out with her, part of something greater, there's always a tension simmering beneath the surface. I watch the others laugh and debate with Ceira, their conversations full of opinions on the lands of Éire and how things should be run. I smile when I'm supposed to, and join in when expected, but I never quite feel like one of them.

As the evening wears on, I grow more uneasy. The tavern's tight spaces mean bodies press close, and I feel the crowd around me shift uncomfortably. One of Ceira's friends begins talking loudly about witches, about how they curse men and bring ruin with their magic. The others laugh, and I force a smile, willing my face to stay neutral even as I feel my chest tighten. I can't let them see.

I feel something slimy on my waist, turning round I find a man resting his hand on me, grinning down with his uneven smile. My skin crawls, and I stiffen, trying to move away. But he's persistent, his breath hot and sour as he leans closer.

"Don't be shy, love," he slurs, his fingers grazing my arm. I pull back sharply, but no one seems to notice, or care.

Ceira's friends smirk from across the table, exchanging glances as if this were some sort of joke. I glance at her, hoping for help, but she's lost in another conversation, laughing and completely unaware of the discomfort swirling inside me.

Smiling back at the man, I turn, trying to hide myself. Placing my hand on his I advert my gaze to the nearest candle and focus on the flame. My magic tingles a little as my fingertips warm. Soon my touch it too hot for this man. He hisses stepping away, not before calling me a *bitch*, or a witch, I couldn't quite hear.

This is how most of our free time is spent now, me, on the edge of Ceira's world, following her lead. Sometimes at the pub, sometimes in her garden or on the wall soaking our feet in the lough.

Ceira is full of strong beliefs, always debating and teaching, but her friends never warm to me. They tolerate my presence at best, their disdain thinly veiled behind forced smiles and cold words. And the rest of the village? They don't see me as one of their own. Some take advantage of my silence, pushing boundaries like the man beside me, while others mutter mean-spirited comments when they think I can't hear. I'm an outsider, and every day it feels more apparent.

# Chapter Six

The sun slowly sets over the castle, turning the clouds deep blue and grey in the sky. I sit on a wall by the lough, waiting for the darkness of night to blanket us all. The town has long since quietened as everyone closed their doors and windows for the night. I watch as fires are extinguished, the smoke from chimneys puffing up into the sky greeting the clouds.

Once I am finally covered in the disguise of darkness, I swing my legs over the wall and jump down onto the soft grass.  The tide is out, further away from the shore than usual. Leaving a trail of slimy rocks and dried seaweed leading to her waters.

Stripping down on the grass, I shimmy out of my layers of skirts, blouses and shawls. Until I am standing in nothing but my undergarments and dagger. The breeze tickles my exposed skin, making me smile. Adrenaline pumps through me, as I take the last of my clothes off, burying my dagger amongst the pile.

 Soon I am wading through Cuan's water. The initial sting of cold water soon disappears as I get deeper. So deep my toes just about touch the rocky floor. Cuan ripples around me as I slip beneath the surface, the world above fading into a gentle hum. Here, in the stillness of the night, I finally feel free. Cuan comes to greet me as her waters hug me tight and I dive deeper through the forest of seaweed.

The water is dark, but it welcomes me like an old friend. I feel it cradling my body, the soft currents soothing my tense muscles as I float, weightless and free. And with each gentle stroke, I release a bit more of the energy I've held in all day, letting it ripple through me like the waves that lap at the shore.

Here, I can be whole. The coldness of the lough sharpens my senses, making me feel more alive, more connected to the world than I ever do on land. The water seems to hum with my magic, the energy flowing from me effortlessly, dancing around me in gentle pulses. It's like the lough knows my secret and holds it for me, keeping it safe beneath the surface.

I glide through the waters for what feels like hours. Never breaking the surface for air. Eventually, I cannot continue and start to make my way to the top to take a breath.

My throat closes over as I see a figure standing by the shore. My pile of clothes at their feet. They don't move. Although, they must see me. I tread water for some time as I contemplate what I should do. No one is out at this time of night. No one in the village, including the Elders, would be brave enough. Only those who can defend themselves would be out in the darkness, or those who people would need defending from. My magic flickers to life again as I start to swim to shore.

The brave part of me believes I can protect myself from any threat. Whilst the logical part of my brain is finding escape routes and telling me to slow down or remain in the water. All while my magic licks and tickles at my chest, begging to get out.

Slowly the figure's details become clear, they are wearing a dress, with long hair. But continue to remain impossibly still. Eventually, a soft pale complexion and blonde wavey hair, neatly arranged around a woman's face come into view. It's Ceira.

I pause, standing on the rocks, the water covering my chest, and take her in. She doesn't normally come out at night, she never comes down to the lough, yet here she is, with not even a shawl to keep her warm from the night breeze.

"Hello," I call from the water.

"Hey," she says back, so softly I almost can't hear her. Walking closer, I take in her face, she seems spooked by something. Her skin is paler than usual, her eyes are wide with fright, they don't sparkle like they usually do. She's not smiling, she always smiles.

"What are you doing here?" I ask as I try to hide myself with my hands as I skirt past her, grabbing my clothes for more protection.

"I could ask you the same thing," she reaches down and grabs my dagger, pulling it from its holster.

"Swimming," I smile at her, pulling on my blouse before reaching for a skirt, "I usually swim at night, I am sure I told you?" I didn't tell her, I don't tell anyone.

"No, you didn't," standing I see she is pointing my dagger at me. Her arm is straight, her feet shoulder-width apart, her chest upright. It wouldn't take her long to plunge the blade into my chest. I know her strength and studied her moves. Yet why would she do this to me? At night, whilst I am vulnerable and unarmed.

"What are you doing?" Now fully clothed I step towards her, but she doesn't step back.

"I could ask you the same thing," her face is demanding now, the fear gone.

"Swimming," I reply sternly. I think about leaving, walking home and leaving her on the shore looking like a fool with my knife. But something about her seems off.

"Was that all you were doing?" her arm doesn't shake, I note. Mine would, my arms would shake from the weight of the dagger and from holding that posture for so long. But Ceira is strong, built like a warrior under her pretty dress.

"Of course, it was all I was doing. What else could I have been doing out there in the deep water?"

"I saw it," she says, her eyes widening in exaggeration. I don't reply, growing tired of this back-and-forth. "I saw you, under the water."

"Because I was swimming"

"No, I saw the spell you made in the water," she whispers, "I saw the lights and the beast you created." It makes sense now. I had always thought I was invisible under the water. There, I can relax and allow my magic to flow along beside me. Underwater I can be me. I never imagined what it must look like from the shore. I always felt safe at night. When the rest of the village retreats to the safety of the inside, no one is out to see me.

"It's not what you think," I rise my hands in defence, stepping back slightly.

"Are you a witch Éabha, like they say you are?"

My heart stops. Droplets of water run off my hair and down my face. I try to blink them away before they crawl into my eyes.

"Ceira," I whisper, trying to control my voice from trembling. "What are you saying?"

Ceira corrects her posture, having slipped slightly, she moves closer to me as she does so. My dagger closing the distance between us. "Tell me the truth- are you a witch?"

I open my mouth to deny her claim, but nothing comes out. If Ceira knows what I am I will be left with nothing. She hates people like me as do her friends and everyone else in the village. But I can convince her that I am truly nothing to be feared, barely even strong enough to grow a tree. Taking a deep breath, I try to ignore the sound of my pulse which is pounding in her ears.

"I am not what you think," I say carefully, "There are things about me you wouldn't understand."

Ceira's expression hardens, "What's there to understand? You created a monster in the lough! I saw it!"

"I didn't. That was me in the lough, there are no monsters here."

Confusion sweeps across her face, followed very quickly by anger. "You are a witch." She whispers.

"I am," I say defeated, dropping my hands to my side. neither of us moves. We stare at each other with a mixture of anger, confusion and for me; liberation. This is the first time I have confirmed, out loud, into the open air, to another person, that I am a witch. But the liberation is short-lived as Ceira's hatred of all things not human creeps into my mind. She may not fully understand but I am determined to change her mind. "But I promise you I am far from dangerous."

"I have never killed, never harmed, never even created anything, let alone a monster in the lough!" I laugh trying my best to soften the tension thick in the air. "I can heal," I explain, "and I make things grow."

Silence falls between us again. My damp hair has soaked through my shawl to my blouse beneath. It clings to my skin like a slug. The sick wet feeling penetrates my skin to my chest, which now hammers as I wait for Ceira to respond, to react in any way.

"I didn't choose this, Ceira," I whisper, "it's something I was born with. I would never do anything to hurt you. To hurt anyone!" She lowers my dagger slowly, remaining silent. Her expression unreadable. Eventually, she drops the dagger, it clatters on the stone, I cringe at the thought of the damage. But my focus remains on Ceria.

Slowly her expression softens, and her eyes relax as she says, "How can I trust you?" tears begin to well in her eyes, but they never appear or run over her eyelid. She remains confident "Witches, they are mallacht an domhain"

A small part of me feels sorry for Ceira. Of her blindness to the goodness she's seen in me over the months, we've known each other. Has she not seen how I care for the earth, protect the earth, fuel the earth? Perhaps her blindness is because she has yet to see.

"Come with me," I turn slightly, grabbing my dagger I make my way towards the wall, "I want to show you something." Smiling I turn, climbing the wall, I wait on the other side. She follows behind reluctantly.

We walk in silence along the road leading back to the village. Our footsteps echo between the houses, making a marching tune for us to follow. Ceira doesn't say anything as we turn down the road to her house. She remains slightly behind me; I can feel her eyes on me. Curiously wondering what I am doing. Finally, we make it to her place, and she follows me around the house into her barren garden. I march right into the middle and turn to smile at her.

"What are we doing here?" She says, nervously pulling at her sleeves.

"Just watch." I don't need to touch the soil. My magic has been reeling to get out since I walked to the shore. I feel it glide through me like soft linens falling over my skin to my feet. It's almost like the earth soaks up my power like water after a sunny day. She pulls at my power, trying to get more and more.

Ceira's eyes widen in shock, as she looks around me. Short spikes of grass erupt from the soil. Bright green and strong. The clusters are random but quickly group together coating the ground in green. Behind me flowers sprout, pinks, blues and yellows dance along the fence. They grow bigger and bigger forming bushes and hedges. At Ceira's feet, a tiny circle of white flowers appears, staring up and smiling at her. She lifts her foot as if she is scared to trample them. But they stay in their little circle.

Ivey claws its way up through the ground and over to the red brick of the back of Ceira's home. It mixes with another plant, which frames the windows and door. Slowly purple flowers unfold, dropping down like drops of rain trickling down the windows.

I stop it there; fearful I have already done too much. Looking around the garden has been transformed. The flowers I spent time imagining over the years now decorate the boundary behind me. Clusters of pink leaves have formed bunches amongst large green leaves. Yellow petals hug each other on long thin stems, surrounded by leaves of jade green. Tiny bells with frayed edges the colour of blue line the bushes, with tall floppy leaves. All my creations are now birthed into life right here. My heart swells with pride and I turn round to face my friend.

I swallow as I let her process the magic which surrounds us. I wonder if she can feel it too. Feel the magic worm its way through the ground, pushing up the grass, plants and flowers as it goes.

Ceira doesn't move, but her eyes flicker from side to side, up and down. Her garden, once a wasteland, is now full of abundance and colour. I wait patiently for her to gasp in awe, for her to call it beautiful and to praise me for my gift.

She doesn't. but her eyes tell me she is pleased, she is impressed, she is happy. Finally, after what feels like hours of tense silence as Ciers takes it all in, she turns to me and smiles, "Is that all?"

# Chapter Seven

I wake to rustling in my bedroom. The sound of drawers being opened and banged closed was followed by the weight of cloth piled on top of me.

Groaning, pushing them off, I sit up to find my grandmother towering over me. Sunlight is streaming into my bedroom, stinging my eyes.

"Put these on," Lifting the clothes she tosses them on top of me again, "The Elders would like a word with you."

I bolt up out of bed, my heart jittering to keep up. "Elders? Did they say what they wanted?" I ask as I start to pull on a petticoat.

"No, but by how panicked you seem, perhaps you know?"

I don't, but being summoned by the elders after they have left me alone for so long is not a good sign. "I haven't done anything, I swear," I try to reassure her.

There is no time for food, as my grandparents wait by the door in their finest clothing. My grandfather in a suit, a cap tucked into his arm and his formal walking cane. My grandmother wears her only coloured dress, a fine thick woollen dress in green, covered by a dark shawl.

My grandmother explains that the Elders want to meet at the temple, as she fusses over my hair, instead of at their lodgings in the village to prevent people from seeing me. I sinking feeling dropped into my stomach, I am not sure what I have done wrong, but I have also felt one day they would gather enough evidence to make something up that anyone would believe.

The three of us walk towards the tower. No one is around. I imagine word has gotten out somehow that I have been summoned. So, they are respecting my grandparents and staying away.

This is the third time the elders have called for me.

The first I was five. If I accidentally used magic as a child, my grandparents or my aunts would slap me, tell me to behave or they would bring me to the forest and leave me there. But my magic was bursting to get out, I didn't understand it then.

So I went into the garden, dug a big hole right in the middle, sat inside it and grew a tree. I was a toddler and didn't think anyone would have noticed it, but the tree grew around me. My grandfather needed to cut it down to get me out. He needed help from the farmers next to us, word got around about the weird girl in the tree.

The second time, I truly believe was uncalled for. The king's guards had just left the village on horseback. I can't even remember why they were here. A cat, we had adopted as our own, followed me up to the village, to watch the parade as they all left on horseback. She got scared of the horses, their hard hooves clicking and stomping on the ground, bringing up dust. She ran straight through them to get away. Only to find herself under one of those hooves.

I remember screaming as the guards left behind my dead cat. Her body was limp when I picked her and everyone watched as I held her to my chest and allowed my magic to pour into her, bringing her back to life.

The elders ruled that my cat be executed.

My grandparents said I should have been hung alongside the cat.

I shiver at the memory as we enter the temple, standing in the cold hall, lined with rows and rows of empty pews.

Footsteps echo down towards us as High Priest Dubhan appears, walking down the aisle. He does not smile as he nears us, only frowns with anger and disappointment.

"Mr and Mrs Ní Chaiside," Priest Dubhan greets my grandparents with a nod of his head before turning to me, "Éabha," My name is laced with venom like it hurts his tongue to say it.

"Hello, Priest Dubhan," We all respond in sync.

"I am sorry to call you here under such disturbing circumstances, again." My grandfather sighs, taking a seat on the nearest pew, already exhausted by the conversation.

"As I am sure you are aware, the communities around Cuan who share in her abundance, have been having difficulties," we all nod in response although this is news to us. The lough has never failed to provide for the communities that live off her.

"Dwindling fishing numbers, leading to lack of food to feed our families. You only have to walk around the market square to see the poverty it has created." He explained, his voice full of sadness, his face trained to reflect the same, as this lie glides so eloquently into the air.

"It has been brought to my attention that Éabha swims in the lough at night." My face gives away my guilt. Most nights I swim in the lough, when everyone has closed up and gone to bed, only a handful of people know where I go at night. And two of them are here with me.

"What I am sure Éabha does not know, is we watch the lough at night." The Elder's lodgings are right in the centre of the village, with no view or advantage point of the lough- impossible for them to see me swimming.

63

"What we have witnessed has been most upsetting. For a child of Cill O'Laoch to produce such a heinous thing. An act of war, one might say!"

"Those are serious words, Dubhan," my grandfather glares up at him. The pair, once friends, now torn apart by their divergent convictions. Their convictions being me. The belief I am dangerous and the value that I must be kept safe within the family.

"Excuse me, what is it you believe Éabha done?" My Grandmother asks.

"She has created a beast in the lough." His words float around us as we stare in disbelief. "She has used her magic to do what all witches do! Create destruction. We have seen it grow throughout the night, glowing underwater, ingesting all of our food!"

Surely, this is made up. A foolish attempt to scare everyone into believing I am evil.

"We worship Cuan for the food she provides us. For the safety she grants us. And you..." Dubhan steps closer to me, reaching out he goes to grab my neck. No one moves to protect me. I don't move out of his grasp either. He drops his hands before they enter the space around me, "You put all of that at risk."

"I have done no such thing!" I declare, finally finding my voice, "I love the lough as much as any other mortal in these lands. I come here every week to worship her, give thanks to her and beg for forgiveness like everyone else. I spend my nights worshipping her from within her water. Giving to her. Loving her!"

"I would never create a monster," I whisper, "You are mistaken, I have no such power."

"Since the day you were born, you have created, changed and manipulated to your own advantage. Do not stand here, in the house of Gods and say you love them and worship them!" Dubhan raises his hands to the Gods, gesturing to the space around him.

"I remember the day you were born." He turns slowly towards me, whispering, "I remember the colour drenching and staining the earth."

"What?"

"High Priest, we have no evidence that Éabha brought on the drenching. She was just a baby! Not even minutes old," my grandmother stutters. Turning to her I demand answers, but Dubhan gives them willingly.

"The high priests gathered and drafted a prophecy. Falsifying the words of the Gods! So, when the colour had tarnished all of Éire, seeping into the oceans to the rest of the earth. We declared it the work of the Gods." He walked to the alter, where on top lay a book. The book of old prophecies and writings. Writing in Gaeilge, a language long forgotten, the language of the old Gods.

Pulling a page from the ancient book he brings it to me. Letters, familiar somehow, were scrolled across the parchment in elaborate and flamboyant writing. I cannot read the word of the Gods. Their language is now long forgotten in our world. But I know the prophecy, the gift the gods bestowed upon us, as a way of thanking us for caring for the earth they created.

They blame me for the drenching.

"Humans are fickle, apologies, but we are. To prevent war we had to preach of security. To stop rioting, we spoke of the gift the Gods had granted us." Dubhan snatches the paper from me, admiring his work with sombre eyes, he turns to return it to the alter.

"The vampires were too drunk on power to recognise. The fae did, they crept out of their holes at night and tried to hunt the witch who attacked Éire with her colour." With a slam he closed the book, it echoed through the temple until silence followed. He stands up there, his eyes fixed on mine, like he is trying to find something within me. Looking for answers in the eyes of a woman he believes to be so cruel.

"And for some reason we protected you. Allowed your grandparents to raise you, as their daughter, Erin, would have wanted."

"Thankfully the green was simply nothing more than just a stain. Colouring in the dull shades of the earth."

"But this beast," he allows the hardness of the word to linger longer around us, waiting for the sound to stop echoing in our ears before he continues, "This is one too far."

My stomach felt heavy like it was limed with lead. I need to vomit. "What are you going to do to me?" I whisper.

"We shall have to consult with our brothers in Béal Feírste. They were the ones who encouraged us to keep you safe as a bae. So, I believe they will remain impartial and provide a fare judgement."

"Thank you…"

"Do not thank me, Éabha, I want you hung."

With that, he turns and leaves. His footsteps echo louder than before. My grandfather stands, his hips and knees clicking as he does. Grabbing me by the back of my neck, he turns and shoves me towards the door.

"Home," He grunts.

We say nothing as we walk the two thousand, six hundred and thirty-one steps home.

My magic gurgles in my stomach. I try to stop myself from retching it out. The thought of it, of my magic, makes me feel sick. I can feel it trying to soothe me, stroking at my insides, trying to warm my heart with a hug. But the thoughts in my head are shouting louder. *Worthless, evil, pathetic, witch.*

I stained the world with my magic. My grandmother may believe it is not true, a coincidence perhaps. So how come I can feel it? I can feel the earth, the lands around Éire call to me, like a song. I have always felt they are part of me and have never known why. Now I know it is because I have inflicted them. I have forced magic upon the earth, colouring it with unnatural brightness. Now it believes we are one.

The world was harmonious before I was born, saturated with calming tones. When I picture Éire before me, I imagine mortals living in peace. The fae, of all kinds, being free within the wildness of Éire. And the vampire's happy with their control.

I took that away.

The priests may have crafted a plan. Driven by the guilt and sorrow they felt for my family; to have cursed so much they lost a daughter and gained a mallacht an domhain, on the same day. This plan may have blinded the mortals. But I know the fae are smarter.

They started to hunt us. The stories and our timeline begin to match up, as we walk along the road home. The Delamont Fae began to hunt us. Cill O'Laoch was their target. We retreated indoors at night. We were told we always did this, always have and always will. But it started the day of the drenching. It started because of me.

"You should leave," my grandfather says, as he almost falls into a chair. He doesn't turn to look at me as he concludes, "Pack your things now and leave."

I turn to head to my bedroom. I won't take much I decide. I own nothing of value except for my mother's dagger. Packing won't take long.

"Wait," my grandmother calls, just as I leave the kitchen, "She cannot leave." She adds a log to the fire in the oven, and begins to fuss around the kitchen, "If she leaves now, they will think we sent her away before her judgement." My grandfather huffs and lumps back in his chair. "We will be convicted for your crimes," she explains, turning to me.

My grandfather turns to me from the comfort of his chair. His eyes narrow with the same cold disapproval I've felt my whole life. The burden of me weighed heavy on his shoulders. The silence between us is thick with unspoken resentment, a reminder that my presence has always been more of a curse than a blessing.

I feel the sharp sting of realisation- running is not an option. As I always felt it was. I always had an escape route if things didn't work out here. But running would only drag them down with me.

I spend the rest of the day in my room. Tracing the familiar grooves in my wooden headboard with a trembling hand. An unwelcome weight rested on my chest like someone had placed a stone there, and then another and another. I feel trapped.

I watch as the sunlight streams through my window and begins to crawl down towards the horizon and behind the trees.

My door creeks open slightly, and my grandmother appears, slipping into the room as if she doesn't want to be noticed. Her tiny frame blends in easily as she stands at the end of my bed, looking down at me. I imagine I looked the most pathetic I ever had, lying on my bed, hopelessly. Her eyes are no longer filled with shame but with sorrow. Her frown has softened only slightly and also her shoulders still looked tense, the tension did not seep out into the room around us.

"What you did, it was a good thing."

"I didn't do it," sitting up I try to make some space on the bed for her to sit down.

"The drenching I mean," she doesn't sit but moves towards my window. The sun is shining through and hits her face with its warm light. "If you did do it, it was a good thing. The world has been drenched in colour. Some people don't like change. But this change brought so much happiness into the world. You're good for us, whatever you are, you're good."

The words hang in the air, almost unbelievable. I blink, unsure if I heard her right. Tears swell in my eyes, not enough for them to spill over and run down my face. But enough for the emotion to clog my throat also. My grandmother doesn't stay, once she has said her peace she turns to leave. Closing the door softly behind her.

I sit on the windowsill, hugging my knees to my chest, staring out at the darkening sky. The soft, muted colours of twilight blend together, and the world outside feels far away, distant from the chaos and fear that's been swirling inside me since this morning. The priest, his harsh words echoing in my mind. I have cursed the land, brought something monstrous into the lough.

My eyes drift over the fields below, now bathed in the deep, vibrant hues I unknowingly painted with my magic. People marvel at the colours, but to the priests, it's an abomination. And the beast they say I've created, the one lurking in Cuan Lough—it wasn't me. Or was it? I don't know anymore. Doubt clings to me like a second skin, suffocating and cold.

I let out a long breath, resting my head against the cool glass of the window. My mind races with questions. What if they're right? What if the drenching was wrong? What if the colours I gave the world were just another form of destruction?

A shiver runs down my spine, the weight of their accusations heavy on my chest.

My mind wanders back to the lough and the beast they claim lives within her. I have swum in the lough at night for years and have yet to come across anything bigger than a seal. Nobody has ever seen me swimming in the lough at night, or they would have mentioned this sooner. Well almost nobody except for one.

Ceira saw me that night in the lough. She never said why she was out. Perhaps others have gone out at night. Or perhaps Ceira told them about me.

The hours pass, as my fear began to shift, morphing into cold, hard resolve. Ceira would not betray me. I feel like we have known each other our whole lives. She didn't run away when she found out what I could do. She understands and loves me for it. I have to know though. I have to speak with her.

It feels like my heart has stopped beating as I slip out of my window and make my way towards Ceira's house. I can feel the adrenaline mixing with my powers which propels me forward. The mixture of dread and determination makes my body feel heavy.

My heart thuds in my chest as I stand outside Ceira's door, the weight of my thoughts pressing down on me. I don't want to believe she'd tell anyone. She's my closest friend, the only one who knows about my secret swims in the lough. But the priests didn't just guess—someone told them.

I take a breath, steadying myself before I knock.

The door creaks open, and Ceira stands there, her face framed by the fading light of the evening. For a moment, we just look at each other, the air thick with things unsaid. I try to smile, but it falters, and before I can stop myself, the words tumble out.

"Did you tell them?"

Her expression stays the same. But I see something flicker in her eyes. Only for a moment, less than that even. She steps aside, motioning for me to come in, but I linger for a second, unsure if I want to hear what she has to say.

"Tell who?" she asks, her voice calm but with a hint of wariness. Or perhaps I am searching for her uneasiness so much I think I find it.

"The priests," I say softly, stepping inside. The warmth of her home feels suffocating after the cool evening air. "About me swimming in the lough. They know, Ceira. They say I created a beast which has been eating the food source."

She's quiet for a moment, and I can feel my heart sink. My fingers brush the edge of my shawl. I twist it around my

71

fingers trying to hold onto something whilst I wait. Wait for Ceira to tell me to wise up and get over myself. Because I cannot hear that my only friend, the only person I trust, thinks I could create such a horrible thing.

"Éabha, no," she says finally, her voice quiet, almost too soft. "I didn't tell them about you. Why would I?" Our eyes meet and I see the sadness in hers. Shame washes over me. "You think I'd betray you like that?"

There's no anger in her voice, just a quiet firmness. But she's closed off, her expression guarded in a way I've never seen before. It stings more than if she had just been angry.

I swallow, my throat dry. "You're the only one who knows. I had to ask." I step closer reading reach out to hold her and try to reassure her, but she steps away. "I didn't come here to accuse you, Ceira. I just... I needed to know. Everyone's looking at me like I've cursed the land, like I created something awful. I'm scared." My voice breaks slightly, and I hate how vulnerable I sound, but I can't help it.

She sighs resting her hand on my arm. "I wouldn't do that to you," she says, more firmly this time. Her touch is warm, but there's still a distance between us that I can't quite bridge. "I didn't tell them. I don't know how they found out, but it wasn't me."

I believe her. I do.

"I do trust you," I say softly, *then why does it feel forced*?

# Chapter Eight

Rot and decay have a funny way of spreading. Like a sickness, it creeps over the vegetables in their neatly stacked crates. Slithering its way up the carrots, rolling over the potatoes, and circling the onions. It only softens them at first, before borrowing deep into their flesh. Blackening their core. Turning everything to mush.

My magic weeps a little, as I toss another crate into the compost. The growing pile of dirt smells foul as I mix it.

It's been quiet since we met with the elders. Not in a good way. Our deliveries have reduced, and vendors don't want to sell our produce anymore. Even the Hamilton's have refused our usual delivery. That's where my grandfather is now, pleading with his daughter. This morning when he left, he looked broken, like a shell of himself.

Walking back up to the house, I hear shouting. My grandfather has returned. Stopping at the gate I catch what he is saying. His voice carries across the garden, thick with anger. I see him there, storming about, kicking at the soil as if trying to beat the earth into submission. His fists clench and unclench at his sides, and his face is flushed with rage.

"They're refusing everything," he shouts, pacing back and forth, eyes wild. "Years of hard work—gone. All because of you."

My stomach tightens as he turns towards me, his cain in one hand and the other clenched into a fist. The guilt settling deep in my chest. I stay by the gate, wanting to run, but unable to move.

"You're useless!" he screams, his words cutting through me like a blade. "Worthless, and good for nothing! The whole village wants nothing to do with us now. And what do we have to show for it? Empty hands and broken pride!"

I flinch at his words, biting my lip to keep the tears from falling. He's never spoken to me like this before. His voice has always been gruff, but never filled with this much venom. I know he's angry but hearing the disgust in his voice shatters something inside me.

"We've no money now," he continues, his voice raw with frustration. *Money.* The sole reason they kept me around this long. I knew that, everyone knew that. Now the money is disappearing.

"The rumours are getting worse, Éabha. Every day, they say you're the reason for the beast, for the curse on the land. No one will even look at me, let alone speak to me. People cross the street when they see me coming—because of you."

His words echo in my ears, and I swallow hard, the weight of his accusations crushing me. It's true. People avoid me now, like I carry some kind of sickness. When I walk through the village, heads turn away, and whispers follow me. No one talks to me, not even my grandparents anymore. It's as if I don't exist.

It started with words. At first, they called me names when I passed—the usual curses about witches. But the insults grew nastier, more vulgar, until it wasn't just words anymore.

"I am not this horrible witch," I whisper, more to the fading light than to him. My voice trembles, almost lost in the wind. "I didn't do any of this."

He stops, his back to me now, his shoulders slumped. For a brief moment, silence settles between us, thick and suffocating, the space too wide to bridge. Then, without another word, he storms back into the house, slamming the door behind him.

I'm left standing in the garden, alone under the twilight sky, the cold settling into my bones. My feet feel heavy as though rooted to the earth beneath me, but my mind is racing. The village blames me, and now my own grandfather looks at me like I'm a stranger—an enemy.

The weight of it all presses down on me, but I refuse to let it break me.

I glance up at the sky, the first stars appearing through the dusk. Somewhere out there, the truth is waiting for me. It has to be.

*

When the sun sets, casting the village into darkness, I make my way over to Ceira's. She is expecting me, I can see her dark shadow sitting by her window as I make my way down the path. The back door is unlocked, and I let myself in.

Ceira doesn't look up right away, her gaze lost in something in the shadows around us. The stillness in Ceira's home always feels awkward and unwelcoming. I try to ignore it as I sit down across from her, feeling the silence wrap around us, tighter with each passing second.

"My grandfather…" I begin, the words catching in my throat. "I've ruined everything. I'm worthless, and I've cursed our family." The admission feels like a stone in my chest, heavy and unmoving. "I don't know what to do, Ceira. If I leave, which I know I should, they will be persecuted. If I stay we will all be persecuted."

Ceira's eyes flicker toward me, and for a moment, her expression softens. But it's fleeting, more of a reflex than genuine empathy. She stands, grabbing a bottle of something from the table and pouring us both a glass of amber liquid. She hands it to me without a word.

75

"I'm sure he didn't mean it like that," she says, finally. Her voice is calm, and measured, but it doesn't reach me the way I need it to. "People are scared. They'll say things in fear they don't always believe."

I stare into the glass, the coolness of it doing little to ease the cold that has settled deep within me. "Maybe. But I've done nothing wrong, and still..."

Ceira shrugs slightly, moving to sit on the edge of the table. "They're small-minded. You know that. You taught me that."

We both drink. The liquid burns as it carves a path down my throat. I try to cough as I gasp a little trying to cool the ache. The silence slowly becomes comfortable as I lounge back into the seat allowing my drink to take affect.

"We can still train if you like?"

"Here?" I ask, unsure. "In your house?"

She nods. "Where no one can see. No one needs to know what we're doing. It'll be safer this way. At night, when the village is asleep. And you can replace it with swimming in the lough."

I want to feel comfort in her words, but they fall flat, distant. It's more a solution than solace, and I'm left feeling like nothing has really changed. My magic still needs an output. She still needs to breathe and feel free. Like when I swim. Still, I nod in agreement, because what else can I do?

"Alright," I say quietly, my voice barely above a whisper. "We'll train here."

Ceira smiles, though it doesn't quite reach her eyes.

I look down at my hands, at the fingers that still tremble from the harsh words my grandfather threw at me earlier. Deep down, I know Ceira is trying to help, trying to reassure me, but the hollow ache in my chest remains. I'm still alone in this—no amount of training will change that.

*

It has been weeks and the priests of Béal Feírste have yet to respond. It feels like time has slowed since I was summoned by Priest Dubhan. Like someone else has placed a spell on me, wanting me to suffer through the agony of not knowing. Not knowing if I would be allowed to live or if I should be executed.

My aunts and uncles visit a lot, providing support to their parents. Trying to appear united. They travel from neighbouring towns and villages. My eldest uncle and his family are visiting from Duiblinn, just south of where the King resides. His wife assures me that no one in the south has heard the rumours of me, yet. Although, my uncle says the king's guards have been sent on a special mission around Éire. He believes they are looking for me.

My grandfather believes the high priests of Béal Feírste are travelling to Cill O'Laoch, to see the beast in Cuan for themselves. It's half a day's ride on a horse at most. A full day, maybe if they are going by sea. Twenty days seems excessive.

I haven't been to the lough.

My magic cries out to me, yearning to be allowed within the freedom that the waters offer us. It pulls and tugs at my chest. I can feel it wrapping itself around my ribs, trying to claw its way to freedom.

I have no output for her. I can feel her now, clawing at the cage I have put her in, yearning to be let out. We can't risk it though. I cannot risk doing something silly, or noticeable, and my family being executed alongside me for it.

I visit with Ceira most nights. She has been training me, and I have been trying to dispel my magic through that. But the rage still bubbles inside me, encircling my heart and lighting a fire there.

Each night, I sneak out under the cover of darkness to her home, where no prying eyes can find us. Ceira's friendship has become a lifeline, a thin thread tethering me to the reality that I haven't completely lost control. She understands I need an outlet. Although she is still weary of power, I try not to use it around her.

At first, it was just lessons—small exercises meant to give me an outlet. But as the nights passed, it became more than just training. We've begun to share our fears, our worries. Ceira listens and helps me understand others' perspectives. Helps me feel part of this world.

"I don't know how you do it," she told me once, her voice low as we sat together by the hearth. "Keeping all that power inside you, hidden. If I had even a fraction of your magic, I'd probably go mad."

I force a smile, but the truth is, I already feel like I'm going mad. "I don't have a choice," I whisper back. "I have already made life, living here, so bad for my family. If I do anything else, even by accident, they could be executed alongside me."

Ceira frowns, her usual confidence flickering in the dim light, "I know it feels like you're alone in this, Éabha, but you're not. You have me."

Her words were a comfort, but even now, as I sit alone in the quiet of my room, I can't help but wonder if I'm truly safe.

With each day that passes, my magic feels more volatile, more uncontrollable. I fear the day will come when even Ceira's training won't be enough to hold it back.

Days have passed, and the house has grown eerily quiet. I spend my time by the window, waiting. Waiting for the high priests to summon me, waiting for the villagers to stop whispering behind my back, waiting for something—anything—to change. But nothing does.

It has been difficult, for everyone, this unfair ostracization from the community. My grandmother doesn't leave the house. My grandfather, wakes early, going from market to market trying to sell anything. Always coming home with everything he left with. We have started cutting down our fruit trees for the firewood.

The weight of it all presses heavily on me. Every day, I can feel the walls closing in, the silence growing louder. On the odd occasion I do leave my home during the day, the villagers won't look me in the eye, and when they do, their gazes are filled with something darker than disdain—something closer to hatred.

And yet, there's nothing I can do.

I watch helplessly as my family crumbles, my magic trapped inside, no longer able to bring life to anything. It's as though the whole village is waiting for us to fall apart.

But today, as the sun dips below the horizon, something feels off.

A crash sounds from outside, and before I can even stand, the front door slams open. My uncle rushes in, breathless, his face pale. Blood is splattered across his shirt and he rushes around, grabbing towels and other things as he does. He doesn't say anything as he rushes back outside, with my aunt, his wife, hurrying behind him with a bowl of water.

Panic rises in my chest. "What is it?" I demand, but before he can answer, I already know.

I feel him. My grandfather.

I push past them and down into the garden, where my worst fears are confirmed. Grandfather lies crumpled in the dirt, barely conscious, bruises are blooming across his arms. His head falls to the side and I can see the damage to his face. He can barely open his eyes they are so swollen and purple. Blood drips from his split lip, and his breath comes in ragged gasps.

"Who did this?" My voice shakes as I kneel beside him, my hands hovering over his injuries, terrified to touch him. He winces, trying to speak, but his words are lost in the shallow breaths he struggles to take. Instinctively I move my hands, resting them on his chest as my magic flutters to life, excited to get to work and sharing in my anxiety also.

My uncle grabs my arm. "Éabha, no, he doesn't want…"

I don't listen to him. I can hear my grandfather struggle for his next breath, the grass is stained with his blood and his heart rate is slowing. If I don't do anything now, we could lose him forever. Pulling my arm free I plant them firming on his chest.

My magic feels almost giddy. I concentrate on directing her into his body, allowing her to spread through him.

Closing my eyes I can almost see the internal damage done to him. Organs burst and bones broken, all bleeding into each other. The pain from him radiated into me. My hands begin to turn pink either through the blood coating them or my magic working harder I don't know. But I feel it—her—moving through me like a river untamed, winding its way into the cracks and crevices of his broken body.

She is a song, a melody of life, humming through my veins and into his. Each note mends a wound, stitches a tear, rebuilding him from the inside out. Where there is darkness, she brings light. Where there is death, she pulls him back toward life, weaving him together like threads of a tapestry, piece by delicate piece.

His heartbeat falters, and for a moment, my own stills with it. But then the rhythm returns, faint but steady, as if my magic is cradling it, coaxing it back.

Slowly the swelling around his eyes reduced. As he blinks them open the cuts on his face close over. The only evidence left from his assault is the blood which soils his skin, cloths and the earth around him.

"Who did this?" I demand again, louder this time, tears burning at the corners of my eyes. But no one answers me. The anger building inside me flares, burning through the helplessness and grief that have gripped me for days.

I stand, but my uncle steps in front of me, blocking my path. "No, Éabha. You can't go. You'll only make things worse."

"I'm not going to sit here while they destroy our family," I snap, trying to push past him, but he grabs me again, harder this time.

Something inside me snaps, a dam breaking under the weight of everything I've been forced to swallow. It's not just magic- it's raw, blistering rage that has been bubbling beneath the surface for days. It claws at my insides, begging for release, and when it finally erupts, it's like a storm breaking free from the skies.

My chest tightens with fury, and I can feel the heat rising throughout my body, like a wildfire spreading uncontrollably. The air around me crackles as my magic surges forward, no longer soft or careful. It's violent and wild, feeding off the anger festering in my heart.

I don't even see my uncle. All I can feel is the rage, like molten lava pouring from me. The fire I sometimes imagine in my chest moves to my fingertips. I can feel it roar to life as my uncle reaches to stop me again. Before I can pull it back, it slashes across his arm, the heat blinding, burning everything in its path.

His scream pierces through my haze of fury, but it barely registers. All I can feel is the unrelenting force of my magic, like a beast unleashed, taking everything with it. The flames scorch his skin, the smell of burning flesh making my stomach turn.

81

It dissolved as quickly as it appeared. My rage. Burning itself out as I look on at my casualty.

I try to say something, explain, apologise, but my words falter as I see the look in his eyes, a mixture of fear and pain. He staggers to his feet, holding up a hand to stop me from coming closer.

"I told you," He says through gritted teeth, "You can't go."

The magic still pulses beneath my skin, hot and angry, but I force it down, biting back the tears that threaten to spill over. I look back at my grandfather, lying motionless in the dirt.

"I'm sorry," I whisper, but the words feel empty. Because no matter what I do, it's never enough.

# Chapter Nine

The hospital is the last remaining place that makes orders with us. Mostly because we are now the cheapest vendor for miles around. The sick and dying don't care if a witch grew their vegetables.

Every other morning, I make the grim trek into the village. Leaving just before the sun begins to rise, I push the wheelbarrow up the hill. Onions, tomatoes and potatoes bounce around in sync with my squeaky wheel. At this time in the morning everyone is still in bed. I can sneak through the village unseen and work my way back home just as vendors start setting up.

I have returned to avoiding most people after my encounter with the elders. The outcome of their discussion with the elders from Béal Feírste is pending. I felt like I was finally finding myself, testing my powers, on a path of discovery. Ceira has helped me become a brighter person. And that has all been dimmed by fear of execution. Execution, my grandparents like to remind me, also includes them! The shame I feel for being me is overwhelming.

Just as I begin to think about my next steps, the how the where and the when. My wheelbarrow bounces off the stone steps of the hospital. I lift one crate out and begin to climb. It feels harder today like my body is weighed down with thoughts and anxiety. As I climb the steps with the final crate the anxiety appears, an icy chill down my spine. It almost feels like someone is looking at me from afar. Turning slightly, I see the sun's rays break through the rooftops and the distant sound of clatter and chatting as the marketplace opens. But there is no one around the hospital yet, to see me. Turning back, I continue up the steps and through the large oak door with its chipping blue paint.

I drop the crate beside the others with a crash, hopefully signalling to someone I am here and need paying. The hallway is dark and silent. The cracked beige tiles and blank walls welcome only the Goddess of Death. Listening harder there is not a sound in the whole building.  The silence rings in my ears as it bounces off the walls. Walking deeper into the hall, I try to find someone. Where are the people who run from room to room, pulling carts with unusual instruments, or people shouting for help or giving demands and instructions to others?

I get to a door leading into another room. An elderly man lies in the bed across from the door. The anxiety returns to my spine. I look back towards the main door, the sun casting a warm glow on the tiled floor. But no one is there. No one is on the stairs, down the other side of the hall or in the room. Apart from the old man.

I find myself walking towards him. The room is warm, heated by the remains of a smouldering fire in the ornate fireplace beside the man. The sun moves higher again and strings of yellow and white light strike through the bay window at the far end. Right beside two more empty beds.

Why is he on his own? His hair is grey, and his skin is so pale and fragile that it's almost see-through. Although he is covered with a blanket I could make our skeletal frame beneath, his ribs protruding out and his hands looked like there is no flesh covering them at all, just the bones connecting it to his wrist. I gasped stepping back as the man moved slightly.

"Get a hold of yourself Éabha, he's not dead," I mutter to myself as I give myself a little shake.

"But he will be soon." Jumping back, I turn to find the owner of the voice. A small nurse stands with a jug of water in one hand and towels in the other. She smiles slightly, as she moves around me to place the jug on a low table. Reaching over she pulls down the collar of the man's shirt and looks back at me. Her face now filled with worry, her eyes pleading with me to understand. I move closer to examine his neck. Right there on the side of his neck now exposed are two red dots.

I cover my mouth to keep in my gasp as I take a few steps back, knocking into the other bed as I do so. The nurse smile sweetly, but not reassuringly and begins to prepare a basin and towels around the man.

With my heart pounding I turn and leave as fast as I can. I can come back tomorrow for payment. There is no need for me to stay there any longer when they have patients who have...

"What were you doing in there?" *What is with these people creeping up behind me?* I turn round on my heels and come face to face with a large woman in a white starched dress and bonnet.

"Sorry, I was just looking for someone," walking backwards, I try to navigate my way to the door, towards my escape. "Just looking for someone to pay me? I left the veg and stuff by the door." She continues to follow me until there is nothing more than a step between us. My back hits the door frame.

She looks at me with her head slightly tilted, not saying anything just looking. It feels like she can see into my soul. And it burns. The security of the door frame holds onto my back. Although as she steps closer the security and comfort of a solid frame dwindles.

"I have your money." A brown envelope slowly creeps into view and pauses just between our noses. She doesn't smile, her eyes are just as blank as the nurses in the room. I attempt to snatch the envelope out of her grip and away from my face, but she holds onto it as it crumples around her fist. "That man," she gestures behind her with a head tilt, "His… injury stays within this hospital."

"Oh, I would never. I didn't mean to," I try to push myself deeper into the door frame. She just confirmed my fear. The only creature to create such a wound and leave a man on the brink of death like that. That man was fed from by a vampire.

"If anyone hears of this man or other patients, I will know it is you," She warns, moving closer if that is even possible.

"Other patients?" She hisses me to be quiet. "I won't talk," I whisper as I manage to slip my pay out of her grip and slide out between her and the door frame. At the top of the steps, I look behind me and watch her turn hurrying back inside.

Stumbling as if I have drunk too much, I land at the bottom of the steps in the market square. The ice-cold prickles tickle the back of my neck at the thought of more than one patient attacked by a vampire in there. I turn to look up at the large doors behind me, one remains open showing the dark shadowy hallway. Slowly I trail my eyes skywards, each window appears just as dark and lifeless as the man in the bottom room.

The unspoken rule of respecting boundary lines appears to have been crossed. With a crash of realisation; *They are coming*.

If they are not already here. Looking around, anyone could be a suspect. I pull my shawl closed, wrapping my arms around myself and begin to march home. To do what, I haven't decided- perhaps leave and let my family go on without me. Take my grandparents to safety? Even though there is no more safety outside of Cill O'Laoch.

I only make it a few steps before the shouting starts. With the sun fully risen the market square should be a hive of happy chatter, traders shouting and children running to the schoolhouse. But the happiness in the shouting is missing. Women are screaming and grabbing children, pulling them into the dark shadows between the buildings. The doors to the hospital and the elders' building are slammed shut with a very clear click of a lock going in place in both.

Large men in the king's guard uniform are pulling stalls down. Causing produce, spices, meats, clothes and more to fly across the square. Traders are begging for them to stop. Pulling at the arms of the guards, only to be shaken off or thrown to the ground as if a spec of dirt landed on their uniforms.

My spine is numb with ice-cold anxiety. I am frozen in place as people run around me, a ceramic bowl smashes at my feet and a woman even collides with me. "Éabha, you of all people should not be here, go!" She urges me as she pulls her baby into her arms and takes off towards the lough.

The guards, there must be about thirty in total. All tall and thick, sporting short hairstyles and the same navy blue military tunics, with gold buttons across the front and black cuffs around the wrists and neck. Black breeches and shiny boots complete the ensemble. If you lined them all up, I reckon it would be hard to tell them apart. All of them have another thing in common. One trait you may miss until it is too late. They are all vampires. Their strength and speed give it away. They are not just the king's men, his army. They are the king's guard.

I need to get out of here. Retreat to the safety of the shadows at least. I need to move but my feet won't let me. I am stuck in place, not breathing, watching this scene play out like I am at the theatre. My mind is screaming at me to flee, but that icy cold feeling in my spine wants to stay. It begins to move up over my shoulders as the shouting begins to subside and the remaining villagers are herded into a bundle around me. It moves over my shoulders and across my chest, morphing into a cool embrace. Encouraging me to stay and watch.

One of the guards steps forward raising his hands in a sort of surrender, but the smirk on his face says otherwise. He sports a red colour whereas the others are black, perhaps some higher-ranking officer?

"I apologise for the early morning interruption," He shouts walking towards us, everyone slowly steps closer together, like sheep facing a wolf, each afraid into stillness. "But we are looking for someone." He stalks his prey a little closer. The crowd goes silent, holding their breaths for his next words. *Looking for someone?* I can feel their eyes wanting to dart to me, wanting to hand me over, but being too afraid to move.

Behind him, his guards find a man hiding a woman under his flower stall. We hear him beg as two guards drag them both out into the open. The officer merely glances and continues to walk around our neatly formed circle of humans.

"I am sorry please let her go," the florist begs, tears streaming down his eyes. "Please, please, I will do anything." He begs. The woman screams, as her guard places his hands over each ear and, in a smooth motion twists, snapping her neck. She slumps to the ground, and I feel the last thump of her heart as she remains motionless on the ground.

"You bastards!" the florist screams, pulling himself to standing and struggling to get out of the guard's hold. The crowd around me slowly steps away from the scene, but my feet remain stuck in place. Almost like a rehearsed dance move the guard turns his back to the florist, whilst drawing his sword and sweeping it across the man's neck. With a little push, he lands right in front of the crowd. We all let out a loud gasp and everyone steps back further, only bringing me closer to the front. The florist clutches his throat and blood bubbles out around his fingers. His eyes are wide with shock and his slowly turns from pink to white. He starts to gurgle and choke on his own blood.

Through the painful sounds of the man's remaining minutes, the officer's voice rings out again. *Was he talking this whole time?* "There are rumours this witch lives within this village." He rounds the back of the crowd. I feel daggers on my skin from people's eyes. we all fear of how swiftly the guards can end our lives. We remain too terrified to look at the officer as he rounds the front again.

The florist on the ground in front begins to cough, blood splashes up and more seeps through his fingers creating a pool of deep red on the dirt floor. No one rushes to his aid to stem the bleeding. No one crouches down to reassure and soothe the dying man. All staring forward too cowardly to even look at him.

The blood darkens as it mixes with the dried dirt on the ground. The gleam of redness staining between the man's fingers slowly fades as it runs out of him. Turning to nothing as it mixes with the earth. My eyes are fixed on his wound. Where his hands still hold his neck, trembling now with loss of energy as he nears his death.

Suddenly I feel like I am underwater. Still able to see and feel around me but my ears can't reach the noises around me. The heartbeats of the villagers, their increased breaths, the steps of the officer as he circles us once more, or his booming voice as he antagonises us. All I can focus on is the man.

Slowly I lower myself onto my hunches and edge closer to him. No one notices, too transfixed on the officer's message. As my magic begins to flutter in my stomach and hands, I know what I need to do.

It's not my magic which drives me forward, it's the anger. The rage I have inside me is perpetuated by the audacity of the

King and his guards. The ancient promise to protect this human land, our last remaining holy place and the descendants of the lough, us, these villagers, has been broken. For what? Sport? To find a random and likely innocent witch to blame for something the King most likely caused.

"As we know, witches are dangerous." The officer comes back into focus slightly as I near the edge of the human forest around me. "They will steal your children, wipe your memories and prevent any crops from growing." My eyes follow him as he circles to my left and out of sight again. Someone moves slightly out of line, Ceira. Her eyes are wide with fear, glancing between the surrounding guards and myself. My only friend knows me better than I know myself as she shakes her head clearly mouthing "No".

My pull to the florist is unbearable as my magic begins to ache with need to mend, to fix and to grow. Gritting my teeth I crawl the short distance towards the man. The life in his eyes is draining, as they begin to turn grey with loss.

"This particular witch is cunning." The officer shouts from behind us. "She has integrated herself into your community with one goal in mind!" I don't pay attention to his words, they are lost on me as I focus on the blood in front of me, now soaking into my skirts.

I place a hand on his shoulder and allow myself to breathe. The blue begins to return to the man's eyes, as a tear escapes. "It's ok," I reassure him, "I am going to try to stop the bleeding." I strain against the urge to place my hands over the man and push to stop the blood. Instead, I shrug off my shawl and place it over the man's neck and chest. From beneath the shawl, I pull the man's hands away and replace them with my own.

A hand grabs onto my shoulder pulling me away, "Stop, leave him, he's already dead." Ceira begs me. I don't even bother to turn to look at her. I can't allow this man to bleed out in the street while these vampires stand and laugh at us. Other villagers begin to notice, I can feel their eyes burning into me. Their anger is palpable around me. The guards look, I can feel their Icey stares, but none make a move to stop me.

"She is powerful, the most powerful witch seen in decades. Her power can be felt from the capital." The officer rounds the back of our little circle, but nothing is stopping me now. I can feel the life returning to the man, as his wounds begin to bind themselves back together.

My shawl is soaked through, its woven fibres now sticky and congealed with blood. Again, Ceira pulls on my shoulder, with more force now, urging me to leave him "Éabha, please he's already dead" she whispers. My hands shake from the pain of my magic surging, trying to hold onto the man, to reach his soul and bring it back.

The other guards begin to notice, stepping closer to look. Simply seeing a human girl attempt to help a dead man. I feel them snigger and laugh with each other at what must look like a meek attempt at revival.

Closing my eyes, I sigh as the trickle of magic seeps from my hands and through the wound. His bleeding stops suddenly, mid flow, mid drip, it stops. I lean back slightly but my shawl follows me revealing the man's woundless neck. I hear Ceira gasp and fall back. Leaning forward, I cover my work with my blood-stained hands, trying not to draw attention to the slow changes in his presentation. The florist blinks, eyes widening, he slowly lifts his hand to my wrists attempting to pull them away, but I hold firm. Wanting the vampires to move on, to turn and look away so I can move him out of their sight and to safety.

"She has come to kill every last remaining mortal, and she will stop at nothing to ensure this!" The officer rounds the corner again and makes his way towards the front. Everyone sees what happened, the villagers begin to whisper and gasp in shock. Slowly all eyes land on me. I can hear their proclamations; *it's her, she's the witch you want, she's a demon, and a fae, it's her, take her!*

I hold my breath in an attempt to remain still. Irrationally believing if I move, the guards will notice me. Slowly a large shadow comes over me. *Don't look up, don't look up.* I plead with myself. The guard crouches down. *Don't look at him, don't make eye contact.* I can feel his icy stare, the heat from his body, I can almost hear him laughing at my fear freezing me to the spot.

"What is this?" says a deep voice with a foreign and unusual accent. *Don't look, don't answer, don't say anything.*

"The man, let me see his wounds." He commands.

"See what? It was just a little scratch, not deep enough to kill him!" *Yep, well done. What happened to saying nothing?* I look at him now. I am met with a large man-shaped shadow with broad shoulders. Although his features remain dark as the sun shines around him masking his front in a shadow, I can still make out his piercing golden eyes.

Everything else around us stops. The other guards all turn to us, the villagers move, encircling us closer trying to get a good view. I can feel them closing in, blocking out the light and looming over me. Panicked, I pull my shawl back over the wound, I know is no longer there. But the guard is faster and rips it from my grasp. I fall back as the mess of blood covering the florist is exposed. And right there in the centre of his neck is the receding slit from the sword wound, closing and sealing, leaving nothing but a line of wet blood.

I can hear my heart jumping against my ribs. My body heats, and with my hands on the ground, I force the heat into the earth to prevent any more accidents from highlighting to the king's guard, whose eyes are boring into me, that I am the witch. Beads of sweat drop down my brow as the guard crouches down, his eyes finally leaving me to observe the florist's neck. The florist also frozen with fear.

Slowly the guard returns his attention to me. My heart stops. But with a thud, I jump into my pleads "It was just a scratch, he wasn't even harmed, look it has healed as normal."

Now no longer a shadow I can make out his features. His dark hair with slight curls on top, straight nose and defined jawline. Cocking his head to the side he frowns, his eyes darkening. Keeping his eyes on me he slowly rises to his feet, simultaneously pulling out his sword and holding the point to my throat. We watch the wound close and disappear on the florist.

"What are you?" he asks, tilting his head slightly in the other direction as if to examine me from a different angle.

I look around at those in my peripheral vision. I see Ceira, stepping back into the crowd whilst others push forward to get a better look. Everyone is waiting patiently for my execution. For the declaration, they have waited on for so long. The vampire holding a sword under my chin tilts it further, making my head move up so I have no choice but to look him fully in the eye. I can feel the sweat drip down my back and my breathing changes. I feel like I am underwater again, this time trying to breathe and only sucking in salty water. I can't get enough air. With every gasp, I take the sword further into my skin, I can feel the slight puncture and warm blood coming to the surface.

"Tie her up." My capture commands, turning away whilst other guards close in. Hands land on me from behind, roughly they push me to my stomach. Dinally find my breath as I scream so loud, I'm sure my grandparents can hear me. Kicking my legs out behind me I thud them into whoever is on my back and feel

93

him fall over. Then someone grabs my shoulders as I begin to push myself off the ground. I twist until I face him, throwing my legs up over my head I knock him to the side. On my knees, I push up just as the tall vampire approaches again. I have no time to stand, no time to run or even scream. He raises the handle of his sword and brings it down my head. Darkness takes over my vision as I pass out.

# Chapter Ten

The rhythm of my throbbing head is beginning to make me feel nauseous. If I squeeze my eyes really tight, the pain moves to just above my eyebrows and is slightly more bearable. Quickly the memory of why my head hurts flashes through my mind. With a groan I focus on where I am- face down in the dirt. Hopefully still in the square. I try to pull my hands to my front so I can push myself up, but am met with the familiar fibrous spikes of rope around my wrists and ankles. Pushing through the pain I roll onto my back. Opening my eyes I am met with the sting of sunshine. I pull forward and sit up. The motion makes my head spin. I can feel dried crusty blood on my face. My hands are still stained red from the florists blood. I wonder if he is still alive. Stretching my legs out in front of me I assess for other injuries. My skirts have browned with the dried blood covering them, but thankfully my limbs are fine, if I can move my legs then I can run. I can still feel the tight hug of my dagger holder around my thigh.

As my eyes adjust to the light I take in my surroundings. The king's guards are lounging around, some are chatting, sitting, leaning on trees, some still have their full uniforms on whilst others have removed their tunics. Turning to my left are four other mortals tired up, all on their knees. Wet streaks mark their faces as if they had been crying. Crying in pain, mostly likely due to the puncher wounds noticeable on their necks and arms. They shuffle closer together noticing my gaze, like I am the villain here.

Beyond them are trees, we are surrounded by trees. *Shit.* We are in the Donard woods. Massive trees with trunks as wide as two men and swirling branches sweeping into the space between, twisting with each other and swooping down to the ground. This pattern of branches continues so high it blocks out all light from the sun. Why is there sun on my face?

Pushing myself onto my knees I examine the tree line. We are not in just any clearing. There were trees here, but they have been cut down. Stumps of the large Doire trees scatter the ground. Some of their trunks and branches even mark the edges of the clearing, stacked neatly with a layer of moss blanketing some areas. This is not a clearing in the woods. This is an arena.

Pushing my blood-matted hair off my face I look back at the group of villagers. They have given up, all slumped together with no hope of freedom. Have they not noticed where we are? Suddenly, the temperature drops. The hairs on my arms stand to attention. But no one seems to have noticed the change in atmosphere; they continue with their relaxing break, basking in the sunshine.

The other villagers are speckled with blood, but I am drenched. My heart beats fast inside my chest, I am surprised the vampires around me don't notice. I can smell the metallic tang of blood coating my clothes, hands and face. The smell starts to become stronger as I kneel in the middle of the arena like a beacon. A beacon in the middle of the Doire woods. Tears come to my eyes as I yet again realise my life is to end in the most brutal way.

We are always warned not to go into Donard forest. And most certainly not covered in blood. They can smell blood. Failinis can smell blood and enjoy playing with their food. They will rip us apart, strip our flesh from our bones and use our remains as toys, these were all stories told to me as a child.

Perhaps it is not true. Perhaps it was just a story to prevent little children from getting lost in the woods. Perhaps my grandparents enjoyed scaring us. Perhaps they are not so big. Perhaps we could fight them off. Perhaps it won't hurt.

A tear breaks free from my eye and trickles down my face. The salt taste awakens my survival instincts. "Why is everyone sitting around, we have to keep moving!" I scream trying to stand up, only to lose my balance and fall back down. I turn to the other villagers and beg, "Please get up, we need to run, they'll come for us, please look at me, let's go!" They don't even react. All are broken by their journey so far.

Pushing up onto my knees I turn to the guards, "Please, you're not safe either! They will rip you to pieces!" They ignore me, some glance in my direction, but no one reacts. "For fuck's sake, untie me, I am not dying in these woods! I will go with you, but we have to go please!"

The vampire, the shadow man, who commanded the others to tie me up, is leaning on a tree, a little distance away from the other guards, sharpening a branch into a spike with a dagger, his golden eyes glance over. Lifting his head he turns to the other guards, then back at me. With a sigh, he pushes off the tree and saunters over flipping his dagger between his fingers. Hot magic fuelled by anger suddenly returns to my body, but I try to push it down. Convincing myself I can save this rage for the fight to come.

The Shadow man stands over me saying nothing. Just looking at me. He has taken his tunic off revealing a cream shirt which is unlaced around the chest and sleeves rolled up. I take him in for a moment. I can see his muscles and veins tense and move in his arms as he twirls his dagger between his fingers. Over and under over and under. The movement has me almost hypnotised.

Pulling my eyes away from his dagger, I crane my neck up to his face and I fix onto his eyes. The gold shimmers in the sunlight, but that doesn't make them any less threatening. "Please" I almost moan. "The Failinis, they find it fun. Sport even. Not even you are safe." The heat in my chest intensifies, I lean to place my hands onto the solid ground to disperse it into the earth. The shadow man doesn't respond. He just looks at me, not blinking.

A snap from the tree line grabs everyone's attention. My vampire darts his gaze from me to the direction of the sound. His dagger held tight in his fist. The other guards stand, hands on the hilt of their swords ready for action.

"Please, I refuse to die without a chance." I hate myself for begging, but I square my shoulders and try to make myself taller whilst still on my knees "Please untie me!"

He looks back at me, his mouth sloping up on one side in a smile. The gold in his eyes shifts slightly as he looks me up and down.

"Sure," that is all he says as he pushes me back off my knees with the rope connecting my wrists to my ankles. Using his dagger, he cuts it and with a little shake my legs are released.

With my hands still tied together I stand, trying to keep my balance. Standing in front of him, I notice how tall he is. Staring forward, I take in his chest. Hairs speckle the triangle of exposed skin, his shirt sits loosely around him but as my eyes track up, I note how it tightens around his shoulders. His neck and chin have a layer of stubble, decorating his strong jaw. Following the line of his straight nose, I meet his eyes again. With a sudden gust, the heat in my body rushes to my face. It is not my angry rage, but something different. Embarrassment, I tell myself, from having to beg this disgusting creature for help.

I bring my wrists up in front of me, holding them out for him to cut free. He raises his eyebrows like he is shocked I would even ask for my hands to be released. He opens his mouth to say something, just at that moment another snap echoes around us, followed by a deathly silence. I turn slowly to face the tree line. Guards draw their swords and arrange themselves in a neat line around the clearing.

Strong hands grab onto my arms, as the golden-eyed vampire easily cuts through the ropes binding my wrists. He stands a step away from me, dagger sheathed on his hip as he too draws his sword. With a circular swing of his blade, he falls into position like the others. Ready for attack.

I pull my crusty skirts up, gathering them on my hip to retrieve my dagger. And take a similar stance as the guards. Golden Eyes turns to look at me, I can feel his eyes burning as they travel up and down my body. Turning my head slightly I meet his eyes. Pleased at the slight shock of his expression. He was not expecting me to be armed and ready to fight.

A few more beats of deadly silence is followed by a guttural growl. The Failinis creep from the darkness of the trees. Creatures I had only seen in drawings, stalk towards us. Their wolf-like bodies remained low to the ground as four legs jut up as they move into their arena.

Clouds cover the sun, casting us in grey light. Eight Failins in total, circle us. Red eyes fixed on each target as they drool in anticipation. As they creep closer, their true height is revealed, towering over the king's guards like fur-covered mountains.

Within seconds, they are pouncing forward diving onto the nearest guards. Their claws dig into their bones, ripping off their limbs and letting them fly off into the trees. Some guards further back have time to slash and stab the beasts were possible. The vampire beside me is gone. I watch him running forward to bring his sword down on the neck of a Failinis who had pinned a guard to the ground with a roar.

To the side I make eye contact with a Failinis, who wastes no time pounding forward. Instinctively, I dropped to the ground, forcing him to barrel over me. He skids to a stop, bearing his teeth, he growls at me, making the ground beneath us quake. He jumps again. This time I bring my blade up piercing his neck and into his mouth. The wolf cries out before his full weight lands on top of me. The air is knocked out of my lungs. I gasp as I struggle to push the brute off. I try to push him off. Lifting him mere millimetres before he crashes back down, heavier than before. Again and again, I push until my arms can't take it. Closing my eyes I need to focus. I need to channel my power, just like Ceira advised. Focusing on my arms, I imagine them growing in size, with new bulging muscles. My arms ache as I push. The pain so intense I scream. My scream giving me the force to flip the dog off me.

I don't have time to stop and get my breath back. Jumping to my feet I grab my dagger and run towards the others from the village. Only to find their shredded bodies and scattered limbs.

I catch a glimpse of Golden Eyes as he kicks a giant dog to the dirt. The turning with inhuman speed and sweeping his sword across the gut of another jumping to attack him from behind. The remaining guards are trying but despite their inhuman vampire strength and speed, they are no match for the Failinis.

Drips of water land on me. Looking up I expect to see the grey clouds about to burst with rain. Instead, I am greeted by the drooling snout of a Failinis. Saliva strings from between its teeth as a rumble sounds from his chest. I run. Darting between its legs I run for the tree line, aiming for refuge behind the logs. The ground is slick with blood and guts, causing me to slide and crash into an unexpected guard, just as he is about to slice through a Failinis' leg. The dog behind me is fast, turning on us in less than a second, his claws crush into the guard's skull, smashing his head into a flat oozing block.

Lifting his other paw, claws extended, he aims at me next. I gasp and roll onto my side protecting my head, but nothing follows me. Jumping back onto my feet, I grab the crushed guard's sword prepared to take my aim. But Golden Eyes has dealt with my assailant. I catch him as he turns to charge after the final dog.

Chasing after him, adrenaline and fear fuel my blood and propels me forward. He jumps, aiming for the beast's heart. The Failinis swipes his sword out of his hands with ease, causing him to land into a sort of roll beside the wolf. The Failinis eyes me running towards him with no plan of attack except to charge and stab. He roars, crouching down preparing himself to jump. But I am faster and jump first. Landing on his head I wrap my legs around his neck tight.

His howl shakes the arena as he thrashes his head from side to side in an attempt to throw me off. I lean forward and with my new sword cleanly cut along his throat. The beast screams in pain and drops to the ground. His blood spills over the dirt as I clamber onto my feet. The sword still in hand I plunge it into the creature's eye, with one last yelp he is gone.

Looking around all that is left is carnage. Body parts are strewn around blood soaking the ground. A mixture of mortal, vampire and Failinis parts scattered around including in the tree canopy.

Only one other person is standing. On the other side of the dead dog. Golden Eyes dusts himself off, not a drop of blood on his clothing at all. Pulling a hand through his dark curls he turns to look at me. His eyes cast over my body, at the shredded sleeve, the dirt and sweat that clings to me and the splatters of blood across my face. The gold in his eyes gleams slightly. Only for a second then it is gone.

Breathing deeply, as I trying to get my breath back, I watch him walk over to a fallen beast. He disappears from view returning holding my dagger. He turns it over in his hands, blood drips from its tip. As the sun breaks through the clouds the gems sparkle and dance. Pulling some clothing off a nearby arm he cleans off the blade. Extending his arm slightly he admirers my dagger in the sunlight, twisting it from left to right as the etching on the blade comes to life in the sun.

I am not sure what he sees in the blade, or what he thinks it is, but he gives me a confused look as he holsters it through his belt on his hip.

Ignoring me he turns towards the area where the guards where resting. Checking through some of the bags, he picks up two rucksacks. Stepping over body parts like it was nothing, he reaches around me and puts one on my back with a soft smile. "Right," he says frowning, then he bends down and grabs some rope off a random arm. Grabbing my arm then the other he holds them in on hand and ties them together with the other, forming a sort of lead.

"Think we better keep moving." With a judder from the rope, we start walking out of the clearing heading west.

# Chapter Eleven

We have been walking for hours. My feet hurt, my legs hurt, my head hurts, everything hurts. And I am cold but sweaty at the same time. My guard has a rhythmic march, even on the uneven forest ground. The beat is giving me a headache. Every time I stumble, or my pace slows, he tugs harder on my lead. I can feel the smile on his face, as I yelp, or stumble forward or trip over my own feet trying to keep up.

I think we have walked all the way through the forest of Delamont and Castlewellan. As the tree changes to towering evergreens, we begin to climb uphill. Rocks jut out of the ground, growing bigger. At times it seems there are paths but they do not last long, morphing into boulders and then dirt. Sometimes light escapes down through the branches casting strikes like lighting across our path. We are on the edge of the Mournes.

A while back, I tried to focus my energy on the rope around my wrists. I visualised it fraying slowly, smoking with each tiny snap. My magic even tingled a little in my fingertips. But all it got me was a tug on a rope as this beast of a man climbs over a boulder allowing me to walk right into it.

Vampires, so I have been told, are sensitive to changes. They can hear like the eagles in the sky, smell like the wolves and see better than any creature on this earth. I wonder if Golden Eyes, leading me by a rope, can sense my magic. Could he hear it spreading through my body, or tingling in my fingers? Could he smell when I warm with magical rage?

Looking around him, I see a clear path, I can close my eyes without risk of crashing. Focusing on the rope binding my wrists together. I can feel the fibres scratch my skin. Rubbing against my skin. Spiking my skin. I picture each little strand of fibre in my mind, slowly tweezing them apart. My hands warm slightly as my magic begins to take effect. But cools suddenly. I try again, concentrating harder, pulling tighter on the strands in my mind. But nothing happens, my energy is spent.

He turns slowly. His brows cast a shadow over his darkening eyes. He doesn't say anything, as his eyes travel down my body to my hands and back to my face. His piercing eyes bore into mine. They soften slightly and I catch the movement of gold flecks in his iris'. He doesn't look like he has spent most of the day walking miles through a never-ending forest. His skin isn't flushed, and his hair remains intact. Some purposely placed loose curls, fall down over his eyes. Suddenly I find myself imagining what he would look like a little bit dishevelled.

Using my lead he pulls me closer. Just three steps are all it takes until I am at eye level with his chest. The scent of fresh rain and oakwood envelopes me. Casting a spell of comfort. A spell, I can only assume is my own making. From memories or fresh mornings, post rainfall walks in the woods. For a fleeting moment, I allow my senses to surrender to chasing the reassurance his sent brings which clings to him like a whispered promise.

A rumble from his chest sounds as he growls, "What was that?"

My eyes dart up to his.

He bends down until his nose is a hair's width from mine. Baring his teeth he states, "Have I captured a witch who can't even escape a rope?" His eyes become molten flames as they bore into mine. Fear steals my voice. His fangs rest on his lower lip as a growl rumble in his chest once again. I can feel his breath on mine, hot and filled with fury.

He can feel it when I use my magic. But how? Can he smell the heat in my hands? Feel the change in the atmosphere? *Deep breaths and stand tall.*

"I can't believe I have the wrong fucking witch!" He growls into my face.

"So, if I am the wrong witch. Why am I still here?" I said whilst taking a step back for air.

"A witch is a witch. I am sure we can make use of you somehow."

For the briefest of seconds, my heart lit up with the hope of freedom. But the bleak reality, *a witch is a witch*, burnt it out. For hours and miles, I had been focused on my sore feet or hiding my power. When I should have been contemplating what awaits me. The Vampire King of Éire and the national hatred of witches. *A witch is a witch.*

Am I even a witch? Witches are described as cruel and dangerous. The ones I have met in the market hold very little power and resort to making and selling their potions and remedies. My only links to my father are my dreams, which really could be any man, and my mother's dagger, which could have been given to her by anyone.

I had not realised we started walking again. Or how long I have contemplated my doom or my heritage. I do not believe I am this almighty witch. How can I be? I am weak. I am worthless. I am nothing.

"What's your name?" I couldn't take the silence anymore. And it is most definitely my right to know the name of the man who has kidnapped me.

"Cian." That's all he says, doesn't even turn round.

"I'm Éabha." He doesn't respond.

"Is this how it's going to be, all the way to Duiblinn?" He doesn't respond. I need to get out of these ropes and away. Looking through the thick trees around us, I consider my options but am torn between logic and the need to just get away from the Golden Eyed Vampire.

The woods are a dark tangle of trees, fallen branches and rocks. With dark corners and ditches, I could hide in. *What else is hiding in the woods?* As if the trees could hear my thoughts, I catch them waving their branches at me, beckoning me closer into the dark. I swear I see them move, following us as we walked alongside them in silence.

My home also calls to me. But what is left for me there? The priests likely sighed with relief when I was taken, saving them the hassle of their own execution. My grandparents, are not free from the burden that I brought to them.

But staying with Cian means facing the King. Who would surely strike me down at first glance for the fun.

My magic flickers weakly beneath my skin, like a tiny hug of encouragement or recognition that she is still with me. I need to escape.

I can hear water, a trickling stream is nearby. The tinkling sound of water hitting and flowing over stones makes me smile. The smell of fresh greenery and flowers that grow near riverbeds attacks my senses, and I suddenly feel at ease.

Cian shows no signs of stopping. He keeps marching forward not even bothering to glance at the water. In protest, I slow my pace, sighing loudly to communicate my frustration. Either he didn't notice or didn't care as he kept on the same pace, not even bothering to glance back at me.

My legs hurt, more than before. Not just my muscles, who most certainly were not used to this amount of walking in a day. But the combination of dirt and hot sweat was causing them to burn. My wrists are sore from friction. Red and itchy. And my feet... the soles of my boots have thinned way down. I can feel each tiny rock and stick I step on. I am not sure how long these boots will last, especially if we are to walk all the way to the King in Duiblinn. I need to get out of here and back home, if home will even have me.

My mind wonders to my lough. How her cold waters soothed my sores, the currents pulling away the dirt on my body and massaging my aching muscles. I would never see my lake again. Never dive into the water through the forest of weeds and back to shore. Never hold my breath and allow my problems to float away like bubbles. Never feed off the magic she gifts to me. I will never go home. I will never feel at home.

I stop noticing the sounds of the water, the steady thump of Cian's boots on the hard ground or the smell of the forest around us. I become lost in memories of a home I didn't realise I loved or would miss so much.

Suddenly I find my face smashed into something soft and hard. Focusing my eyes, I find myself facing a cream tunic shirt, with laces undone exposing a hard smooth chest. Following the exposed fleshed up, I find Cian's stern face looked down at me, those golden disapproving eyes with spots of rich brown judging me. His eyes never leave mine as he pulls my wrists up between us. He pulls on the end of the rope, binding my hands together, untying the knot.

"You're covered in blood, wash yourself and we will rest here tonight." His voice is level and harsh as he drops the rope, my arms dropping with it.

"Rest?" I ask a little confused, I assumed he would march me to the King with haste.

"Rest." He responds pulling the pack off my back.

"Tonight?" I clarify.

"Tonight." He responds, dropping the bags by the smooth rocks to our side.

"Perhaps you are not understanding me. You wish to rest here tonight?"

"I do." He responds, walking away from me towards the water.

"You do?"

He turns to look at me then. And it's a look that says *Shut the Fuck up.* So, I do.

With a frown, he returns his attention to the water. The stream, I heard a while back, has grown into a river with slower-moving water. The space between the trees is narrow but enough to comfortably sit down on the mossy bank.

"Surely you wish to continue," I gesture in the general direction we were heading. Surely, after our meeting with the Filians he would want to continue. *But rest sounds good.*

"No, surely you wish to rest?" He responds, whilst scooping up some water with his hands and splashing it on his face and hair.

"Surely, as a vampire, you can just keep going." He stands, raking his fingers through his curls as he does. I see him stand normally but within a blink, he is right in front of me. Moving with inhuman speed.

"Ah, alas, here in lies the problem," He smiles, and for a moment I am blinded by it, until his face changes into something different, something new, something scary. "I am a vampire. But I am escorting a witch. A witch, who is in fact, no better than an average mortal."

*No better!? No better?!* I scream in my head. If I didn't feel so weak and tired I would show him what I can do. Why am I so insulted? This vampire has shown me nothing but his speed. If I concentrated, I could move just as fast. And if I couldn't, I would move the earth. Open the ground and watch him fall in. I want it so badly I can feel heat from my magic stir within me, as it readies to release.

Just as the land was about to rumble, Cian wakes me from my anger-fuelled stupor; "Wash, rest." With a hand between my shoulders, he pushes me towards the water. I turn to glare and notice his other hand on his chest, rubbing as if it hurts.

The moss on the riverbank is soft, sitting down I remove my boots and stretch my toes into the water. It tingles the skin between my toes, swirling around them and wrapping them in a cool embrace.

Reaching down to cup some water in my hands I splash it on my face, rubbing as much blood off as possible. I doubt I am making any sort of difference, I needed to scrub with soap. But it is so refreshing. I wipe blood and dirt from my arms. Pulling my skirts higher, I do the same to my legs.

Cian is filling up some canteens with water, one eye on me and another on his task.

I should escape. I should rest as he recommended and then escape. Hopefully by then I would have saved enough energy for my magic to help me.

My legs were sore and begging for the cold water. Pulling my skirts higher I move into the middle of the river, just far enough in for the water to come up to my knees. I see Cian move into my peripheral vision. I feel a little twinge to turn and look at him but fight against it. I know he thinks me weird or silly. He just stands on the water's edge and stares at me. I begin to splash water around my legs and thighs with one hand still holding my skirts. Movement catches my eye, making me stop. Cian moves back towards where he placed our bag by the trees. With a bit more privacy I slashed higher. Once satisfied and cooled I stand straight and stretch out my back and just allowed the water to flow past me. I can't help but smile.

She welcomes me, this river, like an old friend. She pushes at my shines and licks up to my knees. Like clear silk cloth falling over me. Lost in the feeling I drop my skirts and let this new friend swallow them. Pulling them down to the bed and back behind me.

I am startled by a grunting noise. Cian clears his throat, with a sparkle in his eyes and a smile on his face. Standing on the riverbank smirking at me. His eyes danced with amusement. He gestures with some folded fabric in his hands, placing it on a dry part of the ground before looking back at me.

"I will give you a bit longer to do... whatever that was. It'll be dark soon." And with that, he turns away, although looking over his shoulder after a few steps and smirks again. That sloping smile of his and dancing eyes is going to really get on my nerves. The faster I get out of here the better.

Getting out of the water, I use my skirts to dry off my legs. Cian has left a pair of trousers and a shirt just like his. Although not warm, it is dry and not blood-stained. The trousers just about covered my bum, and are ill-fitting in the front, but better than skirts.

A twig snapping in the trees close by grabs my attention. Looking through the tree line I see nothing but more trees in the darkness. At least I don't think I can see anything. I can feel my breath stop and my heart slow- anticipating another attack. The more I investigate the trees the more I think I see them moving.

Ice crawls down my spine as I sense something, someone, looking at me.

Cian comes marching into my view, carrying a large stack of logs. I had not noticed him leave. He side-eyes me with this awful lop-sided smirk of his as he walks past.

"What? Scared, little witch?" Cian asks with a tinge of amusement.

"Of you? No," I knew he meant whatever was out there. But I need to make it clear I am not afraid of him. Cian drops the logs beside an already neatly stacked pile of dried leaves and sticks. "Didn't know vampires feel the cold."

Moving closer to the pile, Cian hunched down close, he pulls out a metal block. With a twist of his wrist, it opens on the short side revealing a small spinner. He flicks it, making unusual clicking and grinding noises. Bringing the block closer down to the leaves he replies; "We don't." Sparks emerge from his gadget taking hold of the dried leaves beneath the sticks.

He was making a fire for me? Why would he do that? Vampires are ruthless and show no mercy. But this one is kind? He is concerned I may become cold?

The flames danced to life, casting a warm glow over the clearing. Cian stands, a smirk playing on his lips, and I can't shake the feeling that this facade of hospitality masks darker intentions. As he approaches me, holding a length of rope, I remember—I hated myself for forgetting—I am not a guest; I am a captive.

Pulling on the knot tight, Cian leads me over to a tree. Kicking the fallen pine needles and small rocks out of the way, he pushes me down and wraps the rope around the tree, leaving me there to tend to his fire.

We share the space in silence for some time. I watch his every move—how he walks around the fire with grace, how the fire reflects in his eyes and off his skin. He doesn't breathe much. I count them—every time his chest rose and fell, I counted. I had always thought vampires were like the dead—no heartbeat, not breathing. But he breathes. His heart must also beat.

The ground beneath me is hard and cold. My bum has gone numb, and my hands throb from the tight rope. Every time I try to move, to relieve some pressure from my back, the ropes tightened slightly. Every time the ropes tightened more; Cian smirks to himself. The dickhead and tied me in a constrictor knot.

After this marvellous (not really) realisation, I try to stay still. Fury burns inside me. Warming my chest and waking the last dregs of my magic. Yet it isn't enough to break free. I need to relax and calm my racing heart.

Closing my eyes, I take some slow deep breaths, letting the warm energy pool down my arms into my hands. I let my anger fuel me, as my eyes bored into Cian. Letting it swarm my blood and mix with my magic in the hope that I would regain enough strength to distract him and make my escape.

"What got you into being the king's errand boy then?" Distracting him with questioning seems like the easiest way to do this.

"I am not his errand boy," his tone was level. I thought that would have annoyed him.

"What are you then?" he answered with a look. A look that said, *do I give the obvious answer?*

My magic was growing stronger, I try to focus on the ropes binding my wrists. Closing my eyes again, I picture all the tiny frays of fabric within the rope. Picturing them being pulled soo tight they snap.

"Ok, what is your job then?" Almost a thousand little strings made up the rope, I need to snap each one, silently, and one at a time, to avoid Cian noticing.

"A witch catcher," he says tossing another piece of wood on the fire, it hisses and spits at him, as it catches fire. Turning he smirks, I am sure my face showed a mixed look of fury and shock. Of course, the King had a witch catcher!

"Not really," He muttered, "I am just an old guard." More of the strings and frays were snapping now. My hands were hot from the magic and power rushing through them.

"How old are you?" The frays were loosening, slowly.

"I don't count," he replied dismissively. "After some time, it becomes irrelevant."

"So, you're old old?" A frown creases his ancient features. I could move my wrists a little now.

He takes his time to respond. "Older than time," he murmurs, so quiet I think he hoped I wouldn't hear.

With a silent crack, my bonds snap away. My arms sigh in relief, as I try to hold the ropes in place. If I drop them and run now, Cian will catch me in seconds.

Sitting still on the hard ground, I try to channel my adrenaline into something more useful. I don't need to wait long for my magic to start bubbling inside. Focusing on the ground beneath me, I push it into the earth. Letting it spread and grow wherever it can reach.

I can feel it seeping and spreading out beneath me. I can feel it as wriggling through the root systems of the trees and shrubs around us. And I can feel it as it finds it chosen target.

A breeze flows through our little camp, threatening to put out the fire. Cian saunters over to his pile of logs, adding a few to the fire to keep it growing. Just as he stands looking into the growing flames, the roots of the tallest tree begin to snap. Pulling themselves free from the soil, they spring out of the earth. My magic keeps them silent as it coils itself around the tree's base, pulling and pushing.

I watch on, as Cian admires his fire, as the tree slowly makes its dents. It casts a shadow over Cian, distracting him from his fire. It feels like everything slows down. Yet Cian moves at normal speed. We watch the tree tipping towards us, the birds take flight as their resting place is disturbed. He doesn't move out of the way and simply watches the slow descent.

Turning to me, I catch a little gleam from his eyes. Before he turns back. Now time has resumed at normal speed. The tree is barrelling towards us, threatening to crush us. Or maybe just Cian who is yet to move out of the way.

None of this is my problem, as I seize the opportunity, dropping the ropes behind me, I flee into the darkening woods. I can't risk running uphill, or down so I just run straight. The trees begin to thicken, the ground becomes mossy and uneven with roots. The ancient, towering trees seemed to guard secrets as she ascended into their branches, seeking refuge in the maze of their intertwined limbs. I don't dare to see if he follows but I know he would, I can feel his eyes on me even now. I need to get off the path so he can't rack me.

Jumping for the nearest branch I am surprised at my strength as I haul myself up into the tree. Crawling along the branch gripping its bark tight I close my eyes. In my mind, I see a path made of tree branches forming a straight and unobstructed route through the forest. The adrenaline mixes with magic fuels my body with warm tingles. I slowly stand, trying to keep my balance, as the tree usher me forward. Just as I am preparing to leap onto the next branch in the neighbouring tree, it moves to me. Then the next moves and the next one. I keep running, a new force keeps me upright and balanced. It's the trees I tell myself as the branches form a road for my escape. The trees know now to fear and are aiding my escape.

The feeling of being hunted runs through me. Cian is tracking me. The cold sensation running down my spine makes me sweat from fear of being caught by him again. I hope the trees reform themselves into their usual positions and do not remain like an arrow pointing in my direction.

I cannot and will not be forced in front of the King just to be made an example of. I know in my heart I am not the witch they seek. I harness no such power to end lives, only to heal and grow. I had never the heart to even harm a person, not when I was made an example of in school, feared and whispered about within the village. Nor when my grandfather was tied up and beaten just for being my grandfather. No in those times I only held onto that anger, releasing it into my lake during my cool and lonely evenings.

The trees continue to move and flow as they form my path. Their general humming of encouragement propels me forward and far away from Cian. Their humming matches the rhythm of my leaps and steps through the canopy. I am so focused on the rhythm and my movement that I hardly notice when it changes.

The fae's battle song begins soft, like the breeze rustling through the trees. Then its rhythm changes, like the beating of a drum made of bone and leather, slowly joined by the piercing notes of flutes or pipes, almost mimicking the calls of wild animals.

It's a song meant to ignite fear, a reminder of the fae's ancient power. The haunting, lilting sound of the fae singing to their prey, signally to the forest that death is near.

I stop suddenly, branches form around me to prevent me from falling to the ground. The song's tempo increases, growing frantic as if feeding on the anticipation of the hunt, matching my growing panic. The trees continued to usher me forward, creating their path and waving their branches to beckon me onward. That ice-cold feeling in my spine freezes me to the spot. The song, the song of people's nightmares. The song that signals something terrible is beyond, and it is not Cian hunting me.

A branch above me shacks slightly, letting pine needles fall into my hair. Slowly I turn, looking up to find a tall slender man leaning down through the branches towards me.

His eyes, like glowing stars, stand out against his smooth pale skin, which shimmers, not quite human, too perfect, reflecting the cold light of the night. On top of his head, white hair is weaved into a crown.

I stop breathing as the fae cocks his head to the side studying me with beady white-blue eyes. That fear and panic that keeps me safe never arrives, I am stuck in place. Even the branches of the trees swap sides. They start wrapping their branches around my legs and waist, pulling me back into a bed of leaves and sticks. My unblinking eyes do not leave the man before me, his eyes narrowing into slits as he leans down closer to me.

The tree dips slightly as the man is joined by another, then a woman. My head shoots to both of them as they settle into the tree smiling at their friend. The new additions wear their hair down. Their dark curls bounce around their translucent, glittering skin. Yet all three wear very similar clothing of gold chest pieces, delicately shaped over the smooth curves and ridges of their bodies. It sits on their skin like water, making them look like statues. Rather than trained hunters.

Their bare arms, thighs, and waists are wrapped in intricate ribbons of silk or leather. Some ribbons are decorated with jewels others with sharp knives. I take note of each weapon they carry, five knives between them, a long sword, and two spears.

"What a strange creature you are," The first fae says surveying me closer.

"She is interesting," The other male says stooping closer and looking over his friend's shoulder. He comes down to my side. My body fights to get further back but a sylvan power keeps me still. He sniffs my neck bringing his face through my fallen hair. A wave of lavender envelopes me. Each of my muscles starts to relax with this soothing aroma. Clearly part of this fae's enthralling spells. I shake my body back into reality, ready to fight if needed.

"Is that Fae blood we smell?"

The female comes down now, sliding onto a branch nearest me, "Either Fae blood in her or on her."

All three suddenly look towards the direction I was running from. They freeze, only for a second. As if they should hear something I could not. Cian. I follow their eyes but see nothing except for the green darkness of the pine forest.

They look between each other, as if in silent conversation. The first man, the one with the hair crown, tilts his head, his eyes pierce into me. Slowly he leans through the branches to bring his face a whisper away from mine. Sniffing me just as dramatically as his friend. Again, I am enveloped by flowers, soothing my body back into a state of fabricated calmness.

"Based on the man that follows her, I think the Fae blood is in her," he straightens, relaxing back to where his friends sit within the tree.

With the alluring magic following him back, I begin to pull at the trees holding me still, they tighten and push me closer to the three fae. I try to shove my legs out try to get myself to drop so I can run. But the tree holds firm. The woman comes down, smiling at me, her green eyes twinkling in the darkness. Slowly a branch slithers around my shoulder and up to my forehead, pulling my head to the side. My tendons pull against the tree's force, but it holds firmly, I cannot move. She comes closer resting her head on my shoulder on the crook of my neck she breathes in deeply. With a sigh she rises, stroking my hair away from my face, and wiping the tears I did not notice had escaped. Her eyes were dancing with delight her smile bigger.

"She smells wrong though," her smile turns to a frown "Like salt water." Lifting one of slender fingers she smooths my eyebrow and scraps a nail down my cheek. With a sting that makes me hiss, yanking my head away only for the branches to tighten around my shoulder and head. A flash of darkness passes her eyes, her nails digging deeper into my face. I can hear my skin sizzle as her nails penetrate my skin, only slightly. Gritting my teeth I force myself not to scream.

"Let's take her home, see what she can do."

"Be careful sister," says the tall, crowed fae. His sister merely laughs, straightening she turns and leaps onto another tree running in the direction the tree was guiding me. With my head now released I was pushed into a standing position. The crowned one straightens also, cracks his neck to the right, then left and follows his sister.

The fae left behind smiles at me. Raising his hand, the tree branches holding me pull up at the same rate. He smiles bowing to me and gesturing in the direction his friends set off in. I tense my body to remain where it is. A power pulls me in the direction he gestures. My muscles shake with the force of the pull and eventually, they give up. I follow the fae along the tree.

# Chapter Twelve

The fae trio pranced and danced through the trees for what felt like hours, I relaxed into the pushing force of their magic which pulls me forward. Only for it to suddenly pull away. Along with the support from the trees. I land with a loud smack on the ground beneath. Bruising my hip on a rock. I scream out in pain, rolling off it and checking for broken bones.

Laughter fills the air as my captors glide to the floor like three swans landing on a lough. There are more than three of them now. Slowly more tall and slender figures talk towards where I lay. Some saunter out of the dark tree line, some swing down from the canopy as if from nowhere, and others stay in the trees.

Looking around me, is an intricate network of homes, muddled amongst the trees. The thick tree trunks and branches sprawl out like arms cradling the homes. Some were carved directly into the tree trunks, with balconies of twisted branches and vines covered in moss which glows bright green, illuminating the space around us. Rope bridges connect these elevated homes, swaying gently in the wind, creating a labyrinth of treetop pathways.

My three fae captors are not the only fae dressed in ribbons and gold. Tall slender fae began to encroach upon me, covered in the same uniform. Others dressed in robes remain in the trees. Their skin and eyes shimmer in the green darkness.

Now on my feet, I spin around looking for an escape. But they begin to close in. Their muscular bodies creating a wall, fencing me in and blocking my escape. Their eyes glinted with malice, faint whispers of magic crackling in the air. I can feel my own power flickering, barely a spark compared to the storm they brought with them.

One lunges at me, faster than I can react. I dodge him, but another grabs my wrist, twisting it hard. Pain shots through me like fire. I scream as a bone snaps with an echoing crack. My hand falls limp at my side, useless, while they circle closer, feeding on my weakness.

"Stay back!" I rasp, cradling my hand to my chest, trying to summon any trickle of magic to heal it. Nothing comes. The numbness begins to travel from my elbow to my fingers, but the pain remains.

A sharp laugh comes from behind me. A third fae shoves me forward, sending me crashing to my knees in the dirt. My broken wrist throbs, but something else catches my eye—a bracelet. Black plated string, wrapped tightly around the wrist of the fae closest to me, with a navy-blue stone gleaming in the moonlight. It pulsed, almost alive, as if it had its own heartbeat. My father's face flashes across my vision.

Another blow hits my shoulder, distracting my attention. The blow forces me into my back. Ethereal fae faces look down at me. Disgust plastered across their beautiful faces. My magic reacts, and a fire comes to life in my chest. It's weak though, flickering out just as quickly as it awakens.

A haunting melody slowly trickles through the air. One that makes your heart stop, and your brow sweat. A raven breaks through the trees, squawking to gain everyone's attention. On its descent, grey smoke leaks from the ground, blanketing everything in a thick haze.

As the mist dissipates, three figures materialised – one blonde, one brunette, and one with fiery red hair. Dark dresses with sheer skirts and bodices. Their skirts are made of stars, not embroidered stars. The light in the dark night sky has been captured and stitched into their skirts. I can feel their pulse of life calling out to me. As if they know me, are also part of me.

The women walk around the crowd of fae as the mist begins to clear. Silence captures the fae as the women push through the fence of fae around me. Their skirts brushing my legs and hands as they come close. Sparks of light singe my skin with the contact.

Heat fills my body. I was prepared and anticipating the ice cold of fear that holds me still, rendering my body and power useless again. But this heat was something new. Filling my stomach and head with anger. Anger I could not explain. These beautiful women looked more human than fae. And yet I hate them more than these creatures who should have retreated to the ground.

"What have you brought?" One of the mysterious figures demands.

"We have found a halfling, my queen. She smells like magic," A woman fae with a gold striped cloak declared, she sounds giddy with excitement, jumping towards the new women dressed in stars as if to present me to them.

The three newcomers close in, circling me like predators. I crawl to my feet as they continue to circle me, eying me up and down.

"Oh, sisters, look. Not quite a halfling," I spin round to face the woman who spoke- the blonde one. She smiles reaching out to grab a curl of my hair. Her fingers seem aged, whereas her face seems young. Untouched by time. Her hands are blemished with crooked fingers and sagging skin. I bat her hand away as another spoke behind me.

"Not a halfling at all." Declares the brunet. She stands closest to me. Her features become clear, and symmetrical features with eyes so clear they are almost grey. Identical to the others except for her hair colour. She rakes those eyes over me, making me squirm slightly, backing away from her stare. My stomach rumbles with uneasiness. I breathe in deeply, attempting to simmer it slightly.

"Who are you?"

In unison, they replied, "We are Morrigan."

"The Phantom Queen," I practically whisper. The heat turned to an icy chill with courses through me returning to the range. A growing rage, now I knew who I face.

"She knows of us!" The blonde whispers with a wide smile, making her eyes sparkle. The Phantom Queen. Each sister has a power. Not like my power, or the fae's or even the witches. Their powers are decisions. They decide, who dies, when then die, what happens to them and who lives- Death, Fate and Life.

Anyone who comes across her, either within her three forms or as a raven, does not live long enough to share their story. Yet I am not afraid of my end. I am infuriated at them. They have taken away our free will.

"Sisters, I think this is the part where we explain." The red-headed queen walks forward.

"I would prefer to watch her squirm a little more."

"Or make her work for it"

"Sisters.."

"Éabha." The brunette addresses me directly. Making me spin around to face her. "You were born from two extraordinary people. Of Éire and of the Gods." The fae return into the shadows. Perhaps allowing Morrigan space, perhaps giving themselves more space away from them. "You were born to create something new."

"Alongside someone, not so new."

"I would prefer if you found it out on your own"

"Any yet we have the opportunity to speed things along." They begin to bicker between themselves. Until the redhead walks past me, hands held in front of herself as if admiring the trees beyond. "It won't take long sisters, he is close."

"Close? Who are you talking about?" I ask spinning around trying to keep all three of them in sight. "What are you talking about?"

Without the need for gestures, the Morrigan impose a spell, restraining me and rendering me powerless. Their features clicker between scales and beauty as they look down at me. "No more games, Éabha. You have a task to complete, and we cannot help you with it."

The blonde one lights a boulder with ease. And with a smile, it crashed down on my head. The world around me blurs and darkness claims me.

*

The darkness subsides and my dream claws forward. I know this to be a dream, as I feel like I am floating. Like I am not in charge of my own body. Instinctively I flex my broken wrist, to find it fully mended. Relief brings calmness over my body, and I relax back into the cold ground beneath me.

The dream does not let me remain resting with my eyes closed for long. Hues of green slice through my eyelids, forcing them to open. My dreams always start the same, and this is no different. A battlefield forms around me. Everything is covered in thick wet mist. Flashes of light strike across the space, joined with balls of fire from all corners. Sounds of swords clashing together and screams fill the small clearing.

My father comes into view. Pleading with his kin. The armour which covers his chest is similar to that of the tribe I recently left. His bear arms, like theirs, are covered in ribbons or silk and leather. My eyes trace their way down his arms, to the black rope bracelet on his left wrist. My heart stops, and I stifle a gasp as I note the small navy-blue stone hanging from the plated rope. The similarities to the one that fae in reality cannot be a coincidence.

Just like all my other dreams; my father blocks a blow, turning to find a sword being pushed through his chest. I watch as it punctures his skin, breaks his ribs, slices his lungs and appears on his back. I can not move as his face pales and a woman cries out from above me. My feet are stuck firm to the earth, I am stuck and helpless amongst the carnage.

The battlefield fades into the mist as my father's body lies there, sword still sticking out of his chest. The light dims to a grey-green shadow. A stillness blankets the clearing. Usually, I move towards him, I try to help him, but my feet remain stuck in place.

A young man approaches my father's body. He wears the same gold plating on his chest and similar bindings on his arms and thighs. His hair is long and flowing down his back, dark with a curl—*the same as mine.*

He doesn't speak as he kneels beside my father. The air around us becomes quiet as he bows his head and places his hands on either side of the sword.

It feels like the trees around us are praying for the death of their fallen friend. I can feel slight whispering spreading through their roots beneath my feet. The young man is praying, I think, his lips are moving, but his voice is so low I cannot make out a word.

He reaches for my father's left arm. Removing the bracelet and placing it on his wrist.

Slowly as if the instrumentals are beginning a song, sound returns around us. Above me, I can hear a woman crying, begging to hold him. But I cannot see her, I cannot move to look up into the trees. No one seems to be consoling her, this woman who loved my father so much, she wails for him.

The young man says nothing, as he looks up at her from where he kneels. His eyes are red from tears, yet he does not make a sound. He looks around my father as if he is searching for something. Finally, he finds it, with a soft smile and pulls a dagger off my father's waist.

Standing the young man holds up the dagger, presenting it to the wailing woman. "He would want you to have this. He would want his baby to know he loved you."

I hold my breath as my hand instinctively reaching for my thigh—where the dagger should have been—but it was gone. Panic tightens in my chest.

The man extends my dagger, not to me, but to my mother, hidden amongst the weeping trees. Tears stream down her face as she reaches for it, her sorrow engulfing everything around her. My heart pounds in my ears.

Meanwhile, I could sense Cian—his presence distant, like a shadow misplaced in time, storing away my thoughts, my dagger, somewhere beyond my grasp.

And then it hits me, raw and undeniable, the scream tearing from my throat as the dream shattered around me.

# Chapter Thirteen

## Cian

Éabha has an intriguing scent. It stands out against the damp forest floor and evergreen trees. I follow the aroma of blooming wildflowers and salty frozen air. Her scent somewhat enchants a harmonious symphony that resonates with the magic I know she possesses.

I feel drumming in my chest as I catch another smell. An unwanted smell. Lavender. Stopping amongst the rocks and tree trunks, I cast my eyes from side to side and note the absence of any blooming flowers. All around me is hues of dark brown and spikes of pine trees. When there is no colour around and you smell lavender it's a dangerous thing. The Fae smell like lavender.

Relief and adrenaline course through my veins. I knew the Fae would find her, another collectable for them. But these Fae, the ones that reside hidden in the woods, jump from tree to tree, masking their scent in the damp earth. These are the Fae of the Danu tribe. These are the Fae that are protecting Her.

Drawing my sword, I continue on, as the smell of lavender becomes more intense. Twinkling lights in the distance draw my attention. Slowly I come to a stop. Crouching down I try to get a better look at the direction the lights are coming from. A hand lands on my shoulder halting my advance. I can sense five Fae behind me. Lesser Fae by the smell of them. I stand slowly turning to face a tall warrior Fae. Four more emerge from the darkness shrinking back at the sight of me.

The Fae know who I am. Even in the darkness of the damp forest. The lesser Fae warriors know they do not stand a chance against me.

The hand on my shoulder is strong and pushes me down. This one thinks he has a chance of becoming a legend I see.

But speed is not one of his skills, I note as I quickly swipe my sword up slicing right through his wrist and cutting off his hand. He doesn't scream as I expect, but staggers back to lean on his peers. All frozen in the shadows like wood carvings, still with wide eyes as blood spills down their friend. Slowly I cut them all down, without making a sound. No gasps or grunts as they work harder to take me down. The only evidence of the fight is the blood that decorates my face and sparkles on the forest floor.

My body is stiff. Taking a moment, I stretch my arms and back from the aches of a sudden fight. We have spent months travelling around the north of Éire searching for Éabha. I knew she would be in the last place we looked. I could sense us getting closer to her each day as we carved a path through the north coast and down to Cuan Lough. I had become lazy in my training, assuming we would find her and bring her back to the King dead or alive. Not anticipating I would be doing so alone, and this precious opportunity would arise.

Taking some time, I stretch my arms out to the side, moving my head from shoulder to shoulder and releasing a sigh at the sound of the satisfying clicks from my spine and tense shoulders.

The lights I saw before, begin to dance in front of me. I can sense Éabha just beyond them, although she is weak, she is the witch of the prophecy, and I can feel it. But the Danu tribe can't have her. The stress of having to escort her back to the King without a team of men watching, her weighs on my muscles which begin to pull again.

The trees around me begin to transform with lights dancing across them. Bushes, ivy and longer tree branches open and close in front of me, forming paths and dead ends, like a maze fencing me in. I can hear the Fae music from all directions. The twinkling stars and lights distract me from my goal. I feel drunk, staggering and using my sword as a walking aid. My mind is dizzy. This bloody maze is sending me round in circles and I can't find the energy to fight my way through it. The lights dance, the music twinkles and my path keep changing as the foliage either opens or blocks my progress. Protecting Éabha. I can feel they want her as much as I.

But it is not her I only desire, it is what she attracts. The phantom queen. Morrigan.

Continuing through this bizarre maze of light and foliage the songs of the Fae get louder. It dances from ear to ear, making me jump. But I am ready for any attack, ready to take down anyone or anything that stands in my way. I've waited for too long. Coming close only a handful of times. But I can feel it, this is my chance, this is the moment when I finally confront the Phantom Queen.

Just as that thought enters and leaves my mind, an image of Éabha is blasted into my sight. The Witch that is prophesized to end all. The witch who my King believes will be the ending of all vampires and his reign. The Witch that can harness the power of Éire, to change the world. The Witch with bright blue eyes, hair of the earth and fire in her heart. That fire burns inside me too. I can have them both, I can have Morrigan and the Witch.

Suddenly, I break through the magical barrier attacking my mind. In time to see Éabha pushed by a godly force, she lands on the ground in a heap and doesn't move. I feel a sting in my chest for the briefest of seconds. I'm not sure why, nor do I stop long enough to question it. But I note this strange occurrence and the fact that all my thoughts are stunted by the location of the force which attacked Éabha.

The Phantom Queen, in her three forms, is the source of the force. They speak in low voices before a rock appears. Seconds later that rock lands on Éabha's head.

I charge towards them, silently but with my sword in hand.

"Ah, the old one has joined us sisters!" One proclaims clapping her hands. I aim to cut through her with my sword, but she steps to the side. Without any speed, as if it is I who has slowed down.

"Oh, how fun, both in one place."

"Perhaps he is here to rescue her at last!" They all come together, clapping their hands with glee.

The high Fae dressed in their mystical robes which decorate them like bark and leaves and pine needles, begin to close in, ready to protect their Queens. I can feel the tingle of their powers coming to life as they begin to protect the Phantom Queens. But at a very slight signal, the Blonde Queen stops them.

With the Fae standing down. I continue my attack on the Queens. Jumping with my sword high slashing diagonally, attempting to chop the head of the nearest Queen, the brunette. It's almost like my eyes closed, or I blinked and as I landed expecting my sword to have sliced through her neck, only to find nothing there. Turning I find her scowling at me.

"Did we plan for him to be this strong sister?"

"No, I believe that was an accident."

I could see the ginger Queen creeping up beside me, through my peripheral. Swinging round, I lunge with my sword in both hands and thrust it into her stomach. Only for her to turn to smoke at impact and reappear just to my left.

"That was not nice, sir."

"I hope you don't treat other ladies this way."

Laughter and distant sarcastic whispers spread around me as the Fae note my growing failure. They have crept closer. Beginning to cast illusions of armed Fae soldiers, monsters and barriers amongst the smoke. I dive for each illusion, only to crash to the ground or fall through it coming face to face with one of her- the Phantom Queens forms. Their magic begins to crackle, with the strength required to keep me at bay. Each time I get close to one of Morrigan's forms, I hear the cracks of fire before I am pushed back.

The cracks begin to show as the Fae of the Danu tribe become more visible. My sword feels cold in my hands, its steel gleaming in the light of the illusions cast by the Fae. I slice through a foggy illusion of a Fae warrior before me, only to be met by a high Fae on the other side. He charges, with his long hair and cloak dancing behind him. As he nears, I drop to my knee and slice through his stomach with my raised sword. Glittering blood falls from the sky as his body lands in a heap behind me.

The smoke slowly fizzles away, and the illusions of monsters, beasts and warriors vanish leaving nothing but blank spaces. The group of Fae surrounding the Morrigan appear smaller, as if they too decided to vanish. I expected carnage, a battle, and shouting. But I am met with silence.

The silence I realise is for Éabha. She lays on the ground before me. In the darkness, I can only make out the outline of her lying on her side. Wet from the ground and seemingly asleep.

No one moves, even the air stays still. Everything must wait as I listen for any sign she is alive. Ignoring the sudden fear that she has fallen, and our venture ends here, she ends here, I continue to listen for what feels like a lifetime. *Thump Thump.* Her heart beats.

The earth lets out a sigh, or was that me?

Turning back in search of Morrigan I find the Fae closing in around The Phantom Queen once more. But the tug on my chest pulls me towards Éabha. I look between her and the Queen. As the pull intensifies. Bringing me to Éabha, to be with her.

"Sisters I think he feels it." The Blonde one steps forward.

"She is the daughter of Erin; she is who you truly need." Says the red-head. "Time needs her."

It feels like a spell has been cast, a damn opened, or a tie undone, as the Morrigan speaks. *She is who I truly need, who Time needs.* I take another step closer to Éabha's sleeping form. Only to be interrupted by a burst of blinding white light. A sharp pain radiates through my neck and across my head, as my knees connect with the hard ground, I let out a scream through my gritted teeth. Shockwaves of hot sharp pain run through my body. Gritting my teeth, I turn on my knees to find the source of the attack. Three tall high Fae stand meters from me their arms connected, shielding their kin.

I push my way back onto my feet, but my knees buckle, and I collapse, again I try and down I go. My sword clatters to the ground as I do. Screaming through the pain still cursing through my body, from the blow to my head, I get to my feet. As I steady myself, my eyes fix on the Phantom Queen. Just as she vanishes, one form at a time, into nothing.

Fury bubbles in my stomach as I charge towards the remaining figures. With no plan of attack and no sword, I aim to pull the Fae from limb to limb. But something stops me, pulling me backwards. Looking down, vines have sprouted from the earth beneath my feet, snaking up and wrapping around my legs. I claw and pull at them as they encircle me. Each attempt I make

132

to break free I am met with stubborn resistance. Finally, with brute force, I break free of one vine and another and another. As they fall from my body another one grows and forms a weave around me like a living prison.

I pull and strain against the vines, as they pull me to the ground. Around me, the Fae begin to disappear into nothing, along with any evidence they were here at all.

The vines, remain around me, hugging me, but no longer growing and constricting. I find myself standing alone in the now empty glade. The air heavy with magic. The lavender scent from the Fae slowly dissolves. Leaving me alone.

Shrugging off my prison made of plants, I collapse to the ground. The floral scents that float around me seem to have a calming effect. To prevent my anger from taking over I lay on the cold ground breathing. Breathing in, noticing how my chest expands. Holding it there, noticing the damp seeping through my shirt onto my skin, chilling it. Breathing out, noticing how my stomach collapses with it.

This routine has become an integral part of my life. Anger is a volatile force, capable of distorting time itself. The intensity of my rage can threaten to tear the fabric of the present, pulling me into fragments. To anchor myself, I focus on each breath as though it were a lifeline. In, and the world expands; out, and my fury begins to collapse, retreating into the background. Noticing all the sensations of my body reminds me that I am still here, still now, clinging to this moment.

I lay there, letting the damp earth soak me, threatening to freeze me. The heat from my body is stolen by the earth. I let her take it, let her cool me down.

For centuries I have tracked and planned ways of capturing Morrigan. Thought of wild and creative ways to make her answer for her sins; of what she did to us. Only a few times I have gotten close. Narrowly missing her by a whisper, until tonight.

Tonight was the first time I got close to capturing the Queen. Being that close to her, in all three of her forms, I cannot describe the feeling.

Turning my head, I find the bundle responsible for achieving this closeness to the Morrigan. Lying unconscious on her side. Éabha's heart rate varies like she's dreaming of something. She truly is the Witch we are seeking. Her magic drew out the Danu Tribe. Bringing the Phantom Queen down to meet her. Yet her magic is not quite what I expected. She is weakened by something.

Hopefully, she stays this way.

The red-haired Queen said Éabha is the daughter of Erin, and that Time needs her. I need her.

I know no Erin of importance. And our prophecy states a witch will destroy us. Destroy me. Why would I need her?

The Gaels; they have a way of always speaking in riddles, every word wrapped in layers you have to unravel.

# Chapter Fourteen

## Éabha

My scream gets lost in my throat as I scramble to sit up. Expecting to feel my mattress, pillow and blankets but I am met with hard, cold and damp ground. And then darkness. Slowly my eyes adjust to the dim lighting and the world begins to come back into focus.

I am sitting in a dark opening between the trees of the forest. A dull ache prickles its way down my left side, from my head, down my arm to my hip. Leaning back on my hands I gasp as the sharpness intensifies there. Holding my wrist to my chest, I nurse my injury as I try to piece together how I ended up here. The natural warmth of my magic cascades down my body pulling all physical pain away as it flows out and into the ground.

The last thing I remember is trees and... *The Phantom Queen.*

She was here with the fae. She said... they said...

The fae? In my dream, they looked just like my father. They dressed like him, walked like him, and talked like him. One even had the same bracelet as he wore in my dreams. Morrigan mentioned something about my parents. I can feel it in my memory, but I can't quite get to it.

Wait. Where did they go? The tribe were all here, living in the trees. I stand with ease, as my head and hip still throb. There is nothing there, no sign of anything ever having been in the trees. No evidence of them throwing me around. No footprints on the ground. They must be playing tricks, wishing to mess with me. *I could run*, the thought pops into my head. They may follow and bring me back. But, they might not.

"They are all gone." A voice cracks from the darkness. Turning, Cian slowly emerges from the darkness. Sitting on the ground. He is leaning back on his hands with his eyes closed as if he is soaking in the sunlight. Although the sun has long set and the moom cannot penetrate through the thick tree canopy.

Cian found me. Hopelessness swarms my heart, as I try to fight off tears. Cian found me. I have no hope of running from him again. If he can track me through the magic the fae leave in their wake. The protectiveness in which they shield the Phantom Queen. I have no chance of getting away from him.

He remains sitting though. Leaning back on his hands, basking in the darkness, with his eyes closed. Taking a few slow steps towards him, I notice he is breathing. Of course, he is breathing! I mean he is taking deep breaths. One breath in. Holding. And one breath out. "Are you ok?"

"Yes," he responds in an out breath, making no signs to move or open his eyes.

Perhaps he is so absorbed in his breathing that he won't notice if I leave. Instead of stepping towards him, I step to the side. Then I step again. And again.

All I do is blink and Cian appears right in front of me. His golden eyes, the only light source in the dark forest, burrow into me.

"Where are you going?" He whispers. He stands so close I can smell him. As he leans closer, the scent of damp earth and ancient trees surrounds me. It's the kind of smell that belongs to a place forgotten by time, a wildness that lingers long after he's gone, pulling at something deep within me, like a memory of simpler days.

I try to formulate a response when his hand comes to my chin, his rough fingers hold onto my smooth skin as he tilts my face up towards him. I am lost. Lost in his aroma, his touch and his eyes.

"They could still be out there waiting for you." He moves closer again, so close our bodies touch. My magic screams-reaching for him. A wave of current runs through my body, settling at each part our bodies touch. My heart is begging me to reach for him.

"What spell have you cast on me?" his hold on my chin hardens.

"A spell?" I whisper, "I have no idea what..." I go silent. My magic reacts to him, like she wants to wrap herself around him and hold him tight. Perhaps I have put a spell on him.

"This pull, I have felt for years." He releases me placing a hand on his heart as if it hurts. "It's you. It's you I have been feeling."

He reaches out as if to hold me, but I step back out of his grasp. "I have no idea what you're on about." We both stand in silence. He stares deep into my eyes as if he is searching for some kind of answer.

Ever since I was born my magic has been reaching out across Éire. The drenching, the leaders told me it covered the whole island by the time I was six. By the time I was a teen, it had crossed oceans. And now at the age of twenty-eight, I know, as I can feel her in the earth beneath me, my power has reached all the corners of the world. But I do not tell him this. I do not want to help him. I just want to be left alone.

*Born of Éire and the Gods.* That's what Morrigan had said.

A snap of a twig sounds meters from where we stand. Within a blink Cian is gone, leaving behind the sound of a growl that does not travel with him. A screech followed by whimpers comes from the same direction as the twig. I squint into the darkness trying to make out the source of the sound, or the direction Cian disappeared in. Slowly my eyes adjust. Cian stands between the pine trees holding half of a wolf in each hand. My breath, my voice, my scream all of it at once gets stuck in my throat- he just ripped a wolf in half for interrupting us.

My legs work faster than my brain as I take off running through the trees. I drive my legs further. Push them to move faster. Train my eyes to focus on the obstacles in front of me. My thighs start to burn, my lungs ache and my eyes water but I force myself further. Until one step, that's all it took, one step with not enough force, not enough propulsion, not enough drive, causes me to buckle over my ankle and fall. I crawl back onto my feet, prepared to run again, through the pain of a now throbbing ankle. Stopping for the briefest second as I notice the remains of a fire and bags resting by a tree.

"For fuck's sake," I scream into the air. I thought I had been running away, but I was running back, all this time. Back in the direction we came in, well at least it's downhill.

As soon as the comforting thought of heading back downhill slipped into my mind, I am slammed against a tree. Rough hands push my shoulders and back into the bark. Cian growls down at me, his eyes filled with fury. His hips press against my stomach so I can't move. I choke out a breath, unable to breathe from the pressure as he pushes into me.

He pulls back slightly as I scream, "Get off me!"

"Why, you like being chased, little witch? What's so fucking special about you, witch?" His hand comes up to my chin as he squeezes my cheeks, resting his forehead against mine. His breaths are haggard. I can feel his hot breath on me as he breathes in and out. He's trying to regain composure; I can feel him trying to steady himself. Adrenaline courses through me, as

138

the only thought I can focus on now, is why he is trying to control his breathing like this. My eyes drop to his mouth, his fangs pocking out slightly, resting on his lower lip.

"Why you," he growls.

I try to push him off me, try to move my head away but he holds me tighter, pushes me deeper into the tree. "A witch? A powerful witch that came from nowhere? What are you?" He screams at me.

I can't say it out loud. What I saw, what I felt, what I heard. I can't tell him or anyone what I truly am.

My eyes begin to cry as I fight to push him off me, it feels like he is crushing me. My ribs feel like they are about to give way as he changes his position. One arm across my neck and chest the other pinning my hip still.

"What are you? What makes you so special?" He spits. "Why did they let you go?" His fingers dig into my hip as my body sags from exhaustion. "What did they mean when she said I need you? Eh, Daughter of Erin? Why does Time need you?"

"I don't know what you're talking about," I gasp. I beg myself not to say anything, not to tell him.

"What are you!" His scream makes the whole mountain quake, pine needles fall around us as birds fly away from their beds. He screams again, pushing me into the tree, I scream with him. Pain radiates down my arm from my shoulder. With a popping sound coming some my arm, he pushes off me, causing me to fall to the ground, cradling my dislocated shoulder, my fingers slowly turning numb.

"I don't know! I don't know what I am," I cry.

He grabs me by my broken shoulder, pulling me up until we are face to face. "Why are they so interested in you?" I scream as the tendons in my shoulder and arm begin to snap with the force of his hold and the weight of my body pulling them down. Like strings on a guitar, I can feel each one pluck and snap.

"Please stop this," I sob, but I do not know if he can hear me through my tears.

He shakes my body as the muscles and tendons shatter, coiling back up to my neck. I scream as he tosses me to the ground like a rag. "What are you?!"

"I'm Fae!" I scream back, sitting up onto my knees I cradle my arm. The pain makes me double over. Tears and snot stick to my hair. I try to summon some magic, any magic to heal my shoulder. But I am too weak.

"I'm a fucking fairy." I cry to myself. My cry turns to a gentle sob as I nurse my arm, still folded over my knees. My sobs are all I can hear as I will my magic out of her hiding spot. I picture the bone in my mind and the shredded muscles around it. I imagine it moves back into its socket and the tendons and muscles greet it with an embracing hug. My fingers tingle, still a little numb. The pain turns to a dull ache. And finally, my shoulder is healed.

My sobbing softens as I am met by defining silence. He hasn't responded. I hope for a moment that he did not hear me through my screams and cries. As if he did hear me, he would learn what I have feared my whole life. What was only confirmed to me moments ago. I am a fairy. My father was a High Fae from the Danu Tribe. That is what my dreams have been telling me this whole time.

Looking up at him, I see him standing with his eyes closed, his chest rises and falls sharply. He's trying to control his breathing again. I copy him, trying to stop my tears and catch my breath. After a few moments I can tell his breathing is back to normal, he stands taller, taking his soldier's stance. Looking down at me he cocks his head to the side, smirking.

His hands land on me as he hauls me to my feet. "A fucking fairy," I hear him mutter, shaking his head. I don't know where they came from but I feel iron rings around my wrist, and hear them clicking together, I flinch at the weight of them, and the feeling of the cool metal on my hot and sweaty arms. "Does it hurt?" He asks.

"No," I whisper, it should though, even if my mother was human, my father is Fae, and iron is the only thing we know of that can stop them. It should still hurt me. I expected him to click the chains around my wrists tighter as a sign of who was in charge, but he doesn't. Instead, he comes behind me, and with one hand on my good shoulder, he directs me through the trees.

"Where are we going?" I whisper, my tears return, running down my cheeks, as defeat fills my heart and stomach with a sickening feeling of remorse and regret.

"To the king," He confirms.

"Why?" I ask, sluggishly. "I just told you I am not a witch. I can't be the witch you're looking for."

"No," his hand on my shoulder tightens, just a fraction, and then loosens, softer than before. "I think you're something more than that." His steps soften too, keeping me at arm's reach as he whispers; "I think you can solve a lot of our problems."

# Chapter Fifteen

## Eabha

My face is sticky with tears. My hair has fallen completely out of my braid now, I bet it looks wild. Wilder from Cian's point of view behind me. I lost my shawls somewhere along the way, possibly at the last camp or with the Danu Tribe. All I have is a thin shirt. It doesn't matter, the cold is a nice distraction.

I think a full day has gone by since I was taken. A full day with no food. The thought comes just as my stomach rumbles its angry complaint. But we keep walking. Cian's hand is still on my shoulder, keeping me at arm's reach. I barely notice the weight of him now. I wouldn't say I enjoy the comfort of his hand on my shoulder, however, it is the only sign I have he is still there. He makes no sound. Not a breath.

I feel broken.

I had thought about finding my father many times. As a child, I pictured him as a prince from a different land. An explorer who sailed off before I was born. Once even as one of the old Gods. But I have never considered he could be Fae. And from the most notorious of tribes, I have heard of. My magic makes sense now. My connection to the earth, her land and waters, it all makes sense.

But what does it mean for my future? The fairies were hunted, tortured, and forced to use their powers for whatever man wanted. Most of them fled underground. Leaving behind just a few. Am I to be hunted and tortured? Cian said I can solve their problems- am I now a tool? A resource the vampires can use to continue their crusades. The thought makes me sage slightly. Defeated.

My stomach growls louder echoing around our silent march through the mournes. "We'll find food soon, just walk a bit further." The sound of his voice causes me to jerk slightly. I don't respond to him; he doesn't deserve it. So, we keep walking in silence.

Eventually, we start to notice signs of life. First, a small brick building hidden in the trees. Although it appears abandoned, there is a defined trodden path leading to the front door. Then we find some cattle in a fenced pen, followed by chickens, and a large well. Slowly as the trees begin to thin a small village emerged.

Cian directs me off the path back into the dense forest. We skirt around the perimeter of the grey stone houses with moss-covered roofs. The smell of peat fires fills the air, with white smoke snaking up into the sky. Wildflowers decorate the paths around the houses, painting the village in splashes of pinks, blues and yellows. All leading to a large, tall structure further into the middle of the village.

Cian stops, pulling me back as he does. I stumble into his chest, he holds me there, hand still on my shoulder. We take in the scene in front of us for a moment. The tranquillity of the quaint village. At least I thought we were taking in the beautiful village hidden in the mountains. Until I notice the tension radiating off Cian. It seeps through him and around me, holding me by the neck, my pulse quickens. Cian must have noticed the change, his hand following the same path as the tension over my chest as he holds onto my opposite shoulder, almost hugging me from behind.

-

He sniffs, twice. "I am going to release you." He whispers, I can feel his warm breath by my ear. "I need you to stay with me, ok?"

I nod as he slowly let's go of me, he turns me to face him, and he smooths my hair away from my face. "Something is off," The iron cuffs unlock and fall to the ground with a silent click. "We just need to find some food and move on. Ok?" I nod again.

"We cannot draw any attention to us." He confirms as he collects my iron chains stuffing them into his bag. Standing he looks me over, then down at his uniform. His king's guard uniform.

Shrugging out of his tunic. Snapping off the gold buttons and with a quick pull, the red lining decoration comes off with a shriek. No more king's Guard. He pulls it over me, arranging it slightly so it sits neatly on my narrow shoulders. He fixes my hair again, pulling it behind my ears and smoothing it down my back. It's no use I think, if my grandmother cannot make it sit nice with a hot iron, this vampire has no chance.

"Where are we?" I ask as he fixes his hair, running his fingers through it and shaking out a few curls at the front.

"We are nowhere," He states pulling the bag back onto his back, "The people here," he gestures behind me making me turn to admire the cute little stone brick cottages, "There is something off. There's a smell."

I swirl around to respond, but he stops me, by placing his hand in mine. The warmth makes my hand tingle. The words I need to throw at his face get lost in the sensation of it.

"Regardless of the smell," He pulls me closer as if to shield me from something I cannot hear, "people here don't like people like me, and certainly not people like you, so we need to be discreet." He concludes.

We stick to the trees which form a border around the village until we find a wide cobblestone path, leading straight up to the village. The grey stone cottages are clustered closer together creating a circle around the tall structure right in the middle of the village. The structure is made up of a white block with a small wooden door. On top of it sits a tower, reaching almost as high as the trees. I expect there is a staircase leading all the way to the top, as up four little windows look out across the village. The whole structure is covered in an off-white plaster material. The whiteness of the building is blinding against the dark green forest and grey stone homes around it.

The whole place would have been tranquil. An idyllic little village nestled deep into one of the forests along the Mournes.

But the stench is something from another world. Gasping I am unable to breathe through my nose, only to regret taking in the air through my mouth, which tastes of rotten fruits mixed with bile. Not even the sleeve of Cian's tunic cannot keep the smell away from me. I try not to gag every time I breathe in the putrid odour.

Cian is struggling too. Although, he's trying not to show it. He coughs between periods of holding his breath.

And then we see them.

Not the sort of creatures you would expect to be living in cute tiny cottages. These were large, deformed, figures. From where we hide in the trees, I could only make out their shape. Their twisted forms are barely visible, but their silhouettes against the white clean buildings loom large and menacing. Some have limbs too long for their bodies, their skin like cracked stone.

One of them turns towards us. Its face distorted with exaggerated features—jagged teeth, crooked noses, and horns sprouting from misshapen heads.

146

Cian drops to the ground pulling me with him. I land with a grunt as my hands just about catch me before I hit my face on the rocks. His hand reaches over me pushing me down between my shoulders. My heart is hammering in my chest, trying to get out from the fright. Cian hears it, stroking my back, just once. I think he stops himself from doing more, but I still notice. I can feel the slight warmth from the path his hand took, down a little and back again.

"I don't think they saw us," his breath is hot on my cheek as he moves closer to me, "I need you to stay right here. Can you do that for me?" He kneels taking the bag off and looks around.

"What, you're gonna go in there?" I whisper, pushing myself up just a little higher.

"I don't know when we will next have the chance to steal some food."

"Please stay," he gestures at me like a dog, before turning to leave. "You can make a run for it, but between me and them, I don't think you'd get very far." He laughs to himself, as he stalks his way into the village. Eventually, I lose sight of him from my low level.

I stay crouched low in the tall grass. The cool earth beneath my palms grounds me as I listen to the silence of the still forest around me. The rustling leaves whisper above my head, as the silence becomes heavy as I wait.

Tension builds in my chest, threatening to choke my heart with every breath I take. Listening for footsteps, any sound that would break the stillness, but all that I am greeted with are the soft murmurs of the wind.

My magic begins to buzz in my fingertips. Like a little bee is stuck inside each one. I press my hands into the earth, offering the little bees an escape and letting the dampness of the soil creep through my skin. Calming any anxiety.

But my magic doesn't retreat into the earth as she usually does. She stays in my fingertips, slowly travelling to my heart and pulling at my chest. Closing my eyes I concentrate on the direction of the pull. Where is she wanting me to go?

A rustling sound draws me back. Freezing me in place until relief washes over me as I spy Cian again.

"Right let's go," Cian grabs me by my arm half dragging me back in the direction we came.

"Hey, I can walk on my own," I demand, pulling free before turning back to grab the bag before he has too far gone.

"Come one, we need to move faster now!" He grabs my hand pulling me closer to him. Heat radiates off him like the embers of a glowing fire. I wonder what happened to him in there, why is he so spooked? "We need to find somewhere safe to camp and rest."

*

Cian half ran half dragged me through the forest and mountains until he was satisfied, we were far enough away. He places me on a rock and put the iron cuffs back on, this time with a chain attaching it to a nearby tree. He seems frantic, pacing in front of me, not talking and every so often disappearing into the forest in the direction we came. He hasn't said anything since we ran from the village.

"Here." Cian thrusts a slice of bread with a chunk of butter and a flake of ham my way. I spread the butter out a little better using my fingers before eating it.

"Those... people, back there"

"Not people; trolls," he paces in front of me. A trail is starting to form along the line he marches up and down in.

"Ok, trolls. Why have they got you so... spooked?" he stops pacing turning to look at me. Noting my lack of food – which I inhaled- he begins to make another sort of sandwich for me.

"I'm not spooked. More worried." At least he's saying more words than the last time I asked him questions. He hands me the bread and ham as I stare back at him questioningly. "They don't like the Fae. I don't blame them either." I continue to stare, wanting more, with a sigh he continues; "Long before me, before time, the mortals chased the Fae underground. And the underground world is not pleasant. Some say the lack of sun drove the Fae mad. Others think it was a greater power. But regardless, the Fomorians were created from that madness." I listen to him tell his tail, while he assembles what was needed for a fire.

"The Fomorians wanted to live in the upper world. This world. But the Fae who remained hidden in this world, kept them from escaping. As did the high Fae of the underworld."

With a click of his device, there was fire. He pulls out two bedrolls attached to his bag and lays them on the ground on either side of the fire.

"But they found a way out through the mountains. The Fae were angry. But the Fomorians were hungry, for blood. There were battles, many battles with many lost. Even vampires got involved at one point, although we quickly regretted that." He pauses then, lost in thought. He was there I realise. He was part of the battles and had lost people. Cian sighs before continuing; "There has been relative peace for thousands of years now. But the Fomorians continue to brutalise any fairy they come across. Even those lucky to escape the underworld."

He turns to me now, coming up and crouching down so we are at eye level. His features have softened, and the worry is still there I can see it in his eyes. They dance in streeks of browns now, not specks of gold. "If they caught a whiff of you, know what you were, or could be, they would come for you." He explains.

"Would that be such a bad thing?" I whisper.

"Yes." He stands, tracing his steps back into the forest. Making sure we are not being tracked. This routine he has maintained since arriving at this rock. Why is he so worried, they want me dead surely it doesn't matter how or by whom?!

"What's the plan Cian?" I ask from my stone perch as he adds more large sticks to the fire. Breaking some against his thigh with ease.

"We continue on towards Warrenpoint, over to Carlingford and to the King at Mullach Íde Castle"

"Perfect you've got it all planned out!" I don't even know where we are in the Mournes, yet this man seems to know his way over the mountains, across the lough and down to Dubh Linn, the capital. "And when the King finds out I am not the witch from a prophecy you have yet to share with me?"

He pauses, with a stick half broken against his leg. He hasn't thought this through at all. All this time walking, marching, together, and he hasn't thought about what the King will say!

"What if you are?"

"Excuse me?"

"The prophecy is written in an old language." He pokes the fire with a long branch, "Maybe we translated it wrong."

"What?" I almost growl through gritted teeth. "Let me get this right. The formidable King of the Vampires, the conqueror of Éire, sent out a team of his best, and bravest, to track down and find a witch, matching a profile he wasn't absolutely sure was correct?"

"I know it's you," He declares, "I have felt you for the past twenty-eight years. I have felt every time you use your magic. I

150

watched your magic spread across the world. Tracked it actually. I know you are the witch who the prophecy is written about!"

"And what makes you so special?" I stand, pulling on my chain as I try to get closer to him, "Why can you feel my magic? How can you feel me when we only met two days ago!"

Birds fly from the trees as I scream at him. Chirping to each other in annoyance or perhaps warning others to avoid me. And so they should, because I am seething. I funnel my anger through my feet into the earth.

"Who are you Cian?" The grass around my feet begins to burn, browning and baking. All this time, all these two and throw conversations, yet I have no information, no answers. I am no clearer on what's going on than when I was taken from Cill O'Laoch. The mountain quakes from the pressure I funnel down into it.

Cian jumps, and within a blink, he grabs me, lifting me from the ground like a sack.

"Put me back down now!" I screech through gritted teeth.

"Only when you calm down." He looks up at me, his worried expression causing his forehead to crease.

"Calm down!" A chilly breeze whips around us, as the sky darkens. "How can I calm down when I feel so out of control?" I hate myself for not being strong enough to demand answers sooner. I hate myself for not trying to prove I am not the witch. I hate myself for blindly following this man who is inevitably my escort to my execution.

My execution. My next thought was to knee Cian in the chin so he would drop me, but the heavy load of *My Execution* came with a thud. The weight of it made my body go slack. Like everything fell out. My mind swirls. This was not the first time an execution was floated as an idea to control me. At least the elders of the village wished to put me to death, but I still had the freedom to flee, sort of. Now my freedom is gone. I am shackled to a tree. Possibly being tracked by mountain trolls and guarded by a vampire. Why am I only thinking about this now?

Cian must have felt the shift in my mood as he rests me gently back on my brown patch of ground. His hands remain on my hips, but I cannot feel them. "Are you ok?" a voice whispers, it's Cian, but I can't respond to it. It felt rhetorical anyway.

My fate is set. Just like everyone predicted. I am to be executed simply for being me. My life is worthless, I am worthless, I am hopeless, I will make nothing of myself. As I was born to be killed.

Cian looks to the sky as the starlings, float together morphing into shapes and swirls. They sing to each other, a harmonious bedtime tune, as they glide from one corner of the sky to the next.  As we watch the show the sky, the sun begins to set and a small slither of a moon becomes visible overhead. We must have been watching the birds dance for hours, yet it only felt like moments.

Cain moves towards me, still standing on my burnt ground. He clicks the chain off my cuffs, letting it fall to the ground. "Do you need to relieve yourself or anything?"

"No," I say, defeated

He sets me down on the ground by the fire. His large bag acts as a small back rest, a welcome comfort. The bedroll a warm hug to the back of my legs. I feel a cloak draped over my shoulders and Cian moves out of view.

"You might not know it now. Might not feel it. But you're dangerous Éabha." Cian walks around the fire getting into his bed on the ground.

"So dangerous you'd leave me here not chained up?"

"You're not dangerous to me," he murmurs nestling down into his camp.

152

"Who are you Cian?" I whisper as I copy him, lying down on the ground.

"Commander Conlon. Right-hand man to King Conor. Leader of the King's Guard and Commander of Éira's army."

"So you're like important." He doesn't respond. I roll to face him catching a glimpse of him as he folds his arms behind his head, using them as a makeshift pillow. Staring up to the sky, the reflection of the fire casts an orange glow on his face. I can only see the side of his face, but as he looks into the dark cloud-filled sky, he seems lost in thought.

"So how did you become the king's loyal servant? Did you kill your way to the top, or are you generally always this obedient?" He sighs through his nose closing his eyes, yet does not respond.

"I bet it's a fascinating story," sarcasm oozes out of me. "The hot vampire saves the King from the mountain trolls, and the Fae and the witches." I recite my story with zest. "Once he proved himself righteous the king sent him on a mission to recover the most feared witch of them all. Only to find out she's a worthless halfling, who was about to be run out of her village anyways." Resentment gurgles in my throat, leaving a sore and bitter taste.

"Enough, Éabha," He sighs from behind the fire. "Go to sleep."

"What about your family? Oh, I bet it's a fascinating story. Do tell." Although I lay on my back looking up as the clouds move around in the darkness, I can feel Cian clench his fists, trying hard to maintain composure.

"Enough, Éabha." Nerve found, now strike.

"Do you even have a family? Do vampires have parents? Or children of their own? Do you think they are proud of you? Assuming they're not still around,"

"Can you please just stop!" I turn around to shout back at him, but he is gone. His bedroll is a little tasselled and his sword lay to the side. There was no sign of Cian. He hasn't followed his path back towards the trolls. I can't hear him stomping his feet on the ground, or his frustrated sigh.

"Cian?" I call into the darkness, rendering no response. Not even a tweet from a bird or a scuttle from a rabbit. Vampires move fast, maybe he just ran, he'll come back.

"I am assuming you need some head space, so I will leave you to it," I reassured myself mostly, with a soft voice, hoping his vampire hearing would pick up on my calmness. "I will just go to sleep, I promise I won't ask any more questions and I will be quiet."

I manage to shuffle down into my makeshift bed. Pulling the cloak tight around me and hugging my legs to my chest to keep warm. The fire crackles and hisses, but around me is silent. I did not hear if Cian returned to our minicamp. Perhaps he crept back to his bed silently hoping not to disturb me in case I had lied and did have more questions for him. Finally, exhaustion overtook me and fell asleep.

# Chapter Sixteen

## Cian

"Fuck," I crash land on hard ground. Usually, my arrivals are better planned and it is more like taking a step. But when my journeys are fuelled by emotion- in this case exhaustion and frustration, they are a bit bumpy. Part of me wants to lay on the cold, wet ground and hope I return to the present. But anything could be wandering around hungry or ready for a fight. Looking around, I don't think I have gone far. Perhaps even in the same part of the Mournes. I haven't gone forward then. When am I?

The village we passed was not far away. If it is still there, I can perhaps work out how far back I have gone. And hope there is no Fomorians lurking around.

Zigzagging my way towards where I think the cottages are, were, will be, I find a small dirt trail leading deeper into the thick pine forest. There is nothing notably strange about this little trail, which disappears after a short while, into the darkness, but I get a strange sense of familiarity with it. So I follow it.

The trees thicken and the little light provided vanishes. Along with the trail. My memory feels foggy, I can picture myself here. Myself and my brothers. When we were younger, a lot younger. I just can't quite focus on the picture long enough before my memory fades, taking it with it.

Ahead of me I see the light of a fire. First it is a small orange dot floating in the trees, then it slowly grows into a crackling blaze. Three figures stand around the fire. Women, I note, in long gowns. Confused, I slow and drop to a crawl. Why would women be out in the mountains at night dressed for a ball? In my crouched stance, I manoeuvre myself closer and into some bushes for cover.

That's when I see them. Morrigan, in her three forms. The memory comes flooding back of the first night we met them. We were hunting in the Mournes, and came across three beautiful women; one blonde, one brunette, and one with fiery red hair. They invited us to drink with them by their fire.

All three wore the same gown, yet we never thought that was unusual. Dark dresses with sheer skirts and bodices. Their skirts were made of stars, like light in the dark night sky had been captured and stitched into their skirts.

I can feel their pulse of life calling out to me, even now as I look on. The stars are calling to me, begging me to take them home.

Morrigan moves around their little camp. As they move out of my way, I can make out three men lying on the ground. I know these men, I know this scene, my two brothers and me. I freeze dropping to the ground. On my stomach, I can peer through the roots of a bush and just about make out my brother's bodies.

This was the night we woke to be the monsters they created. When we lost everything.

I lay frozen to the ground. I have tried time and time again but have always been unable to return to this night, this event. I want to stop it, perhaps that's why I can't go back. Eventually, I gave up trying. Embraced who I am and forgot my old life.

For a brief second, I think about getting up, taking them by surprise, and cutting them into six equal parts. Until I realise, my brothers lay motionless on the ground. The deed is done.

"Sister, if all three slumber, which is our Chronos?" I hear the angelic voice. The voice that used to haunt my dreams.

"Should we wait until they wake?" Their skirts, flow over our bodies as they walk around.

156

"We will know with time sisters!" One sits down next to my brother. I hold my breath, an automatic fear reaction, I note. Fear, I don't usually feel.

"Should we explain? He needs to know why. He has an important role."

"No," the authoritarian of the three commands. "We have not chosen a girl yet- what is the point?" Her voice now reassuring.

"It needs to happen naturally, they will meet," Another skirt joins the one on the floor. Together they smooth my brother's hair, and fix his clothes slightly.

"What if they wake and are...something different?"

"It is a chance we take sister." They all stand. Moving out of my view. Their skirts skimming over my body laying peacefully by the fire.

"What if something goes wrong and they end up not meeting?" They sound further away now; I chance a peak over the hedge.

"It has been written! They will meet." The blonde sister announces, causing her sisters to step back slightly. "Father Time will meet Mother Nature, and they will restore the world to glory."

Father Time and who? I have no time to contemplate this statement as they all move back towards us. One standing at the feet of each resting figure on the ground.

"He will travel to many times in his long life. He will understand his role and he will wait for her." The ginger sighs, peacefully admiring my brother before her.

They say no more to each other. With a sweep of mist and magic, the ginger sister pushes herself into her blonde sister, the brunette following on the other side. The remaining third of the queen stands smiling down at my brothers and me. Grey mist creeps up her legs, wrapping around her arms like it's dressing her. Her shape changes to that of a crow, which takes off into the sky. I stand, my fear being replaced by anger, and I breathe through it, just like I have mastered.

*Breathe in, hold, breathe out.*

The fire is still warm, and my brother's whiskey remains by his legs. I take a swig, allowing the liquor to burn my throat as a swallow. We look like we are asleep. I always assumed they did something more brutal to us, distorted and violated our bodies in some way. But they just put us to sleep. We look happy and peaceful. Although we are now all frozen in time, Cillian somehow looks more youthful and Connor, well Connor always looked old. I smirk, we were always best friends growing up, following each other everywhere. Connor joined the king's army, and we followed. I got a wife and Cillian needed one too. We did everything together. Apparently, that included turning into vampires.

But I am more than a vampire. What was it they said? "Father Time will meet Mother Nature, and they will restore the world to glory. He will travel to many times, and he will wait for her." What does this mean?

My brothers do not hold the same power I have. Cannot move between past, present and future. They cannot create as I have created. Cannot manipulate and twist as I can. I have infected and diseased so many people.

Surely if Father Time is me, then Mother Nature must be…

Éabha is the Witch set to destroy us. That is what we have read. That is what the prophecy says.

"Unless destroying us means restoring glory?" I whisper to my past self, lying on the cold ground.

My heart aches. It pulls towards her, as it has done since she was born. Pulling me towards this path to find her. I need to return to her.

# Chapter Seventeen

## Éabha

The fire is still going, I could hear it crackle and hiss. Until a slight breeze blows it out completely. The cold air runs through me, weeding its way under my light clothes. Pulling the cloak closer didn't help, as it isn't big enough to cover my whole body. Cian had yet to return, I glance over to his abandoned bed every so often, just to check. I hope he is in the trees, creating distance, watching me. But I can't feel him watching me. He must be in the forest, being stubborn and waiting it out until dawn.

When you stare at something for long enough it almost looks like it moves, even though it's staying still. I stare into the forest, at its tall trees, the low hanging branches, the roots creating tiny mountains in the ground. The trees look like they are moving towards me, growing thicker with each step. When I squint my eyes, I can almost make out the shape of people. But it must be the branches creating weird shapes in the shadows.

When I relax my eyes, I see nothing but darkness or darker darkness. I squint again and see them. They move slowly, keeping to the shadows of the night, in the blackness of the forest. Six in total, I count them as their forms began to appear amongst the trees in front of me.

Ice chill runs down my back making me sweat. It freezes me to the spot. It must be trees, and I am overtired; I try to convince myself. But a voice in my head is screaming at me to run. The rest of the world is so quiet and at peace, why would I run when there is no danger?

Sitting up on my knees, the damp earth seeps through my trousers staining my knees cold. The six trees that look like people have grown in size, like they have gotten closer. I hold onto a nearby tree for stability. Its rough bark digs into the palm of my hand as my grip tightens. Slowly, I blink, and eyes appear. A pair at a time. Blink and another appears. Until there are six pairs of white eyes staring at me through the darkness.

My magic burns, I can hear the wood of the tree on my hands sizzle, but I don't let go, afraid if I let go, I will fall. Cian will come back now. He will rush in and attack, cutting them down one or two at a time. So, I wait. I wait for my executioner to come and rescue me from the darkness.

More time passes as the figures inch closer with every blink of my eye.

And still, I cannot move. The hot rage of my magic churns inside me, whilst the ice cold of fear sticks me so I cannot move. *Run Run Run*, I scream at my feet. But I don't move.

Before I can figure out how to get out. I blink again and they are feet from me. Another blink and they are surrounding me. Their heads tilt to the side slightly simultaneously, taking me in. Pale skin stretches over thin delicate bones, giving them an almost ethereal fragility. Their heads are completely bald, the fire light bounces off them.

But their eyes. They are haunting. The whites glow with an unsettling luminescence, casting soft light onto their hollow, expressionless faces.

These creatures, not quite Fae not quite human, move in unison, their bare feet gliding across the ground without a sound.

A hand comes down over my mouth and I scream, but it is lost in the thick darkness. I am pulled against the owner of the hand as another's arms come around my chest holding me still.

Their skin is so cold it almost feels wet against my clothing. I begin to twist and kick, managing to yank the hand away from my mouth, screaming "Cain!". It echoes through the trees, but no one comes in response.

My heart beats like the deep beat of a drum calling people to war. Two new people grab an arm each and hold them out like I am a cross. Their cold, slimy skin coats mine as I continue to kick and twist away from them. I feel my feet connect with something firm, a head I hope, but no sound comes in response to my attacks.

I can feel their magic as they move, like the bubbles just under the surface of nearly boiled water. In a blink, we are within the forest, another blink and we are in the village. I try to drag my feet, to slow their movements, but with every blink we get closer to the tall tower in the centre of the village. They begin to march, the ones carrying me move in sync following the one in front.

Others join our parade. Fomorians line the cobbled stone path. All lining the street in an unusual silence.

A white stone altar sits below the tall tower. Its clean smooth surface glistening in the dark, almost like it glows. This is their destination.

The hand leaves my mouth allowing me to breathe deeply. Whilst the other four held out my limbs to each corner of the altar. Lowering me down slowly. I feel the unforgiving bite of ice-cold stone along my back. Frantically, I pull each limb free only for it to be captured and held down again.

Tears blur my vision, but I refuse to let them fall. I try to pull my head up to look around for any help or escape. Seeing nothing but the same figures, all dressed the same with the same sombre expressions. My breaths become ragged gasps, as I choke in air, my chest heaving as I fight with the rising tide of panic.

The darkness closes in around me. As these expressionless blurs of people look down at me. *Give up*, my mind whispers to me. I can't. I need to get back to Cian. My heart pulls and screams for me to fight. I can't die like this. I want to fight. I want to live. I want to find the prophecy, my legacy, my father. I need to keep going to finish my story.

The quiet defiance that always burns within me now blazes like a beacon in the night. Summoning every last remaining bit of strength, I begin to twist and kick again, this time getting loose.

Jumping to my feet on the altar, the people step back in shock whilst the Fomorians step forward in defence. Yet no one makes a move towards me. Three beats of my heart were all it took for me to spot the best route through the crowd and into the trees where I could hide.

Jumping down to the hard ground. Cold, wet hands reach out for me, but I am too quick. The adrenaline courses through my body as I run towards the first gap in the crowd, but it was quickly closed off by more people. Turning left I spy another gap and leap for it, only to crash into a body at the last second. They are closing me in, creating a fence around me and the altar. Hurding me back towards it.

Pushing at their dense bodies, I try to break through, only managing to push my arm between two bodies. They come in closer together, I scream, as the force of two people pushes my arm almost crushing it. Pulling my arm back, I try to run at them. Hitting them at the seam where one person meets another. They don't move to stop me, they don't look like they even care or feel me as I crash into them, only to bounce back off. The stone of the alter hits the small of my back, as they step closer again. Climbing onto the altar I can no longer see the buildings of the village or the trees of the forest. All I see is darkness. The darkness is working to their advantage, blocking my escape.

I am left with only one plan... I dive right over their heads and forget to plan for my landing. I fall onto my hands, my wrist giving way. The sharp pain spikes through my bones rushing its way up my arm. Quickly, I scramble to my feet and run in the direction I believe the forest is. Holding my wrist tight to my chest I can feel the hammering of my heart and the ragged sound of my breaths.

It was almost like they allowed me a taste of freedom. They don't shout after me or even move towards me as I run for the forest. But as soon as the tree line comes into focus, I am grabbed from behind and lifted off the ground. A Fomorian lifts me with ease. Its thick muscles and lumpy grey arms wrap around my waist, tucking me under his arm and carrying me back to the altar.

"Please stop this, let me go please!" I beg, thrusting from side to side to try to get away. Unsuccessfully. My tears fall from my eyes. "Put. Me. Down!" I scream.

It only takes a few steps for the troll to bring me to the altar. And this time it is prepared for me.

The rings that decorating the sides, now had ropes looped through them. They take a limb each and tie thick rope around my ankles and wrists, securing me to the table so I cannot move. I can't stop my tears as they stream down my face, the salty water stings my lips as I plead with them to let me go. "Please don't do this, please let me go, *Please!*".

A deep hum builds. Coming from the back of the crowd. It grows deeper and louder as it ripples through the mass towards me. Slowly words begin to form. I recognise some words, but I don't know how. The sounds become clearer and clearer. The crowd is chanting. Using the ancient language of the first Gods.

"Don bhandia, scaraimid cumhacht, Ina dorchadas, brisimid an teaghrán." They call out to the beat. The rhythm matches my heart as my mind translates; *For the goddess, power we sever, In his darkness, break the tether.*

My powers were simmering the louder they chant, bubbling at the back of my throat and sizzling on my palms. This tingle and warmth travel up my arms to my heart, red-hot anger fuelling it. The chanting gets louder and louder as I get hotter and hotter. Fear usually turns me cold, but this hotness only comes with anger.

"Please stop!" I scream, but it is only heard in my head. I try to breathe deeply, as the fire in my soul churns a path of destruction trying to find a way out. Just as I saw Cian, breathe in, hold, breathe out. But I can't get enough air in. I gulp trying to find the air around me, but the heat evaporates it before it can reach my lungs.

The chant continues, following the rhythm of my rapid heart. It's a spell, I realise, their chanting is manipulating my emotions.

*For the goddess, power we sever, In his darkness, break the tether.*

Laughter begins to flood out of me. It ripples down my ribs pulling at my muscles. "Please, don't do this. You have to stop." My body quakes as the ripped turn to waves flowing through my body. The movement only make the ropes pull tighter, constricting me further. My laughter floats louder than their chant, but they continue.

*For the goddess, power we sever, In his darkness, break the tether.*

They are sacrificing me to a Goddess? I laugh at the irony of this. I laugh because I know in my heart, I have nothing left, nothing to live for, nothing to return to. I laugh because the voice in my head wants to let them sacrifice me. The sain part of me wants to let them, just to prove I am not the witch everyone believes me to be.

I can feel the inferno in my chest. Ripping at my ribs and tearing through my lungs. They have summoned a rage. My laughter dies down as my ribs crack from the heat. It feels like my skin is being torn apart. "Stop! Please stop this!" I scream, but the words are lost in the painful shrieks to follow. My ribs are breaking apart down the centre of my chest. I can hear them snapping, feel popping and cracking all the way down to my sternum. Sweat drips into my eyes as I scream out in agony, pulling at the ropes which only pulls my arms and legs down tighter.

The chanting slows to a stop. Taking my pain and the inferno inside me away with it. The silence feels thick, almost tangible in the air. Hooded figures step towards the altar.

Their eyes set deep in their hollow sockets, they glow with an unsettling luminescence, casting soft light onto their hollow, expressionless faces. One on each side of me, and the final at my head. I can see their pale faces framed with the dark shadows beneath their hoods.

From within their hollow sleeve, each pulls a long knife. They twinkle in the night, reflecting off light that doesn't exist. Their handles are made of worn wood, whilst their sharp slender blades appear new, sharp and polished.

Although the pain from the fire in my chest retreated, I can still feel it's flames. They lick at my skin, tickle my damaged ribs, trying to weasel their way out. I breathe in deep through my nose, making the flames relax slightly. And I realise; they may have brought on this inferno inside me and awakened the flames I tried to keep at bay. But they only listen to me. The flames flicker in response. Stroking along my heart, in a seductive reassurance.

They raise their blades above me. One at my throat, another at my stomach, and the third above my heart. I close my eyes, as they call to each other; "For the goddess, we sever power."

"From head to heart, to stomach," My power, the flames, beg me to let them out. Let them dance freely over these people who want to destroy us.

"In his darkness, we break the tether."

The flames consume me, flooding my body and I cannot contain them anymore. I smile up at the man as his knife descends on my throat. A flicker of shock in his eyes is my response. My flames smile back at me readying themselves.

The flames flow into my veins, I can see them glow through my skin. They surge through each vein and artery, lighting up my body into a beacon. The men stop, their blades almost touching me, as they note the light pouring off me. For this briefest of moments, I feel relaxed. I feel at home within my own body. I feel good.

Closing my eyes, I sigh. The ropes tying me down begin to smoke, then sizzle, and finally, they snap off, falling to the ground. The blades stay still, millimetres from their puncher sights. They don't know what to do. They thought they were in control. Thought I was weak. Thought I was worthless. But they awakened something in me. Something I have been pushing down for years. And now we want to be free. I push my feet up and flat on the alter, using it as leverage along with my hips I pulled myself up into a crouching position. The hooded men with knives, reach to grab me, grabbing onto my clothing and pulling me back down.

The crowd begin to chant again. In an attempt to slow me down.

But it is too late, they have brought forth the fire and only I can control it. I stand on the altar, pushing my shoulders back and looking around. The Fomorians have pushed through the crowd their grey muscles and arms bulging, their misshaped heads standing out high above the rest.  There were now several knives pointed at me. More people have stepped forward from the crowd to join the original hooded three. They move closer pointing their blades at my legs, ankles, and knees. The Fomorians are tall enough to reach my chest and head.

They swipe and stab, but I can see all the movements happening before they make contact with me. Dodging their attacks from the top of the altar. I fear if they cut my skin, the fire will seep out. Which I want, but I want to control it first.

"Stop!" I scream, but they do not. With a frustrated scream, I clench my fists. That is all it takes. The three men with knives drop back, clutching their heads and screaming in pain. Some fall to their knees, others lay on their sides. Slowly others in the crowd begin to fall from the same affliction. Three beats of my heart is all it takes before the whole village is screaming in pain.

They start to crawl towards me, reaching out as they scream. Blood oozes from their ears, painting their face in vibrant reds. Clenching my fists tighter I try to stop them, trying to do more of whatever I just did. But it doesn't work, and they come closer, reaching up to me on the altar. Their screams echo through my mind reverberating between my ears and making me dizzy.

Some of them manage to climb onto the edge of the altar. Reaching for me, grabbing at my trouser leg, trying to pull me down to them. I flick them off, kicking them in the face, they fall back, landing on another behind them.

169

The flames inside, flicker in response, pleading with me to release them. But I don't know how.

Someone grabs hold of my ankle from behind me. They aren't strong enough to pull me down but their nails dig into my flesh as they try to anchor themselves there. I reach to them to push them off, but this is the last straw for the flames, as they waited so patiently my whole life. Fire erupts from my hand and attacks the person holding my ankle. He bursts into flames, letting go of me instantly, his screams are muffled by the roars of the fire that consumes him. Like a wave, the villagers and Fomorians catch fire, one after the other.

I can't see their faces, but I can hear their screams. They gurgle as the fire catches hold of their throats. Emitting a smell of crisping flesh, like a burnt animal carcass.

They stop reaching for me. Instead turning to each other, seeking support, help, possibly even to say goodbye. As we recognise at the same time, these villagers, these creatures, are dying. Dying by my hands.

Taking a step back, I reach the edge of the altar. I am killing all these people. The shock loads my body down in an overwhelming crushing pressure on my chest. I throw my hands out again trying to recall the fire, trying to stop it before everyone dies, but it doesn't listen to me.

"Stop, stop, stop," I beg my magic to calm down. To burn out. To finish.

I can't breathe, the smoke from the flames begins to suffocate me.

From beyond the fire, I see others rushing out to help, but as they get closer, they too catch fire. Women and children, run to their loved ones, only to meet the same fate. Death by fire. Death by me.

As more arrive to help, the fire reacts. Creating a circle around me, around the altar. Covering everyone and protecting me. I can feel its pride, pride in my ability, pride of my strength. But I do not feel strong, I feel weak, weak for not being brave enough to fight long ago, weak for killing innocent people.

# Chapter Eighteen

## Cian

I am prepared for my return this time, landing on my feet beside my bedroll. My eyes go straight to Éabha. But she's gone. Her cloak lays in a pile on the ground. The fire is out and stone cold. *How long have I been gone?*

Then I hear screaming. It's faint but it sounds like she's in pain. I take off running in its direction.

The screams of agony get louder and louder like it is coming from more than one person. Reaching the village, I can see fire everywhere. And there in the centre of it is Éabha. She's standing on an altar surrounded by lumps of moving red-hot flames. People are lying on the ground either dead, writhing in pain or crawling towards her.

"Stop, stop, stop!" she screams.

I stop.

Éabha stands on her white stone altar. Her long hair falling around her, almost as dark as the shadows behind her. Her eyes gleaming in the darkness, and specs of fire reflect off them like the night sky. She looks furious, murderous even, as she controls the fire, making it do her bidding. She doesn't shake, doesn't sweat or quiver in any way as she controls the fire. Creating a protective circle around her.

I don't know what Mother Nature is supposed to be. Or even if she is linked to the witch I am hunting. But I know in this moment that she must be Éabha. Éabha has to be something more, as she stands there with the grace and power of a Goddess.

The fire slowly dissolves leaving Éabha standing alone and depleted on the alter. Tears fall from her wide eyes as she looks around the carnage of dead bodies. I don't even notice myself moving towards her, but something pulls me. A primal urge to protect her, to hold her. Éabha looks up as I approach, a flash of panic appears on her face, until she finally recognises me. She takes a deep breath like she's sucking her power back inside.

"I didn't kill them," She whimpers. "I don't think I did. I just... I don't know what I did," she trails off as I reach the altar. Crushing the burnt remains of whoever is beneath me I silently nod, holding out my hand to help her down.

"Eve," I whisper to her, as she places her hands on my shoulders, allowing me to softly lift her back onto the ground.

She looks up at me through her wet thick lashes. Her blue eyes glow in the dark light, reflecting off the last of the flames flickering around us. I can feel the power flowing through her. Ripping through her hands.

"I didn't know where you went. I turned around and you were gone. I tried to escape; I thought I could run," she rambles.

Without looking away. I stepped closer to her, until her chest presses against my body. I don't know what she sees when she looks into my eyes, but she frowns. Slowly a trickle of something hot and sweet flows from her heart to where we touch. I don't think she feels it. But I do.

"They said... they were singing," she trails off again, not finishing the sentence. That little pulse of power begins to get fainter and fainter, and I begin to wonder if I imagined it. Tears appear in her eyes, and she suddenly looks scared. Scared of who she is and what she's done. She wasn't aware of how strong her power was until now. She truly didn't know.

"It's ok," I reach to her pulling her head to my chest and holding her close for a second. How could I kill her? But also, how can I keep her safe? Her body turns from hot to cold as I release her. "Come on, let's keep moving." I turn still holding her and walk us towards the forest again.

It was like Éabha was in a dream as we began to walk out of the village, not going back to our belongings but towards the King. I have no idea who she is, what she is or how she is connected to Morrigan. But I am more determined than ever to find out.

# Chapter Nineteen

## Éabha

He didn't tie me up this time, the chains forgotten somewhere in the wild forest. But he keeps his hand in mine.

Soon the sun begins to rise. The muted colours of the forest were left behind as we broke free into the wild plains of the mountains. The wildness pushes and pulls me along the mountain rock paths. My legs and brain refuse to communicate with one another, making the hike challenging and slow.

The untamed wilderness of the mountains is breathtaking, however, lost on me as I need to focus on keeping on foot in front of another. The earth is wet, from the soft peat, making the ground feel like a sponge one moment, then hard as rock the next. The scent of heather and wild thyme, was sort of calming, allowing me to focus on the journey and not on myself.

We begin to ascend rocky paths, keeping the ancient Mourne Wall to our right, for shelter from the determined winds. The terrain becomes a mixture of steep granite slopes and green and gold hills. Now and then we pass craggy outcrops providing shelter for sheep, who bleep and flee at our approach. Small mountain pools reflect the sky like a mirror, or when the wind caught it, the waters danced like a dress in the wind.

Halfway down the side of a mountain, I stop, my legs no longer having the strength to continue.

For three days I have been walking with Cian. Three days filled with violence. And now on this day, all that echoes around my mind was the chant that caused my power to explode out of me. Decimating an entire village.

*Don bhandia, scaraimid cumhacht, Ina dorchadas, brisimid an teaghrán.*

*For the goddess, power we sever, In his darkness, break the tether.*

Cian said I was dangerous, and I fear he might be right.

But I can also do so much good with my magic. I can heal with just a touch and spread goodness throughout the soil. If I hadn't pushed it down all these years, I would be practised in using it. I would know the extent of my magic and could control it. I could bring life back to the lands and destroy all the creatures who threaten the lives of the mortals. I could be their saviour.

Those creatures, not quite humans not quite Fae. They needed me dead so much that they called for the Fomorians. Mountain trolls. To come to their aid.

Cian tugs on my hand, urging me to continue. But my body refuses to move forward.

"I can't do this anymore," My muscles were aching from walking, bending over I rub my calves, but this did nothing to soothe the burn within them. "I'm sorry, but my feet hurt, I have blisters. I am filthy, I haven't washed in days. I smell bad. My hair is so greasy it has changed colour!" I miss my home, I wanted to cry, I miss my bed and my bath and my clothes. I yearned for the comforts taken from me.

All this time I avoided looking at him. Expecting to feel his frustration with my minor problems in comparison to the catastrophe I had created back in the forest. When I do look up at him, he stands gracefully in his shirt, trousers and shiny boots. Not a wrinkle in his clothing, not a trace of dirt. My eyes travel the length of his body, and I wish that I hadn't, because his face, is sculpted and clean, with only a trace of some stubble. His hair remains neatly placed, some curls purposefully falling forward whilst the others remain obedient on top of his head.

"And you!" I shout, "You look like you have just stepped out of a portrait! Like we haven't been walking and sleeping in the forest for days!" He looks down at himself, and smirks.

"Please," I beg, "I know we need to get to the King so he can kill me, or whatever he wants to do." I don't finish my request. As I catch a glimpse of something in Cian's face, something close to remorse or embarrassment. It's fleeting, gone before I get a chance to fully register the look.

Cian looks around. The rocks form steps leading down the mountain, we can see them turn into a stone path. The gradient levels out slightly as it makes its way back down into the trees again.

"Caisleán Ruaidhrí," He whispers, *Rory's Castle* I translate in my mind. I had never spoken nor read the old language of Éire before, and now, I translate it with ease.

Following his gaze, along the path, which grows small and blurry in the distance, as it disappears in the trees. The trees are tall, sheltered by the mountains from the winds, they are full and luscious. Beyond them is an open space, greying abandoned farmland. That is where Cian's eyes rest. As I look closer, the greying grounds, begin to form into buildings. Or a single building, its walls crumbled, its roof having given in years ago. Roscair.

I have only read of the tales from Roscair. Once an ancient city, the hub of the north is now abandoned and avoided. They say it is home to the Fae who protect the door to the underworld. However, I have also read the door is a cave in the mountains and a cavern in a lough somewhere south. Curious though, how Cian stares off in the direction of the fallen castle.

"I think I know somewhere," Cian turns and starts off down the mountain towards the ancient town.

*

I drag my feet through Roscair Forest. The forest is scattered with stone homes, long abandoned, some still have their four walls, some only one, and some only have a row of rocks along the perimeter left.

If this forest is the opening to another realm, then the eery feeling that something is watching us, following us, makes sense. Cian doesn't react to the little noises within the trees, the giggles, the cracks, the squeaks. All noises that shouldn't belong within a forest.

Through the trees appears one of the most complete houses we have seen so far. Its roof remains, and even its door and windows are intact. Perhaps the ivy, which covers it, holds everything together. The whole building is wrapped in bright green ivy, its vines so thick they appear more like tree trunks. A curtain of ivy falls from the tree, blocking my view. As we round the front of the building, following the path deeper into the forest, its front door comes into view.

Cian keeps looking over his shoulder at me, checking on me, as we near this building. He holds the curtain of ivy of it back to allow me to pass through.

"Where are we?" I finally ask, "Did this used to be a village?" He doesn't respond, just checks over his shoulder again and keeps walking. "Cian this place feels a little abandoned. But abandoned for a reason." I duck low to avoid a branch he pushes up out of our way. "Eery, I think eery is the right word?"

"Yeah, eery seems like the right word. This is Rosciar. No one has lived here for..." he stops and turns to me, running his fingers through his wavy hair. "No one has lived here in a very long time."

We come to a low stone wall. Tight curls of purple flowers cluster over the stone while the ivy has weaved its way across and twisting around the iron gate, held together with rust and greenery only. Cian stops with his hand on the gate. After a moment he pushes it open with ease, the vines all snapping off. He turns to look at me, the gold in his eyes is muted, no longer glistening with excitement like something has dulled them.

Looking past Cian sits a fully intact grey brick house. Its brown door looks like it has been used more recently than the rest of the forgotten village, as ivy only climbs around the frame, not blocking the entrance. The windows, however, were blanketed with ivy. Its thick roots climbed up the stone walls into the eaves of the cottage.

Stepping up to the house I reached out to pull the plants from the window to see inside. Before I could touch anything, the ivy begins to retreat, slipping down the walls and back into the garden. I gasp, it was my power that moved the ivy, yet I felt nothing inside me. No warning, sensation or pricking heat. Like my power rests outside of me now.

The windows are covered in a thick layer of dirt from centuries of being covered in ivy. Cobwebs decorate the frame, so thick they appear like greying cotton. Spiders large and small skitter away, hiding at the sudden light shining on them.

A soft grunt makes me turn. Cian shoulders the door, forcing it open. It creaks as the hinges, stuck with rust and dirt, give way. Its wooden frame, slightly swollen with damp, cracks, stopping the door from opening past its threshold. Cian uses his knee to push further, letting the door swing open. It crashes against the inside wall, revealing the dark entry of the cottage.

I linger by the door as Cian marches around, pushing and pulling on the windows, before moving deeper into the home, checking behind the doors and furniture. Satisfied the home is secure, or nothing is hiding within, Cian turns to me with a smile. His eyes glistened briefly before the dullness returns to them.

He stands, like a beige light in the middle of the dark space. I remain by the door for a moment, before stepping over the threshold into the home. Light shines past me, highlighting the dust Cian had disturbed as he moved around the cottage. It dances in the light. The aroma of damp wood, mixed with the earthy scent of old musty dust, attacks me, as I step further into the space.

I can feel Cian's eyes follow me as I walk around the small space. Through the door is a living area, dusty and tattered sheep skins are draped over the wooden sofas. A glass front cabinet stands against the side wall behind them, it seems out of place compared to the décor. The dark wood hosted some ornate carvings. Covered in a thick layer of dust coats the grooves and carvings, making some parts of the wood appear grey.

Inside its contents are preserved, protected from the passage of history and the wear of ages. Metals line one shelf, in velvet cases, open, and shining in the dim light. Another contains children's wooden toys, a horse and a boat. The remaining paint flaking off, indicating their age. Finally, on the top shelf, sits two small delicate paintings. The dark colours are difficult to make out, but they are two young girls. Lying beside each portrait on the glass shelf, are long lengths of purple and pink ribbons.

Curious, I move further into the room. To the back is a brick fireplace, with a cast iron fire basket sitting on the stone service, covered in soot. A pile of cut wood piled high on either side. All covered in cobwebs and likely the home for many a tiny creature.

"We can't light a fire in case someone sees the smoke," Cian informs me, he remains in the middle of the room, tracking my every move.

The mantel of the wide-open fire is a thick slab of rock secured into the brick chimney. Some small portraits rest on top. I wipe the dust off with my sleeve, to find paintings of people. The detail of these paintings is immense, making the people look so real like you were staring at a live person. The people in the image I picked up are dressed in casual clothing, trousers and short shirts, all resting on a low wall in front of some water. They look happy, with their arms around each other and smiles making their eyes crinkle. Right in the middle of the group is Cian. His wavy hair looks messy, falling around his face, his smile was the widest I could almost see the sparkle in his eye. Beside him sat a woman, I didn't realise as she was dressed similarly to the men in the picture. Her eyes are on Cian, and she holds the look of someone in love.

Suddenly I felt like I was intruding on a personal moment. Realising these were Cian's personal items, I was handling them without thought. I carefully place the picture back on its place atop the stone shelf. I glance around at him, but he did not seem to mind. He simply stood still, his eyes on me. I wish I knew what he was thinking, why he would take me to this place, his home perhaps.

Just to the side of the fireplace and wood pile are two doors, both open. The first is a small bedroom with nothing more than one bed and a short cabinet. The second door is a bathroom, nothing special. I am sure the damp smell was coming from one of these rooms, so I turn back to Cian in the kitchen.

"There used to be a second bedroom upstairs. But the timber rotted a long time ago and it was easier to take it down than replace it." He explained.

"I see." Moving around him I wander into the kitchen area. "Who lived here?" I ask as if it was not obvious.

The kitchen is open to the living space. A large wood-burning oven takes up most of the space. It sitsin front of another chimney with shelves on either side, filled with pots and pans of various shapes and sizes. The deep ceramic kitchen sink, which housed many crawling insects, took up most of the space on the adjoining wall. Its tap, a dodgy-looking bent copper pipe, jutted out of the wall with a leaver rather than a twisting nob.

My mouth waters at the thought of fresh running water. With a bit of force, I pull the handle up. After a clunk brown water begins to flow from the makeshift tap, quickly turning clear. Bending I drink straight from the tap. It was ice cold just like the water of Cuan at night, but thankfully tasts more like water from a well.

As I rose a hand comes round me and turning the water off. Cian is standing so close to me that our clothes brush together. "Not sure we could get away with lighting the oven either."

Slowly, Cian appears to relax. Leaning against the counter he crosses his ankles. Then he turns to me. A lock of hair falls forward and he pushes it back on top of his head. His eyes shimmer slightly, and I wonder what about this house dulled them earlier. What about me being here made him anxious?

"Who lived here?" I ask again wiping drips of water off my chin with the back of my hand. Looking at me he explores my face as if searching for an answer. When he meets my eyes, I feel him sigh slightly. Not a deep sigh, or an exhausted sigh, but a little expel of air.

"My parents," he says, "and me I guess". Pushing himself off the counter he moves towards the bathroom. "You can use the bathroom first; I'll find you something to wear."

The bathroom is quite small, housing a toilet, sink, and narrow bath. The room is tiled, which is unusual as older houses- particularly in abandoned villages- tended to keep the stone walls and floor. Cian turns the taps to the bath letting the water flow, golden brown then clear. "We will have to stick to cold water I am afraid". He frowns as he tests the water with his hand as if checking for hot water to appear from nowhere.

"When did you live here?" I asked as Cian moves around the bathroom, opening the cupboard under the sink.

"Does presently count?" He says pulling out a towel and a bar of pink soap. He rubs his does the front of his shirt, cleaning off the dust which leaves a pinkish-grey smear. With a smile, he hands them to me

"No," I reply with a grumble. "Your home is..." Taking the soap and towel I look around me at the unusual bathroom within the old and slightly rotten cottage, "...Strange?"

"Are you asking me if my home is strange or telling me?" he checks the taps on the sink, elegant silver faucets, with twisting handles. Again, the water comes slowly with a thud, running brown and then clear.

"I am not sure," I decide, his home is strange. Holding only a few shelves of personal items and an array of pictures, which are too real to be paintings. Then with this bathroom not matching the rest of the home. It is tiled, light pink tiles, along the floor and the tiles travel up the walls to a panelled ceiling. The fixtures and fittings appear glossy and new, whilst also old with their style being from a different time. This bathroom may be fully equipped, but the kitchen sink has a simple makeshift tap.

"I will leave you to it." Sweeping past, Cian gently closes the door, and I am alone in the bathroom.

# Chapter Twenty

## Éabha

I hope I didn't insult him by calling his home strange. Can you call this your present home if it's covered in dust and cobwebs? Moving closer to the bath I find a door, hidden in a little alcove. The only place it could lead to is the bedroom. I decide not to check, but to make sure it is closed properly from this side.

Kicking my boots off they immediately fall apart. I peel off my shirt, the only layer I have left after our journey through the Mourne Mountains. "Fuck," I mutter to myself, "How embarrassing." My shirt has become more see-through than when I first put it on. Which is fine, as I am sure the yellowing sweat stains and thick dirt marks would distract a person from my likely exposed chest. Tossing it in a pile on the floor alongside my underwear and stolen men's trousers. I am too scared to check my body in the mirror, however, as I reach over to turn the tap off, I catch a glimpse of my reflection in the mirror.

My hair is wild. With my tie lost it was free to do as it pleased in the wind on our journey here. It's wilder than I have ever seen it, the curls tying themselves into knots along the ends. My skin is pale and sulkin-looking. Smudges of dirt and dust are smeared up my arms and along my face. Heavy purple bags pull my cheeks down to my crusty dehydrated lips. And my eyes. My eyes are red around the bright blue of my iris. Making me look haunted and inhuman. Quickly I turn away from my own image.

Dipping my fingers into the water I wince, not expecting the water to be just that cold. As I swirl the water around, I picture water boiling over a fire. Just like outside my magic no longer flows from me, but simply is. The warmth moves throughout the bath, as I use my fingers to encourage it to all depths. Before long the mirror and dirty window become covered in steam as the water heats the room.

Easing myself into the warmth I grab the bar of soap and washcloth and begin to scrub my skin. I scrub my skin until it turns red and move on to another part of my body. The water turns just as muddy as the windows of the house. My eyes swell with tears. I can't even say why I begin to cry. I don't notice until they begin to run down my cheeks into the water. The tears drop into the water immediately cleaning it and turning it clear. The grime seems to dissolve. Each drop of my sadness holds a purifying power, as it replaces the water with translucent clarity. There must be something oddly poetic about this, I think to myself. Hoping that the tears will also find me a path of renewal and clarity.

A quiet guttural cry escapes my mouth before I can stop it. I take a deep breath as the tears continue to run down my face blurring my vision. I refuse to allow Cian the pleasure of seeing me cry, refuse to allow anyone to see me cry. And I refuse to give up. To be made an example of. To be exploited and manipulated. But most of all I refuse to die! I will kill the King if I have to.

I drop the soap and cloth into the water and watch them both sink. Once the water calms, the silence in the blush-pink-tiled room becomes deafening. Pulling my knees to my chest I wrap my arms around them and hug tight. The hollow feeling of loneliness returns to my chest, which was once so familiar. I expected to finally feel relaxed. Invigorated maybe, at the sudden revelation I want to fight and not die. That strange niggle at the back of my head reminds me that I am not alone. Cian will stand by my side and fight with me, for some reason I am sure of this.

Yet, I still feel lonely. This old, unwelcome friend slides over my shoulders and around my back like a cardigan. It's quiet, yet it fills my thoughts with loud, cold, persistent emptiness. I remember this weight. I remember how it presses down on my chest with a slight ache. Just enough that I can still move, still smile, still say that I am fine. It brings with it emptiness. Once I thought the emptiness was physical, so I filled it. Filled it with anything, reading, gardening, swimming, eating.

The warmth of connection was the only thing that allowed me to remove this cardigan.

Ceira. My friend. She helped me find myself. Told me how to be in our world. She filled the emptiness within me. I yearn for that feeling again and hope to be with her someday as this all returns to normal. Or someday have new connections, strong enough they too fill the emptiness which burrows away inside me.

I lie back in the water until my head just bobs above the surface. The steam swirls up around me, the swirls start tight, close to the water, then gradually get looser as they rise then before disappearing into the air.

Much like my swims in Lough Cuan, when I am in the water I can float, relax and forget. I feel at home in water, safe and protected. If anything happens to me in the next chapter of this journey, I wish for my body to be laid to rest in my lough. That way my soul, if I have a soul, can float and be free at last.

Taking a deep breath through my nose, I duck my head under the water. Ignoring the water that spills out over the sides flooding the floor. With my eyes closed I stretch out my legs and arms as far as I can within the constraints of the bath. Underwater you can hear nothing, feel nothing, only weightlessness and the sound the water makes as it hugs you close. I feel myself smile as my fears dissolve into the water. But my magic, my new strong powers, wrap itself around my bones, fusing itself to my body but it felt right. I breath in allowing the warmth into my body. The feeling of weightlessness, just like in the lough, wraps around me, hugging me and protecting me.

Suddenly something grabs my hair and the back of my neck, yanking me out of the water. I gasp as my face breaks through the water. Hands move to each side of my face holding me up. I can't blink the water away fast enough but can make out the shape of a man leering over me. Fear keeps me still. My vision clears and I can make out Cian. He is standing in the bath, a foot on each side of me. His face is inches from mine and his eyes are blazing in gold.

"What the fuck are you doing?!" I shout, trying to pull myself out of his grasp but not getting very far as his grip on me tightens like he can't let me go.

"What the fuck am I doing? Eve your heart stopped!" I frown up at him, as his concerned expression holds firm.

"No, it didn't," his vampire senses must be affected by lack of sleep, "I was just underwater".

"Your heart stopped," He breathes. His hold on me softens slightly as a hand moves to hold the back of my neck again whilst his thumb on his other hand strokes my cheek. The gold in his eyes relax, the glints of gold returning. We stay like this for a moment, staring at each other's eyes, both searching for some kind of answer. Then I realise, I am completely naked, fully exposed in crystal clear water. I wrap an arm around my chest as I cross my legs and cover myself with my free hand.

"Your heart stopped," He repeats himself. He searches my eyes waiting for an answer, searching the depths of my soul for anything to explain what happened.

"Cian…" I begin to ask him to let me go. His clothes are soaked through, but he seems unconcerned as I twist myself to maintain some level of dignity. "Please let me go." He drops his hands and falls back onto his heels as I push myself back against the tub. Bringing my knees to my chest I try to cover myself. There isn't enough space in the bath for both of us, so his knees push against mine as he continues to stare with a mixture of concerns and confusion.

His worry for me feels like a cruel joke. He is bringing me back to the King, and we both know the King will want me dead. I have had enough of this, this journey, the endless cycles of guilt and survival. I don't need Cian to save me, what I need is to be released! But I need to prove myself to the King, to Cian, if I am to have any sort of peace in my life.

With the bitterness of clarity in my mouth, I look across to him, "What does that even matter- return her dead or alive remember?"

"Dead or alive," Cian muses, his eyes turning to stone, as he stands climbing out of the bath. "Éabha, there is something about you, I need to keep alive."

Turning he stares at me again, this time it feels like it strikes my soul. And in that moment, something in my chest clicks. Cian frowns, looking down at me, crowding myself into the corner of the tub, protecting the last of my modesty. He frowns, feeling it too.

*

I peer through the door leading to the bedroom. Cian is not there, and the other door is closed. Stepping in I spy some clothes neatly folded on the bed. A dark green knitted jumper, which looks new, a pair of dark breachers and a cream cotton shift with some socks and a belt. He thought of everything. Quickly drying myself I pull on the clean, warm new clothes.

Sitting on the bed I look around the room whilst combing my hair with my fingers. There was nothing in the room except a bed and a chest of drawers containing mostly linens. The walls appear to be lime-washed with the textured surface holding onto dust and dirt. It seems to have become a home to several spides over the years. The bed is surprisingly dust-free, and the sheets smell freshly laundered.

With my hair neatly braided down my back, I return my towel to the bathroom. Cracking the door open slightly, I see Cian. I watch him from the crack in the door as he stands by the sink staring at himself in the mirror. His towel is wrapped loosely around his waist, clinging precariously to his hips. My eyes travel up his back, admiring is a network of strong muscles, perfectly sculpted. His shoulders are slumped and round as he leans on the sink, eyes fixed on his own in the mirror.

The mirror appears more like a painting of a god rather than a reflection. His chiselled torso, smooth and unblemished skin stretching over sharp pectorals, followed by the ripped muscles on his abdomen. A drop of water falls from his damp hair, tracing a path down his chest, and disappearing into his towel. My eyes follow its journey when I spot the muscular lines revealing the defined V-shaped lines leading down from his abdomen.

His eyes flick to my reflection in the mirror. I freeze, like a rabbit, frozen in fear. I must have looked petrified as at that moment, he smiled. That stupid lop-sided grin grew into a smirk. Adverting my eyes, I step back into the room closing the door behind me.

Sitting on the end of the ben I stare at my feet waiting for the embarrassment and shame to pass. I can hear the door reopen. Looking up, Cian was there, leaning his shoulder against the door frame, his towel wrapped more firmly around his waist. His arms are crossed over his chest, only emphasising his pecks and biceps further.

"I'm sorry," I mumble.

He doesn't respond, instead asking, "Are you tired?" I shake my head. "Hungry then?" I nod, looking up to meet his eyes. The gold flecks which disappeared have now returned.

"Alright," he responds as he pushes off the door frame and turns back into the bathroom closing the door behind him. with a distinct click he locks it.

I wait on the soft bed until I hear Cian leave the bathroom into the living space before I follow him out there. I find him on the sofa, pulling on his boots.

"There isn't any food here, so I will go find something," He explains as he finishes off tying up his laces.

"Did this place use to be a farm?" I ask moving into the kitchen.

"Yes, but a long time ago. There are no animals here anymore."

Smearing some dirt off the window behind the sink, I peer outside. Just as I thought, a very overgrown garden. "No shit," I grumble moving towards the small door at the side of the house. Pushing with all my force, I am unable to make it move even slightly. "Good thing your parents fed you vegetables as well."

Cian leans over me with one hand on the door he pushes it open effortlessly. Overgrown vines snap as he pushes it further open.

The side of the cottage was overgrown. With vines of floppy-leafed flowers growing up and over what used to be a pergola. The only thing keeping the wood up is the overgrown garden. The air smells damp, not the same dampness as inside the house, more like within a glass house. The canopy of trees above contains a climate perfect for growing almost anything. Stripes of light fall from the treetops, highlighting various parts of the ground.

There, trailing along the ground as the back, are the little yellow flowers I am looking for. Kneeling, I cup one in my hands breathing in its slightly sweet scent, which brings back memories of my garden at home. The flowers begin to glow and twinkle. Slowly the rest of the flowers light up like bugs in the night sky. Placing my hands in the earth beneath them, magic pours into the soil, spreading around me. Tomatoes begin to bulge out of the leaves. First green, then yellow, then finally turning red. Plucking the nearest one off, I hold it up to Cian who stands behind me in what I can only assume is stunned silence.

He takes the red fruit from me with a suspicious frown, bringing it to his nose he sniffs it once, looking up at me with raised eyebrows, he pops it in his mouth. He's impressed... I think.

"I bet there are potatoes in those barrels," I point to two barrels made of rutting wood barely holding their shape. Cian approaches them and kicks them over. Their roots have grown through the barrel and into the ground, but this doesn't stop him from pushing them over with ease. Soil falls everywhere, but, sure enough, amongst the mud and rubble, are large cream potatoes.

"Fucking witches," Cian mutters to himself thinking I can't hear.

# Chapter Twenty-One

## Cian

Éabha made a soup. Soup may be a bit of a stretch; it was more of a tomato and potato stew. A bland stew. I watched on in fascination as she effortlessly used her magic. When she uses her magic, I feel it tingle inside my chest. It's a familiar feeling, I have been getting for the past twenty-eight years. And it is captivating to watch her magic happen at the same time.

The pull I have to her. This magic connection. I thought it was a warning. However, looking at her now and seeing her vulnerability and power, I think it is something more. We were meant to find each other.

Every time I plan our entrance to the King, any time I think of torturous or quick and painless ways to kill her- I ache. And it's a familiar ache. The kind that stabs your heart with an arrow when loved ones leave.

I think of the Morrigan, the Phantom Queen, and the prophecy. I hope we have mistranslated it. I plan to return to the King and find the truth.

I let my soup go cold as I watch Éabha, sitting with her feet up on the opposite sofa. She's curled up with a throw around her. The weave in her green jumper matches the one she has done to her hair, which hangs over her shoulder. Her eyes appear brighter. Glistening like the night sky. Sparkling like Sapphires. Dark hair and blue eyes. She looks perfect, I think to myself.

"You don't seem afraid anymore," I ponder aloud.

Her lashes swoop up as she gazes at me. Eventually, she responds setting her mug on the floor. "I was afraid. Then I accepted my fate. And now…" She doesn't finish that sentence, but I still wait hoping she will involve me. She looks around the room, at my dusty random collection of furniture. The things my parents left behind have long since gone. Now all that remains is some things I have collected on my travels. From many different times and many different parts of the world. Nothing works together, my youngest brother would always complain. I have neglected the house, over the past hundred years. We worked hard to get Connor on the throne and keep him there, I had no time to return.

I watch as Éabha tucks the throw tighter around her legs. She's cold. I should really light a fire. But the smoke might signal to someone, or something, that we are here. And I can't have that. I need this time, to think, to plan. Just one night. One more night with her.

"I didn't realise I was so dangerous," Éabha whispers, as if she is only talking to herself. "My whole life my grandparents have been strict with me using powers, I only use them to grow plants, light candles, maybe make things move to scare people. But I have never killed people. I truly had no idea I was powerful."

Éabha's eyes travel to the cabinet behind me, where my most precious treasures are stored. Kept behind glass and protected from the world and its decaying power. Her face is unreadable like she's not even here anymore. I don't know where she has gone but I will wait for her to return.

"I knew I was powerful," Her shoulders relax. I hadn't noticed they were tense until they drop a little. I can hear her heart beating in her chest, the rustle of her clothes as her chest rises and falls with each breath she takes. They both slow, slightly, almost unnoticeably. She's found confidence, wherever she went in her moments of silence, she brought it back with her.

"I created the drenching," Her eyes glow as flares of magic sparks behind them, "I was born, and on that day, colour seeped out of me and into the earth. Staining all of Éire and the lands around her. I did that. My magic did that."

I feel my face drop and I process this. We were not in Éire when this started. But when we returned to crown Connor the King, the island was shining. Colours we had never imagined decorated these lands. A team of men were sent to find the Fae who had done this. Because it couldn't only be a Fae to want something as beautiful. But none were found. I tracked the colour all over the world. The world rejoiced about the changes. Thank the Gods for the gift. Eventually, we continued as if this was normal.

Now sitting here with Éabha, and feeling the power which courses through her veins, I kick myself for not making this connection sooner. Perhaps there is something in the silly jokes about vampires being dim. I truly felt it then.

"That was the first time I said that out loud," Éabha confesses, "Now I can create pain in people's heads without even trying. I can create fire which burns people alive. I am too powerful and need to be stopped." Tears form in her eyes. turning the deep blue into a darker shade of navy. Like the night sky. She doesn't let them fall over the brim of her eyelid, wiping them away before slouching back into the sofa, defeated.

"Do you know what we believe the prophecy to say?" lifting her head her eyes meet mine. A storm of desire hits me full in the chest. Striking me deeper than any pull or connection I have felt with her before. Although overwhelming, I try not to react, she doesn't always know when she is using her magic.

"The Witch of mortal and earth people. Will bring destruction of all creatures, living and non-living"

"Cian…"

"But I think that's wrong, we misunderstood." I want to explain that I went back to the start. How I saw Morrigan change me and form their plans. How can I tell her without revealing who I am? *Father time will meet Mother Nature, and they will restore the world to glory. He will travel to many times, and he will wait for her*. This is what Morrigan said.

"I think it should say 'the witch of mortal and earth people, will bring glory.' Not destruction."

Éabha sits in silence. I let my words float between us, hoping she heard me, hoping she understood who she is, and what she can do.

"This prophecy is about you Éabha. But I do not believe you will bring destruction." *Not anymore.*

"Cian, I don't know who I am anymore. I really cannot be the witch of this prophecy. It was only two days ago I found out that my father was from the Danu Tribe. A Fairy. And now my magic is acting differently. Like those people in the mountains awakened it. I know I am powerful; I can feel it. My magic shimmers inside me. Sometimes it thinks for me. But I am not a witch who will cause destruction or glory."

"The prophecy doesn't say much about the Witch's power, but elders talk about her power. How we will know when she is born as we will be able to feel her power from anywhere,"

"Cian, it's not me," she tosses the throw aside to get up.

"But I can feel your power," stopping, she falls back down onto the sofa, "For the past twenty-eight years, I have felt your power. Like a pull in my chest. Like you have latched onto my heart. I can feel you. I can feel you no matter how far away I am."

I can see her mind working. Behind her eyes, I can see the thoughts that float around her head.

"If I am this witch. This powerful, dangerous witch. The King will kill me," her lips begin to tremble as tiny sparks of glittering tears fall from her eyes. She doesn't attempt to hide them from me this time. She lets them fall down her cheeks, creating a pathway for the next tear which follows. "I don't want to die."

I don't prompt her to continue. I always knew she didn't want to die, and she will fight. I saw it in her eyes when I pulled her from the bath. I am sure I saw it in the Doire woods when the Failinis attacked killing all my men. And I see the confidence now. She sits uncomfortably with it. Like it's been stitched into her skin.

We sit in silence for some time. Moments, perhaps hours, I am not sure. We sit while her tears dry on her face, while the bugs outside quieten, while the moon rises in the sky casting a warming glow, slowly moves around the room.

"I have a question." She announces as I slouch back onto the sofa, crossing my ankle over my knee. Éabha readjusts herself so she is sitting squarely. Her long hair falls out of her braid slightly, around her like a waterfall of night, which she tosses over her shoulder.

"Where did you go?" she asks. "In the village that night, where did you go?"

I turn to look at my photos on the mantle place, of the people I used to visit. How do I tell her what I am? When the mortals have spent hundreds of years afraid of anything different. She too will fear me. There was a time when they worshipped me. They had temples and statues of tall, muscled men they assumed resembled me. Those times have since gone. I am sure Éabha isn't even aware of the stories of me. Of my role in the world around her.

"You told me to shut up then suddenly you were gone." I look back at her, realising I must have been silent for some time. "I assumed you had just gone into the forest. You're fast, so maybe I just didn't see you go. But you would have heard them when they came."

She was afraid. I lost control and I left her. I am not sure I regret it. Although, I am consumed with guilt for what happened to her in the mountains. If I hadn't left, I would never have found out. Never realised this link between us. She would have never found her power, the strength within her becoming free. She must have been so afraid.

"You were gone for so long..." I won't tell her, she won't understand. It's too much.

"Let's just get some sleep," I say standing up and moving away from the sofas.

"I am probably going to die tomorrow, Cian!" she exclaims, standing by my side. "I almost died back there!" Her hands grasp my arm as she turns me around to face her. "At least tell me what's going on, a dying girl's wish?" she smiles, and I freeze. *So beautiful*.

"I thought you decided not to die?" I retort.

She looks up at me, through thick eyelashes. Her hand is still on my arm, her warmth spreading down to my hand. How could I possibly tell her, what should I tell her, where should I start, what should I avoid?

I pull away reluctantly, perching on the arm of the sofa. With a sigh, I rest my face in my hands, breathing in and out. I decide not to look at her, I do not want to see the panic and fear in her face. I don't want that sort of rejection from her.

"I was the first" *I am the first*. That is all I decide to say looking up at her stern yet concerned face.

200

"The first what?" With a sigh, she sits back down on the edge of her sofa leaning forward slightly. Her floral scent envelopes me, I get lost in it for a moment.

"Vampire. I was the first vampire."

She doesn't say anything, she doesn't even blink, I think she's breathing. I have never told anyone this before. I am not sure how long I have to wait for a person to process this information.

"I was born mortal," I explain. "In a time when it was mostly just mortals in this world. There was Fae too. I was hunting with my brothers. We met a group of Witches. It was the Phantom Queen actually. They welcomed us and shared their food and drink. We fell asleep and when we woke up… we were different."

She doesn't need to know the pain I caused my family. The heartache and torture I continue to go through just thinking of them. She doesn't need to know the destruction I created. She doesn't need to know about the other things I created. About how the sun shines in the sky during the day and the moon glows at night. How the Gods appeared and moved to their planets in the sky. She doesn't need to know my role in any of this. Éabha doesn't know a time before night and day. When Éire was the heart of the world because there was only vast emptiness everywhere.

"And a thousand-plus years later the world has been tipped on its side and here we are." I fall back into the seat of the sofa. She hasn't moved. Although she is frowning now. Hopefully processing and thinking. Usually, it's my age that takes people a while. I can feel my face drop the longer she stares at me with her brows pulled together.

"Not the reaction I was expecting, I was thinking you'd say something mean, assume I was joking and storm off." Her face relaxes, as she edges slightly closer to me.

"You're over a thousand years old?" I nod. "Does the King know you are the first vampire?" I nod again. "Did you... make the King into a vampire?"

My connection to the King is complicated, she doesn't need to know. "No, I didn't turn the King into a vampire."

"Why aren't you the King?" she tilts her head, studying me as I respond.

"I don't want to be King- I am over a thousand years old. I am tired".

"But..." She trails off. I see her search my eyes for something. She doesn't find it, "This doesn't explain where you went."

As if attempting to rescue me from this conversation, or perhaps giving me a sign that now is not the right time to tell Éabha everything; the eaves of the house creak, stretching and settling in for the night. Éabha gasps standing up and searching around her for the source of the noise. I laugh standing with her, placing my hand on her shoulder, sweeping my fingers through her hair.

"It's just the house settling" I assure her.

We find ourselves looking at each other, I realise we do this a lot, like silent communication but neither of us speaks the same language. I feel the tickle over my heart and search to see what magic she is letting out. But all I see are eyes like sapphires.

"I have seen stones the colour of your eyes," I whisper, not realising I have said this out loud

"Stones?" she breathes back

Clearing my throat, I stand straight, taking a step back I drop my hand. Catching the soft curls of her hair, as it falls. "Maybe we should both get some sleep. Tomorrow, we will make our way over the Carlingford lough, where I am sure the King will send assistance."

"So, we do not even have a full day left?" Tears swell in Éabha's eyes. For what reason I am not sure. Does she feel the same pull for us to remain together or is she back to believing she will die tomorrow? I move towards her, to catch the tears before they spill over. The candlelight begins to flicker as the breeze outside changes and seeps into the house. It casts a golden glow on her skin. Making parts of her eyes appear white and her hair like fire. Placing my finger along her bottom eyelid I catch the first tear, the salty wetness runs across my fingers and lands on the floor. I hear the thump and splash much like anyone else would hear a pale of water being upturned. When the water settles, I hear her heart. Its steady beat almost flutters as her eyes swoop up to me.

"We should get some sleep," she advises.

A gentle twinge against my chest again. What is she using her magic for?

"Do you feel that?" she breathes.

"I feel you, your power touches me here," I hold my hand against my chest.

She frowns, her brows pulling together. Her hand reaches out as I drop mine from my chest. Her fingertips graze my shirt. I can feel the heat radiating through to my skin from her touch. Like she is full of stars, which burn in the night sky. My eyes flutter closed as her fingers continue to float across my heart.

"I only feel it when you use your magic," I say as covering her hand with mine, pressing her palm flat against my heart. "I think you use it when you do not even realise." I snake my other hand around her waist pulling her closer.

"I feel it too," she says as her breath catches when I tug her even closer. "My magic." Her hands move up my chest and wrap around my neck. "I am aware I am using it." Her lips form her words so perfectly. "I think it is you," Her thumb sweeps across my jaw and I lean into the touch. "I am trying to understand," Her voice has dropped to a whisper, and I realise just how close we have become. "This feeling," she says, as I finally press her body to mine. Her heart rate increases, I can hear the lub-dub sound playing softly in the background. Running my hands through her waves of umber hair I expose the softly tanned skin of her neck as she says, "You feel it too?"

She leans her head to the side exposing her neck further. I glide my fingers down the prominent vein as I contemplate my response, "I feel…" I inch my face closer desperate to smell her. Like the aroma of blooming wildflowers and salty frozen air, almost makes my knees weak. Breathing her in I find hints of crisp pine needles. Her skin is smooth I cannot resist any further, I skim my lips over her neck and murmur against her, "I do not understand what I feel."

Her finger begins to play with the hairs at the nape of my neck as she pulls me closer. Between breaths she says, "I feel a pull." Placing a kiss on her neck I trail up to her jaw, planting tiny kisses as I go. I can feel her body press flush against mine. Her curves align against the firmness of my body. Her chest rises and falls with each breath.

She pulls back, hands still wrapped around my neck, she says, "Like both our hearts are tied together."

I feel vulnerable in her arms. I would let her do anything, take anything from me. I want to tell her, how it feels. How I feel about her. What I need at this moment. But the words get lost. Her eyes twinkle as my heart tugs again. Magic, I think, is she using her magic on me?

I hold her head in my hands, my thumb stroking her cheeks as I watch starlight twinkle in her eyes. "The longer I am with you the stronger it becomes," I confirm. Then without meaning to I speak my fear, "Is it a spell?"

I feel her taking a step back, grabbing her waist again I hold her in her place, right up against me.

"You think I have spelt you?" she demands, "You think I have such power?" The soft relaxed planes of face crease with her anger. But are quickly replaced by a slight glimmer of surprise as my hands lower to her hips threatening to venture lower.

"This feels…. Too good" I slide a hand to her bum, whilst my other brushes through her hair. Grabbing some hair in my fit, I hold her there, "It has to be a spell."

Starlight twinkles in her eyes again, for a second, I believe it to be real, but the flickering candle changes direction and it's gone. "Cian," she sighs as if she was realising the stars she kept hidden in her eyes, "believe me, I hold no such power."

"Then this is something bigger." I graze my fingers over her breast, "Born from something greater." Cupping her face again I examine her eyes, "You are something greater, we were meant to meet. For what I do not yet understand."

Her eyes are as blue as the night sky with all its stars, I should have said this instead of stones. I should have described their beauty and sparkle not compared them to the ground.

"I am nothing Cian." She mumbles, turning her face into my hands. She looks like she is trying to escape but the little kiss on my palm is reassuring to kiss is soft. "You cannot look at me and believe that?"

"I look at you and see," I cannot find the words. Cannot translate the vision I see before me into speech. Perhaps there are no words to describe her. I lean into her as her eyes close.

Kissing one eye I say; "I see the future" I kiss the other; "I plan to find the source of the prophecy to translate it properly." Her eyes remain closed, her lips slightly parted. I turn my head slightly and touch my lips to her, "I cannot let you die".

Her lips are as soft as they look. I feel her go completely still as I pull her closer, wrapping an arm around her waist again whilst my other holds her neck. She opens her mouth further and I slide my tongue inside.  A small moan escapes her as my chest warms with encouragement. She tightens her hold around my neck- an electric tingle shutters through my body, where our skin touches.

I explore her mouth, as she melts into me. She is nervous in her movements, anxiously moving with me. But her hands say something different as she pulls at my collar trying to get closer. I can hear her rushed breaths through her nose and the blood rushing through her veins as her heart rate increases. I match her movements, letting go of her hair to tangle my fingers through it. Crushing my lips to her, I kiss her with more urgency now. Like I am chasing something I cannot see. My stomach tingles, it glows and expands to my chest, with a warming sensation.

*This feels like magic.*

I break our kiss. Her eyes glow, filling with questions, as she looks up at me. I am out of breath; I note as I must not have breathed throughout our…embrace. Resting my forehead against hers, I take in everything, trying to find the questions she has from behind her eyes, trying to find answers for her.

"Go to bed," I whisper, our chests still heaving as we try to relax our hearts. We remain like this for a moment, my head resting on hers. Our eyes not blinking. Our hearts calmed slowly. Eventually, she lets go, stepping away from me. She enters the bedroom, silently closing the door behind her.

It takes me a moment before I can move. Before I can form coherent thoughts. I find myself moving to a chest near the kitchen. Inside lays a dark wood guitar. She feels light in my hands. Her wood smooth is soft compared to my rough hands. My guitar has been kept in that chest for almost thirty years. Strumming it once I cringe at the horrendous sound of untuned strings.

My mind drifts back to Éabha, as I twist the pegs to tighten the strings, checking now and then to make sure the sound matches the correct note. I could feel her magic as we kissed, feel the pull tighten around my chest and stomach. It feels real, it cannot be magic. My mind is torn between the need for her, this unrelenting urge to go to her and hold her, and the unsettling questions, which catch in my throat, that these feelings are merely a spell she has placed on me.

I lay back on the sofa. My mind reeling. Softly I begin to pluck the strings of the guitar. Playing a tune from my past. A song that will never leave me. I smile at the memories of an easier time, letting the song flow from me.

# Chapter Twenty-Two

## Éabha

I take the side of the bed by the window. An escape route, I assure myself. I trust Cian. I trust he will keep me alive- until we meet the King. And I trust he will hand me over. What happens after is left up to me, I suppose. I braid my hair off my face and climb under the covers. A shiver runs down my spine as the cold from the sheets seeps through my clothes to my skin.

Pulling the duvet up to my chin, I think of the reasons to stay alive. It's hard to find true reasons when everything that was worth living for doesn't want me anymore. My grandparents, my friend, my life by the lough. All gone.

I need to convince the King I am not the witch from this prophecy. I need to discover who I am. I need to find out who my father is or was. I need to get a hold of my magic and work out why it has changed, and why it feels different from before.

Music drifts through the crack in the bedroom door. Soft gentle plucks. A slow melody. The smooth loops of tunes, flow over to me, washing away all thoughts.

The sound is a stark contrast from what just happened out there, the urgency of need that came from us both. Came from nowhere, in my opinion. My lips feel swollen. I touch my fingertips to them, noting how it felt when Cian had his hands on me. The tingles that ran through my body, burst through my veins, leaving a warm glow all over.

Focusing on the music, I try to get some sleep. Try to stop my mind from racing. The serene stream of sound creates a calming effect on me. Like a spell. The song he plays feels warm, as I snuggle deeper under the duvet. I don't notice when it stops. I sense Cian moving closer to the door and close my eyes. He creeps in silently, climbing into the bed so softly that if I was asleep, I would not know he was there.

As if by instinct my hand drops to my side, the side closest to him. Slowly our little fingers inch closer and closer until they are holding each other. Neither of us speaks, I don't believe we are even breathing. As the sensual sparks of something new grow up my arm to my heart.

I can feel his eyes on me. That prickly feeling on the back of the neck demonstrates it. Rolling over to face him, I find him already on his side propped up on his elbow looking down at me. His golden eyes have softened, yet I can still feel them capturing every moment of me, every part of my soul.

I don't move as Cian's warm hand moves up my arm to cup my face.

I blink, and he has moved closer. He moves closer again, only slightly but purposefully as if to ask permission. I close the gap, bringing my lips to his. Our lips move gently against each other. As Cian pulls me closer, grabbing my thigh and cradling my head in his arm.

Pulling back slightly to catch a breath Cian pulls my head closer, sucking my bottom lip between his. His sharp fangs scrape across my lower lip as a moan escapes me. As embarrassment floods my blood, he forces his way into my mouth. Inciting another moan. Pleasure sources through me, from my core to my legs, resting in my stomach. I don't know what my body is trying to tell me, but I need to chase this feeling, I need more. I need Cian.

I copy his movements. We explore each other and he moans, I smile, pulling him by his hair to get closer.

With speed, he rolls onto his back, pulling me on top of him. I can feel his arousal beneath me. He makes no moves to hide it, in fact, he tactfully shimmies me down, so I am right on top of it.

Reaching up behind me, he pulls free my braid, allowing my hair to fall around us like a curtain, blocking out any further glimmers of light. He doesn't say anything as he combs his fingers through it, twisting it around his fist, and admiring it. My dark hair with its straight parts and curly parts. I take in his face as he does so and catch him smile. Smiling at my hair. He doesn't say it, he doesn't need to, but I know, somehow, I know, he thinks my hair is beautiful.

Swarmed by the sudden affection I lean down to kiss him again. His hands move to my hips, and skirt up my waist. grabbing the hem of my shirt, he pulls it off. I sit back, clutching my chest with my arms. My movement makes him moan. For a moment or maybe not even that long, I fear he'll push me away. Tell me how silly I am, call me fat or ugly, and laugh at me for thinking we could be like this, here, together.

But he holds me in place with a firm grasp on my hip. While his other hand skirts over my stomach and up to my chest. Pulling my arms away, his fingertips lightly graze around my nipple until he is holding my full breast in his hand. He palms my breast sending a surge of warm energy through me, resting between my legs.

I want to tell him I don't know what I am doing. I need to explain that I am clumsy and unpractised. But I realise I don't need to, as his grasp on my hip loosens slightly, just enough for him to rock my hips back and forth. The length of him rubs against me. Warmth gathers as the friction affects him. His eyes close as he frowns. Closing away the gold I have come to find comfort in.

"Eve," he whispers with a moan, before sitting up so fast that it makes me jump. He captures my breast in his mouth. I hold his head there, watching as my fingers get lost in the dark curls in his head. I am struck with the urge to touch him, I need to feel his skin, to see his bare chest. So, I pull at the collar of his shirt until he releases me.

In a smooth motion his shirt is gone and I am faced with the landscape of firm muscle and smooth skin. Resting my hands on his shoulders he lets me explore the smooth mounds of his chest. Tracing the area with a faint dusting of hair, rising subtly with each breath he takes, creating soft whispers beneath my fingertips. Palpable and intoxicating heat radiates from him. My palms begin to tingle as the heat reacts with my magic. His skin is warm, almost feverish, as though he carries the sun within him. Each beat of his heart pulses against my fingers, like the storms within the sun, grounding us in this moment.

I close my eyes briefly to focus on the touch, to centre my magic and reach for the sun. I open them to find him on top of me. My body is scorched where our skin touches. His eyes follow his hand as his fingers skim over my shoulder, to my breast, igniting flames in my chest which scream out with need. His fingers continue over the soft swell of my stomach to the waist of my trousers. They linger there as my breaths quicken and my blood is swarmed with uncertainty and embarrassment yet again.

I can't speak as his hand follows the seam of my trousers. I can't stop him as he pushes his fingers between my thighs. I can't move as he rests his full hand over my centre. I can't do any of this because it feels right. It feels good. It feels perfect.

"Cian I..." I attempt to explain my inept performance as he cups me through my trousers.

Leaning down he captures my lips, taking away my anxious words. "Tell me to stop." He kisses along my jaw to my neck. "Tell me to stop at any time and I will," I moan as he deepens his kiss on my neck. I can feel his fangs resting on my skin, threatening to puncture through, but I know he won't.

I trust him. I trust Cian with everything I am. With my whole body. I don't tell him to stop. Instead, I unbutton my trousers and help him remove them, with very little grace.

Leaning back on my hands I try to cover myself by crossing my legs. His eyes never leave mine, the gleam with what I believe is lust, sparkles as he stands and removes his own so fast, I don't even think I saw him move.

Finally, my eyes leave his, as they travel down the length of his body. I can feel my face redden as my eyes go too low. A quick reminder of our awkward encounter earlier in the bathroom. But he doesn't react the same, his face remains unreadable as he kneels on the bed by my feet.

Holding my ankles in his hands as he whispers to himself "Beautiful," his eyes travel from where his hands rest along my legs and body back to my eyes, leaving a burning trail in their wake. "You're beautiful."

I don't understand it, but I need something, I need him. I reach for him. Pulling him down on top of me again. We tangle ourselves with each other. Our lips once slow and deliberate, now are desperate and fast. It feels like every nerve in my body comes to life, as my fingertips trace the contours of muscles along his back, over his shoulders, down to his thighs. I memorise the rise and fall as our breaths mingle.

Cian shares in this journey, with my own body. Caressing my breasts, squeezing the flesh on my sides, holding my hips still as he tries to get closer to me. Finally, his hand skirts over the soft hairs between us. Pulling back, I take a breath as the nerves there spark to life, like a flickering fire.

Cian leans away from me, as my legs fall open of their own accord. He watches as his fingers skim over the sensitive skin. pressure rushes to the area he touches. It feels like magic, but not my magic. It feels like sparks and fire and stars, are fighting for an audience with him, from within me.

Looking into my eyes he presses a finger against my entrance. My hips move of their own free will. Willing him to push further. He responds by stroking the bundle of nerves I did not know I had there. Shock waves course through me. I grab hold of his arms, as a soft scream escapes me before I can stop it. Once the waves subside after travelling down to my toes, I am left with little sparks where his hand continues to stroke and explore. As if the stars got what they wanted.

"You're so wet," he coos as I begin to pant, digging my nails into his forearms.

"Cian, I need...please," I plead with him to continue but he doesn't. A pang of hurt hits my heart as he moves away from me. Positioning himself between my legs and kneeling back on his heels. He is sat there like a God. Soaking me in and binding me in place. As if he were the night sky, and I, a star captured by his primal power.

His hands rub up and down my legs, from my knees to my ankles, then my ankles to my hips. With each stroke towards my thighs our tender parts touch, causing us both to sigh with need.

He holds himself in his hand as he continues to trace my skin with the other. As if he is mapping every part of me. Every dent and lump under my skin. Every stretch mark, or blemish or hard fat. He maps it all, as his eyes turn from sparkling lust to smouldering desire.

These eyes, these touches, and these feelings are new. A little voice in my head demands I hide, cover myself, push him away, distract his gaze. But it feels nice. It feels nice to have a man desire me. To map my imperfections as if they are perfections.

"You want me to stop?" leaning down he kisses just below my ear.

I breathe like I can't get enough air. Like I do when I feel panicked. But I am not panicking, I am waiting. I understand the pleasure that is waiting. Or perhaps the pain everyone warns us of, is waiting for me. I feel him caressing my entrance, not with his hands. "Don't stop."

He pushes inside me. It feels like I am being stretched apart. I hiss, as my hips rise to meet his. He makes a similar sound as he lowers his head to rest against mine. Slowly I adjust, and I can feel my body relax around him. Cian, however, remains tense. His eyes are squeezed shut and his hands formed into fists beside my head. The creases by his eyes soften as I stroke them. Slowly they disappear as his eyes flutter open. I sprinkle kisses on the parts of his face I can reach, - his lips, his chin, his nose. He responds with a slight smile.

Sweeping my hair off my face, he holds me there. His whole hand supporting my face. Stroking my cheek with his thumb and leaving a warm trail under my eye. His other hand, barely touches me, as it snakes down to my hip. He holds me there, keeping me in place, as he begins to pull out. Stopping when I gasp, and then pushing his way back in, dangerously slow. With every thrust our breathing becomes more intense, the heat between us grows, the sparks of fire and stars flicker everywhere we touch.

I try to hold onto him, onto anything that I can touch. The sparks follow my hands, twinkling up from beneath his skin wherever I touch.

Cian grunts with every thrust, sometimes talking. Whispering in my ear or against my lips as we kiss. He whispers about how good it feels and how beautiful I am.

Soon we are both panting. Both of us trying to chase our breaths, capturing it from each other's lips. The sparks turn to hot fire between my legs. It begins to radiate out pleasure all over my body. My legs begin to shake, and then an overwhelming convulsion shockwaves through me. I bite my lips to prevent myself from screaming his name.

With the last shockwave of my climax, I jerk, opening my eyes. To find myself lying under the cover of the bed, alone. Fully dressed, my hair a little messed up but still in a braid. It takes my eyes a moment to adjust to the darkness. I don't remember it being this dark before. Once I can see I sit up, hoping to find Cian beside me. But he is not there. The bed on his side is not even slept in. There is no sign he has even entered the room at all.

Perhaps I passed out. This act is unknown to me. Cian may have gone to fetch a drink. And yet I am dressed?

I creek open the door and peer into the living area. To find Cian, asleep on the sofa. His feet resting on the arm and his guitar on the floor beside him.

It was a dream.

# Chapter Twenty-Three

## Éabha

Stripes of sunshine decorate the room. Dust dances and swirls through it, swooping up and down and around. I lay and watch their performance, transfixed on it.

The space beside me is cool, although the imprint of Cian from my dream remains. I tossed and turned all night. Unsure of what I feel or what I want anymore. I know I want freedom. Freedom to be myself somewhere where nobody cares. But I think I want that with Cian.

Cian, a man I do not know. Yet, my heart calls to him. Like an unearthly bound. Like fate. But fate would not be so cruel as to match me with a man sent to execute me. I picture Morrigan, and I believe she would. She would enjoy the sickness of the joke. She would laugh at our struggle to love yet be drowning in the desire to kill each other.

As my fate is set, my fate to love and be loved by a man sent to kill me, a vampire, an old one too. I must accept it. Face my fate and break free of it. I must kill the King. This is the only way to release me from my sentence. This is the only way I can gain my freedom. For Cian to start afresh, with me.

I leave the security of my bedroom to find Cian with a guitar, placing it neatly in a chest near the kitchen. Hearing me he turns, with a sombre look on his face, "Are you ready to go?"

*No* "Yes."

Locking the chest he says, "Once we get to Carlingford, king's guards will meet us to escort us the rest of the way. It will maybe take us another half day."

"Escort us?" I slump onto the hard sofa.

"Yes, I imagine the King would have some questions about what happened on the way to him."

He is different from last night, more reserved. Like he is keeping something from me. He doesn't look me in the eye as he moves around the small space, filling a bag with some clothing. I watch as he stops to take in the paintings of the young girls in the cabinet. Slowly he opens the doors, pulling out the ribbons. Long pink and purple ribbons fall through his fingers. A little frayed at the ends but otherwise untouched by time. Gently he places them back exactly where they lay before. I turn away not wanting to be seen watching him in this vulnerable moment.

I was vulnerable with him. I allowed him in last night. And now, it feels like our roles have returned to how they were two days ago in the village. I know my dream was not real, but our conversation and kiss before bed was real. We both felt the pull on our hearts, the connection that was formed. My throat feels clogged with shame. Of course, he feels indifferent to me now. I am truly nothing to him. Nothing to anyone. No one fought to keep me in the village, no one came after me. No one cares that I am to be sentenced to death by the King. Perhaps I am still as worthless as I was before.

Without meeting my eye, he hands me some new boots. I lace them up slowly. Savering the time I have in the peace of this home.

Finally, I stand. Cian stands by the door, watching me. His handsome features seem soft and tired. As I walk towards the door to leave, he stops me. Holding out his arm across my stomach. Looking down, in his hand is my mother's dagger. *My father's dagger.* It's heavier than I remember, it holds a bigger story now. I take it, strapping it around my waist and under my shirt- hidden from sight.

He says nothing as he turns to leave without looking back. I cross the front door into the outside, it feels still. Stiller than yesterday. On our way in, it felt like tiny fairies were watching us, as we moved through their space. Now, it feels like they know where I am going. And they remain silent, mourning for me.

Cian waits by the door, locking it when I leave with a key he did not have before. He leads the way through Rosciar. A few steps ahead of me, never looking back to check I am still there. He knows I am still there, I have to face my fate.

As we leave the forest, life returns. Birds chirp as they fly overhead, sheep and cows graze in their fields. Bugs buzz around leading us to the waterfront. We follow the path that edges around Carlingford Lough for some time. The cool salty air licks at my face, taking away the burn of my shame.

Looking across the lough I see Carlingford itself. Its small hills decorate the coastline, overshadowed by the Mournes to my other side. I once read of a battle there, hundreds of years ago, between the witches and the vampires. Thousands of mortals were killed, assumed to be witches, the vampires slaughtered everyone. Wiping out the witching population to almost extinction. Now they only survive by laying low. Keeping their magic hidden. I once felt akin to them, part of their ancestry. Another part of me that is false.

For two hours we walked in silence, through the forest and along the lough shore. Until we come to a small harbour town. Cain walks through the town with conviction, and I willingly trail behind him. He leads me to the harbour wall. Fishing boats of all shapes and sizes are moored against it. Wooden crates of lobster and fish line the side of the wall. The smell fills the air, the warm sun turning it pungent.

At the end of the wall, where it drops off into the lough stands a group of men. They stick out in their clean crisp uniforms- kings guards. Cian greets them, shaking their hands as I follow behind.

"Commander," One replies, "Thank you for sending word ahead. We are ready to transport the prisoner."

"You sent word?" I reach out and squeeze his arm affectionately, trying to get his attention.

"This morning," He confirms, returning his attention to his men. "Which is your boat?" They lead him towards a small sailing boat, its sails are pulled down and neatly folded atop the boom. I can't see it clearly from behind them, but there appears to be a small cabin through a hatch door.

Two guards grab my upper arms. Their fingers dig into my skin as I try to pull myself free. "Get off me," I scream as I twist, but their grips are firm, "Cian, tell them to let go," I beg him, but he has already resumed the role of the faithful soldier. Looking through me like I am nothing but a piece of rubbish left out in the wind.

"Bring her on board, no need for chains. Iron doesn't seem to work." They drag me to the edge of the harbour wall. Both men holding under my shoulders, they lift and lower me down onto the boat where another guard grabs a hold of me. I let my body drop and push all my weight into the men hauling me around. I won't run away; I will go willingly. Cian knows this, so why am I being locked away?

Last night, whilst I fell in love with the dream of him, of what we could be together, he decided I was worthless, a dangerous fairy who needed to be executed.

What I thought was a hatch door leading to the decks below the boat, was a wooden crate, used to ship animals across seas. I didn't fight as they shoved me carelessly inside, slammed the door shut and secured it with a padlock. I push on the door, just to make sure they had locked it. It doesn't budge, doesn't wiggle open even a little. Through the gaps in the wood panels, I catch a glimpse of Cian, as he climbs down the ladder onto the boat, greeting the rest of his men.

Moving over to the gap in the next panel, I see Cian helping catch the ropes which are tossed from the top of the harbour wall. The boat slips away into the waters, as Cian wraps up the rope, using the space between his thumb and fingers and the end of his elbow to do so. He tosses to someone and moves out of sight.

My crate sways slightly, as they begin to raise the main sail. I hear them shouting orders to each other, turn the rudder this way, pull this rope, mind your heads. Eventually, the sail is up, I sit in my wooden box at an awkward angle as we set off across the lough to Carlingford.

I've lost sight of Cian. Perhaps he's lost sight of us.

# Chapter Twenty-Four

## Éabha

The sail to the other side of the lough doesn't take long. From there my box is lifted onto a carriage. I don't scream or shout for help. I decided I wanted Cian to think I had submitted. In truth, I am thinking of all the ways to kill a vampire. To kill the King. And maybe Cian, this is the only way to untether our fates.

The rhythmic clops of the horse's hooves, become the beat of my anger. I know I could break out of this cage, I can feel the fire inside me rumbling again, begging to be let loose. But, these men, foolish men, are bringing me right to the King. I will choose my time, the perfect time to attack. My magic knows this and smiles in response, warming my chest. For hours, I sit there, swaying back and forth, contemplating when is the right time for my attack. If right as I enter the palace is a good time, or when the King makes his introduction, or wait until the day of my execution, when more vampires are likely to get caught in the crossfire. So many options, I smile.

The cart lurches to a stop. Looking through the gaps in the wood, I try to find Cian. Trying to get one last look at him. Part of me hoped this whole journey was a ploy, and he hadn't changed his mind. But I can't find him. I move all around the small crate, watching guards and stable staff run around getting the horses taken care of and preparing the cart for my dismount. The door opens abruptly, and I am pulled out by a rough pair of hands, tossing me on the gravelled ground.

Before I can look at the careless guard or even the castle behind me, a sack is pulled over my head. Iron cold chains are clicked into place around my ankles and wrists. Their meaning seems pointless, as I am simply dragged up stone steps and down a hall, before being placed back on my feet, as they wait for doors to open.

With no warning, they let go of me. My knees hit the smooth hard floor, and pain shoots over my knees from the impact, causing me to fall forward with a grunt. The chains clink along with me, scraping off the floor as I try to kneel up. The sound of static clicks in my ears as the sack is removed, pulling my hair up with it.

My eyes adjust quickly, and before me sits King Connor. Lounging back in his large throne. He is tall and broad, clearly the throne was built for his size. The grey stone of his seat rises high up his back, with decorative arches sitting just below a gold crown inset into the grey stone. His golden eyes glisten in the light from the candles, arranged around him, but did not shine as bright as the gold of his crown. His hair is pulled back into a bun with a few golden-brown curls falling down to frame his face.

All I can hear was the beating of my heart. Silence falls around the room. His eyes bore into mine but I refuse to look away. Until I notice the tattoos on his neck. Wings appear from beneath his golden collar to his neck, his thick short brown bread obscuring the view of the bird who owned the wings.

My eyes travel down to his hands, which are gripping each arm of the throne. It looks like he is gripping the stone head of a bear to his left and a wolf to his right. Resting on pillars decorated with etched knives. Although he appears relaxed and cool sitting back on his throne, I notice every time he clenches his hands over the heads of the stone animals. They clench to the rhythm of my heart.

A movement to his left catches my eye. Cian steps forward from nowhere and stands beside the throne. He has changed his clothes, his black leather boots shine in the candlelight, his breeches tucked in neatly. Three simple gold metals with red ribbons on his chest, decorate his commander uniform. His hair has been swept back, no curls fall into his eyes, which appear stern, their glitter gone.

He doesn't look towards me, keeping his eyes fixed on something at the back of the room. He looks taller, as he stands with his shoulders back and head high. My heart aches, sorrow and anger mixing together. I push it down, squaring my shoulders like Cian. I sit taller on my knees and wait for the King.

Almost as if Cian's arrival was a signal of some kind, King Connor pulls himself forward on his throne. His eyes narrow in on me as he stands. He is taller than Cian, only slightly. He rolls his shoulders back and cracks his neck from left to right. I am not sure how, but the adjustment makes him taller. His eyes finally leave mine to turn towards Cian. He looks him up and down with a frown.

"I hear you took the long way," Connor's voice is deep and carries down the room. I am not sure who he is addressing as Cian does not respond.

Turning to face me, The King descends the short steps, which elevate his throne, "Witch" his eyes turn into a storm of browns and gold as he looks at me; "I sent a league of my best men to capture and transport you here, and yet all who remain is Commander Cian."

He waits for my response, but I have none. My eyes are fixed on Cian his are fixed on the back of the hall. The King follows my eyes, turning over his shoulder to Cian, to study him again. The two meet eyes for a second, Cian averts his eyes first looking back towards the back of the hall.

King Connor clicks his tongue, drawing my attention. The silence becomes deafening within the hall. Bouncing off the grey slate floor and brick walls. My heart is still hammering in my chest, the throbbing of it echoes in my ears, so loud I am sure they could all hear it pounding against my ribs. I remain on my knees, straightening my spine slightly to appear taller. The King will not scare me into submission. I think he thinks he's already won. He sits back on his throne, adjusting himself so his back is flush against the back.

This silence lingers around us. It's a game he plays. Intimidating, with silence. Showing off his power, through his size, making himself bigger. But I am bigger and more intimidating, he just hasn't seen it yet.

"Well witch?" he demands, leaning forward. "What did you do to my men?"

I turn to Cian, expecting him to interrupt, to provide clarity to his King. He hasn't moved, eyes unblinking. I scream at him in my mind, calling him names and begging him to look at me, as if he could hear me his eyes flick to mine. And stay there. I let out a breath I hadn't realised I was holding. Cian's eyes return to normal, little gold flecks dance across them in the candlelight. My heart flickers alongside them.

The King watches us from his throne. His eyes jumping between me and Cian, taking in the exchange, sensing the changes within his commander. I continue to beg Cian to respond with my eyes, he hears me, I can feel it, but his eyes are pleading with me, saying something I cannot translate.

King Connor gestures with his hand and suddenly hands are on me again. Suddenly, the hard end of a sword handle strikes me against my temple. I collapse into the cold stone floor. I hiss at the pain that cracks across my head. Sitting back up, I note

Cian has stepped forward, taking just one step before stopping himself.

Without warning I am being dragged back down the hall. My eyes remain on the King, as he stands, stretching, appearing even taller than Cian this time. His eyes finally leave mine as he turns to Cian.

"Commander, a word please," he strides away from his throne as I am finally pulled out of the hall.

# Chapter Twenty-Five

## Cian

I watch Éabha allow the guards to drag her out of the hall. Her wrists and ankles chained together with iron. Her eyes inciting a war, as they remain on me. I felt her calling to me, begging me. I had no time to explain. No, I had a lot of time to explain, just not the words. The King needs to think he has captured her. He needs to imprison her, to give me time to find the answers. This needs to happen, I scream back to her, but I have no magic for her to hear me.

Connor stands tall, stretching his back and raising his head to appear even taller, this is his intimidating move, I know it well. Only when she is halfway down the hall, still glaring at me, he says, "Commander! A word please," he turns on his heels and marches into the antechamber behind the throne. I wait until he is in the room, with the door closing slowly behind him before I turn to follow.

The antechamber is dark, with only a few candles lit. A large wooden table takes up most of the space, decorated with maps and scrolls. A set of soft chairs flank the fire in front of me. Connor has relaxed into the furthers chair. At least he looks relaxed.

"Brother, you are playing a dangerous game here," He lifts a glass of amber liquid to his lips, sniffing before he takes a taste.

"I don't know what you mean, *My King*," my response is laced with sarcasm as I help myself to whiskey and join him.

"Oh, Cian. That Witch is set to destroy us! And yet you reach to protect her." Connor's eyes turn molten gold, if you aren't looking at the right moment you almost miss it, but they gleam brighter. I can tell he is trying hard to refrain from jumping from the chair and grabbing me. Physically trying to shake some sense into me. I opt not to reply, staring at him from where I stand at the small bar. He slowly relaxes back into his chair. I know my brother well, rattle him too much and he'll pounce, remain quiet and still and he will settle down, like a lion or bear.

Once I deem it safe to do so I respond, "She is not the Witch you seek, brother."

Connor's laugh is dark, lacking humour. "You never were good at lying." With that, he gets out of the chair towards me. Lifting the bottle he pours himself another drink.

Closing my eyes for a brief moment, I sigh with frustration for my brother. So lost in the fear his crown will be taken from him, his world ripped from beneath him, his power dissolved to nothing. "I don't think she's a threat, she's harmless".

"Harmless!?" he whorls around slamming his glass on the table "Do you not think I know what she did in the mountains!? Did you think you could walk away from that without me finding out?"

"I think with the correct guidance and nurturing she can learn to use her powers for better. She could strengthen our cause." I remain calm, and level as his temperature rises.

"We have no cause! I am the King. I am respected and loved. What we do have is a threat!" Connor takes a breath and stands straight, "The Witch of mortal and earth people. Will bring destruction of all creatures, living and non-living."

My commander stance is gone now, moving closer I try to reason with my brother. Needing him to understand. The prophecy is wrong, it had to be. I consider telling him of my visits with Morrigan, but decide now is not the time. "That's not the correct quote."

Connor turns away from me, downing his drink in one. "We've misread it. It should read, 'The Witch of mortal and earth people, will bring change.' See you think this means she has come to kill us all. But she's here to cure us all"

"Cure us from what brother!? Eternal life? Being Gods? Living at the top of the food chain with nothing to fear?" He stabs his finger into my chest, "You have always wallowed in the guilt of what we are, but this," Connor gestures between us with his hand, stepping away he continues to wave his hand around the room, "This is not a plague we need to be cured of, this is power."

Rage runs through me now, I breathe through it to keep myself from disappearing. Connor, the oldest brother, has always chased power. From our mortal life to now, it's all he has wanted, but once he gets it, it's not enough. His mind is riddled, it impacts him being able to see the wider picture, "And you," I control my voice, if I shout I know the guards will come to his aid, or at least listen in, "You are a power-hungry demon set on preventing the world from evolving, from moving on, from growing."

Suddenly Connor has me pinned against the wall with a knife against my throat. "You may be the maker of us," he spits, "The first one, the time turner, Chronos or whatever the fuck those mortals worship." The knife pushes further into my neck, I hiss at the sting but don't push him away. "But you are nothing but a farmer's son who killed his family and ran. You are nothing Cian." The knife against my throat pushes up towards my adam's apple, I can feel the skin breaking and the blood sliding down my neck.

I smirk through the pain and the anger, "A farmer's son? What does that make you, *Your Highness*?" I laugh, making the knife rub against my throat more. "Remember who you are talking to brother, you are only here because I allow it." I push my face closer to his, causing the knife to dig deeper into my neck, I do not flinch from the pain knowing it will be gone with no trace of the mark in seconds. "You may be the oldest, the obvious choice for a King. But I hold the power here, and I can remove it all just as quickly as I have provided it." I spit these words at him.

Connor pushes off me taking the knife with him. My wound is already healed by the time he re-sheaths his blade. "The girl dies." And with that, he turns to leave, as I glare after him.

*

This castle is a fucking mess. For the past twenty-eight years, Connor has focused on nothing but finding Éabha. Obsessing over the tiny fluttering of energy I felt, gossip from the travelling Fae and the prophecy. Nothing else in his world has mattered. As a result, the castle is in complete disarray. Ancient tapestries hang on the wall, moth-eaten and fraying. Windows are cracked, and some of the frames have rotten through. Damp creeps up the walls, making the place smell like a swamp.

The library covers three floors on the west side of the building. I stand in front of its heavy wooden door, once decorated with fine etchings and carvings, all of which have been filled in with a nice fluffy layer of dust. My thoughts quickly jump to our mother, she longed for an intellectual son who would read poetry and write a masterpiece. All the books she once bought were now lost in time, their stories forgotten, and language no longer spoken. All my mother got was three brutes who are older than the sun and the moon. Shaking my head to remain present I push the door with ease, its hinges protesting.

I can immediately smell the knowledge contained within the rows and rows of books before me. Unfortunately, it's musty, the windows rarely being open on this side of the castle. Rows of dark leather-bound books flank me as I take the first aisle, hoping it leads me to where I need to go. Thick layers of dust, coat the space in front of the books at the edge of the shelf. No one comes here to read. Not in Connor's court anyway.

I don't know where I need to go. But I know what I am looking for. The prophecy. The original copy. It should be in a glass cabinet, sealed away from Time- sort of.

A scratching sound echoes through the aisle towards me. Like a mouse scraping at the wall trying to find its way out. I wouldn't be surprised. But this scratching comes from parchment paper being etched by a quill. The smell of ink is faint but distinctly recognisable.

Following the sound I find the source, hunched over a small desk, an oil lamp hanging on a stand beside them. Whoever they are, they don't look up at my approach, either so absorbed in their task or not used to having others in the library. I clear my throat loudly, but they don't even look up.

I approach closer, standing over them. "I see you, Commander, please wait further back."

Taking a few steps back, I wait, patiently. I have maintained my patience for days. Tension builds up on my shoulders. Three days, that's all it's taken to turn my life on its end. I flex my back and shoulders as the tension rises.

Taking in the man before me; his head bent over his writing all I can see is his bald head. With blue and purple veins spreading across his skull underneath his white skin. White, almost translucent skin, you would think this man has not been in the sun for many years. I think that is correct judging by the iron cuff around his ankle attached to a long lead of chain. Scrolls and crumpled-up parchment litter the floor around him. Behind him are shelves filled with rolled-up scrolls, open books, maps, and more evidence of his frantic writing.

He places his quill back in the ink and looks up at me, resting his hands together on the paper before him. I try not to react when I notice his ears. Pointed, this man is a Fairy. His frame, dressed in a simple shirt appears almost skeleton, his fingers greying from lack of skin with green fingertips. His eyes, are grey like his fingers, he doesn't blink at he looks up at me. "Commander, what brings you to my office?"

"Office?" I enquire looking around at the mess surrounding us, at the cot hidden in the back corner, and his long chain of iron.

"Office, prison, much the same these days," he rests back in his chair.

My brother had once discussed capturing a Fae and forcing them to work in the library, helping with translating the prophecy and other writings surrounding it. But I never thought it to be true.

"You're here about the prophecy concerning the Witch your brother, our dear King, is obsessed about." The Fairy confirms. He gets up and moves around his desk, his chain dragging behind him. He's short, barely making it as tall as my chest, I note as he walks past me. I follow him towards the glass cases I was seeking.

The cases are long, spanning the length of the room. Inside are an array of artefacts, all stolen by the King, and locked away in this dank, dark library. I follow the Fairy down the aisle of relics, some are books, maps, and weapons. But I find some glittering stones, diamonds and rubies, alongside glass vials with cork stoppers and large rocks with lines and crosses etched into them.

The Fairy stops at the artefact I desire. I remember it, it's yellowed paper and damaged edges. We found it in an iron chest buried in the peat bogs in Ciarraí. During Connor's fight for the throne. That story doesn't matter. What matters is what this paper says.

ᛏᚺᛗ ᚹᚪᛏᚺᛗᚱ ᛟᚹ ᛏᛁᛗᛗ, ᛏᚺᛗ ᚷᛟᛞ ᛟᚹ ᛏᚺᛗ ᛋᚤᚾ ᚪᚾᛞ ᛏᚺᛗ
ᛗᛟᛟᚾ, ᛏᛗᛗᛞᛋ ᛏᛟ ᛋᛗᛏ ᛏᚺᛗ ᛗᚪᚱᛏᚺ ᛁᚾᛏᛟ ᛗᛟᛏᛁᛟᚾ ᚪᚾᛞ ᚲᚱᛗᚪᛏᛗ
ᛋᛏᚪᛒᛁᚾᛁᛏᚪ ᛒᛗᚹᛟᚱᛗ ᚺᛗ ᚲᚪᚾ ᛗᛗᛗᛏ ᛗᛟᛏᚺᛗᚱ ᚾᚪᛏᚤᚱᛗ, ᛏᚺᛗ
ᚷᛟᛞᛞᛗᛋᛋ ᛟᚹ ᛏᚺᛗ ᛗᚪᚱᛏᚺ. ᛋᚺᛗ ᚹᛁᚾᚾ ᚲᚱᛗᚪᛏᛗ ᚾᛁᚹᛗ ᚪᚾᛞ ᛏᚺᛗ ᚲᚤᚲᚾᛗ,
ᚹᚺᛁᚲᚺ ᚲᛟᛗᚲᚾᛁᛗᛗᚾᛏᛋ ᛏᛁᛗᛗ. ᛏᛟᚷᛗᛏᚺᛗᚱ ᛏᚺᛗᚤ ᚹᛁᚾᚾ ᚱᛗᛋᛏᛟᚱᛗ ᛏᚺᛗ
ᚹᛟᚱᚾᛞ ᛏᛟ ᚷᚾᛟᚱᚪ. ᛒᚤᛏ ᛁᛏ ᛁᛋ ᛏᚺᛗ ᛏᚪᛋᛗ ᛟᚹ ᛏᚺᛗ ᚺᚤᛗᚪᚾᛋ ᛏᛟ
ᛗᚪᛁᚾᛏᚪᛁᚾ ᛏᚺᛁᛋ ᚲᚪᚲᚾᛗ ᚪᚾᛞ ᚾᛟᛏ ᛏᛟ ᛋᛩᚤᚪᚾᛞᛗᚱ ᛏᚺᛗᛁᚱ ᚱᛁᚲᚺᛗᛋ.

The Father of Time, the god of the Sun and the Moon,
needs to set the Earth into motion and create stability before
he can meet Mother Nature, the Goddess of the Earth.  She will
create life and the cycle, which compliments Time. Together
they will restore the world to glory. But it is the task of the
humans to maintain this cycle and not to squander their riches.

I look down at the small parchment, which holds so much power. The writing of the Old Gods remains intact, but the damaged edges make me wonder if we are missing some of it. The ink used is brown, a dark burnt colour- dried blood. The writing is deliberate as if this is not the first draft. But the final, sealed with the power of the Gods themselves.

"Not many people speak this language anymore, my Lord. But some can read it." His long fingers graze the glass as he moves across me, finding the catch and opening the display. "The King, claims to be able to read in this language, although I take it many years ago." He muses, as he delicately lifts the parchment from its bed, turning to lay it on a velvet table. "And you, my Lord," He moves gesturing for me to come closer, he pulls out a small stool for me to rest in front of the prophecy. "Do you read the language of the Old Gods?"

I take in the scroll, and its distinct smell of blood, and must from the ageing paper. I recognise the lines and etchings before me. I can pull out a few words like God, Sun and Moon. But many become unfamiliar. I sit still, trying to remember my lessons as a child. Memories which are faded, and fragmented. I have learnt so many languages, spoken, read and written around the earth. But my first has escaped me. I speak the words out loud; "God of Sun and Moon. Goddess of Earth." The words feel uncomfortable in my mouth, my tongue tries hard to work with the noise, but it comes out wrong. I read the end, unable to decipher the middle, "Restores the world's glory." These words have been spoken before, "That's what they said," I whisper to myself, forgetting I was not alone.

"The Phantom Queen?"

I turn to find the Fairy standing by my shoulder. He is standing so close to me that I can feel his cool skin through my uniform. His grey eyes are so white at first glance you would think he had none. They bore into mine whilst he waits for his answer. But he needs none.

"You went back to see her, didn't you?"

"How did you?" I push back from the scroll turning to face him square on. I remain sitting as I look him straight into his creepy little eyes. He doesn't say a thing, as his smile grows, wider and wider, showing all of his spiked teeth and the dark inside of his mouth.

"Did she not tell you?" He quirks his head to the side, "Or did you hide?"

Instinctively I reach out and grab his skinny neck. My hand almost closes around it as I squeeze. He squirms a little but his smile doesn't falter. The purple and blue veins in his head begin to bulge out as the blood can't move around his body. He starts to claw at my hand trying to worm his bony fingers behind mine to pry me away.

"Please, Commander," He begins to struggle for air now, "I can show you the real thing, I can send you back to the start."

Standing I toss him with ease across the small space. He crashes into the cabinets, though he is not heavy enough to break the glass. He climbs to his feet, glaring at me. His eyes have darkened although remain almost translucent grey. He fixes his rag which just about provides him with enough dignity.

"Show me," I growl at him, my patience with Fairy Folk dwindles with every encounter I have with them.

"It will be my pleasure," He smiles up at me. Without hesitation, he lifts my stool, and with enough force to tackle a Droimeann to the ground, he smacks me right in the face with it.

Everything goes black, as my head hits the floor. Slowly I open my eyes, expecting to see the ceiling of the library and preparing myself to jump up and grab the throat of that ridiculous Fairy who thought it a smart idea to hit me over the head.

But I am lying on dark, damp grass. The sky above me is different, I can see the planets, nestled together on the horizon. The red glow of Mars creates a dark burning reflection on the ground around me. Venus sits to the right, her flames licking out into the ether every so often. She sits there like she's staring down at me, at Earth. Jupiter looms behind the two. Their stripes swirl round, so slowly I have to focus on them to notice.

This is the sky of my childhood.

Before I was born, the Old Gods, ruled Earth. Governing together. But they fought, mortals, getting caught in the crossfire. Eventually, they grew bored of each other, and their own games, retiring to the planets where they now sleep in the sky. They left behind all their creation, the Fae, mortals and the Phantom Queen, Morrigan, whom they left to ensure that Life would continue, Fate kept things interesting and the mortals in line, and that Death was always inevitable.

As if on cue, I hear them. Morrigan is here, "Our ancestors scoff at us sisters." I get to my feet to find them standing on a cliffside. Their tall, elegant frames silhouetted against the light of the planets.

"Can you hear them laughing?" I move closer, their gowns, aren't made of the stars. Like when I met them recently. This time, they appear to be wearing water. Is that possible? Their skirts flow and lap over each layer, I can hear the slight sound of trickling water, as I move closer.

"They laugh because we are weak. I do not blame them." They can't see me, I don't think.

The fiery red-headed, Fate, turns to her sisters, "Then we shall have to start again- We need to create another God".

The sisters mull over this idea for some time. I admire the planets as they move around the dark sky. Wonder if they, the Old Gods, are part of this. If they return to set this right, the world will be restored to how it was before.

"The Earth's core," I hear the voice in my head, the sisters have not moved, have not spoken, yet I can hear their voice. "We can use it to create a new God. One that will haunt the mortals for us." They appear giddy at this idea, yet continue to stare at each other, not speaking, their internal monologue continues.

"We can pull the nutrients from the Earth. These elements are needed for the darkness and the lightness within him." They move now. Towards a stone table that had not been there before.

"This God will be able to move the Earth. As the Old Gods move their planets." They seat themselves across from each other, and I join them, standing by the shoulder of the blonde sister, Life.

"He must be able to move the Earth from here, create land and destroy it. He will use the water to shape their path, burn the land and scorch the living elements." The dark-haired sister, Death, leans forward, frowning, emphasising her statement.

"If he can do that, he should be able to create elements and restore balance to his destruction. Otherwise, we should remain here, to govern all." Her sister counters.

"The God," Life confirms "We will create, will create and end."

Silence falls between us all.

"That is a lot of power for one God to bear." A whisper comes. The sisters think, I can see their faces crease, and their eyes remain stern as I walk around the table. After some time, the whispers return to my head, "Two Gods. Two Gods will be created and will eventually come together. One to control the movements of the Earth, its darkness and its light. A God who can make these changes seamless and mould them together, making it all appear natural."

"Time," I join in the whispers. The first I have spoken since arriving here, they don't hear me.

"The second, will harness the elements of the Earth and create changes on the ground." Fate stands, her red hair falling down her back as she sweeps past her sisters, grasping both by their shoulders. "They will support the darkness and light. Then, when these Gods come together; devastating the landscape, they will bring joy, fear, life and destruction to the Earth and her inhabitants."

Slowly they all stand together, holding onto each other, as they smile, realising the brilliance of their creation. "The love that Time and Nature will have for each other, is a double-edged sword. Like a scale that harnesses the power to heal or harm or unleash destruction. This balance could tip our world in ways we cannot yet imagine."

Éabha, they speak of Éabha and me. I know I am Time. I am Chronos. I have spent thousands of lifetimes creating the seamless cycle of the rotation of the Earth, placing the Sun in the sky to redirect the Gods and our Earth, and finally the night light of the Moon. I know I am the God they speak of.

Nature must be my balance. A God who can heal and unleash destruction. A God who will balance me.

"Time sisters," They whisper, "He is a warrior." An image of myself flickers through my mind. Me as a young man, a soldier, a farmer's son, set out to protect my village.

"Nature is trickier," several images of men and women jump through my mind, as the sisters consider candidates for this role. "She will need to be the blood of the Fae," they identify, "and of the mortals, as she will need soul." The power of the Fae and the soul of a mortal. "She will be harder, but we will find her."

They all stand in agreement. Grasping hold of each other they embrace. But my eyes remain on the table, as a scroll appears. A parchment scroll with the same etched lines and strikes as the ones I left in the library.

As they finish, the wind picks up, wiping at my shirt. I turn to avoid the worst of the attack, holding my hair in place. It's hard to stand in place as it pushes against me, I take a couple of steps back before turning to find myself alone. Morrigan has vanished. The wind, continues to pull me, making me turn around again and again.

On my third turn, I find myself back in the library.

# Chapter Twenty-Six

## Éabha

My head is throbbing, and my vision is blurred from tears. I couldn't fight against the hands that grabbed me. I let them drag me away from the King and away from Cian.

I was thrown into a small cupboard-like room, with no window, the only light comes from under the door. Sitting against the wall, my eyes are fixed on the line of yellow light, noting when large feet move across it. Two guards are standing outside, I can hear them muttering to each other and laughing at their shit jokes.

Rage bubbles inside my chest, sparking flames in my throat. It warms my body, like in the mountain village. I can feel sweat slipping down my spine and my brow. Moving to wipe it away my chains clink. My magic is so powerful now I do not need to concentrate too hard to achieve what I want. And as I rest my hands on the stone floor, the iron melts away. Soaking into the grey stone beneath me. I don't react, however, I am too exhausted.

The King thinks I am a witch. The same dangerous witch Cian thinks I am. I still hope he is out there, trying to convince the King that I am not the witch of this stupid prophecy. Yet here I am! In a cupboard, guarded by two guards.

More determined than ever to prove them wrong. Or right. Perhaps proving them right would be best, I can kill everyone and return to my sorry quiet life by the water and live in peace.

Life without Cian. The thought jumps into my head and skips out as quickly. Cian, the Spineless Commander. Letting his guards attack me, drag me off, lock me up, me the woman he…

Well, the woman he nothing, really.

My dream of him has warped my sense of reality of the situation—maybe not just my dream of him. I ponder on whether my attraction towards Cian is fated or simply because a part of me is mortal and he is a good-looking man who has saved me more than once.

Remembering our kiss, Cian called it a spell. My heart clenches with the shame of Cian believing I had to place a spell on him for a kiss. I know I have no such power. If I could make people like me, love me even, my life would have been full—filled with joy, contentment, and love.

I hadn't noticed how tense I had become, glaring at the door. Dropping my shoulder, I sit up straighter and stretch my back slightly. Stretching out my legs I notice a tug and laugh. Laugh mainly at myself and of course at the guards that put me in here. My dagger is still attached to my waist. Concerned muttering comes from outside the cupboard, but I can't seem to stop laughing.

I pull the dagger out of its harness. Its stone handle weighs it down. I try to balance it across one finger and watch the light jump off the gems as it sways from side to side until I can find its perfect centre. Grabbing the handle, I spin it around my thumb and forefinger, watching the bright silver and glistening gems merge in colour. My vision blurs again as I focus on the colours in front of me; the white silver, the dark gems with purple tones and the yellow light from the hallway outside. The colours begin to blur together. As the flames in my throat tickle me.

My laughter stops as a plan forms in my mind.

Gathering around the debris in my little cell; dirt, dried leaves, straw and dust, I bring them together into a small pile. The amber of fire flickers to life over my tiny mound. I concentrate hard on my creation, letting it grow bigger and bigger.

"Help!" I scream, "There's a fire, please open the door!" I bang on the door, pulling dark smoke towards me and pushing it under the crack. I continue to scream and beg them to open the door as the smoke thickens, squeezing its way through the gap.

"Please don't let me burn in here," I cry to them with a smile.

The door swings open and a wave of water is tossed over me, putting out my fire. I stand there, my shirt tight with wetness, my trousers sticking to my thighs, looking at the guard smart enough to find water to put out my source of escape. "There you go, love," He smirks, "All sorted now." The door slams in my face.

Depleted, I turn, sliding my back down the door, and hit the floor. At least he didn't notice my dagger. I smile as I spin it around and around in the water. I mindlessly play with the water around me, splashing at first, then swishing it, trying to make whirlpools with my fingers. Then I realise there is a lot more water on the ground than just a bucket full.

"Shit," I jump to my feet, the water covers the entire floor's surface. I can make water.

With a finger, I trace a line along the wall, feeling the coolness and the rough bumps of the stone under my touch. I think of water, its flow, its power. The walls begin to weep, as water oozes from the cracks in the stone. Appearing as droplets at first, then slowly turning into small streams that fall from the stone walls. Soon water gushes from every crack and crevice, filling the room.

I can hear shouting outside. Panicked voices shout at each other trying to find the source of the water.

The water licks at my shins as I stand in the middle of my small cell. And it keeps rising. Crawling higher and higher up the walls. "There's a burst pipe or something! I can't swim! We'll drown!" my voice is laced with fake desperation.

The door slams open, and four guards spill into the cell, their boots splashing in the knee-deep water. They look around, bewildered, their eyes scanning the walls, the ceiling, as if searching for the source. I shrink back, pressing myself against the wall, hiding the smile tugging at my lips.

The water rises to their waists now, swirling and churning, growing wilder with every passing second. One of the guards turns to me, his face pale, "Where is it coming from?" he demands.

I raise my head, meeting his gaze, my expression turning cold. "It's not coming," I say softly, "It's already here."

With a wave of my hand, I summon the water higher, and it surges up, a relentless tide that crashes over them, swallowing their screams. The tallest guard struggles, his arms flailing, but the water takes him too. It presses against me, but I remain rooted, calm in the eye of the storm, as the guards gasp and thrash. Their fear fuels me, the sight of their helplessness a bitter satisfaction.

They begin to choke, their movements slowing, their eyes wide with panic. I watch as one by one, they go still, their bodies floating, suspended in the dark water, like leaves caught in a stream.

The room falls silent, the water holding the weight of their lifeless forms. I take a deep breath, feeling the power thrumming through me, the magic that has brought me to this point, to this moment. I close my eyes, willing the water to drain, to take them away, and as it recedes, it carries their bodies with it, leaving me alone, drenched and exhausted, but victorious.

The rush of water follows an eerie silence. I can't wait here, I need to move. I need to find the King.

With my heart pounding in my chest, like a war drum, I make my way down the corridor, hoping to find a staircase or some signage to direct me. Shivers run through me, as my cold wet clothes cling to me, slowing me down. I discard my jumper as I near a corner. With my dagger in hand, I peer around, finding another corridor, leading to a narrow set of stairs. They creek loudly as I hurry up, taking two steps at a time.

The top of the stairs leads to a deserted landing, with a few doors leading off in all directions. Thread bear rugs clothed the wood floor, and aged oil paintings hung on the wall, coated with a thick layer of dust. After a moment of silence I sigh, this part of the castle is abandoned, no one may even think to follow me here.

I start to try each door, the first few are locked, another is open, but stuck closed through years of congealed dirt. Finally, I find a door which opens into another long corridor. Candles are lit along the wall, casting orange light on the grey brick walls. Further down I can see a brighter light, perhaps made by a fire. Hoping this will lead me to the King's quarters, I tip-toe towards the warmth of the light, keeping my back to the wall, and my dagger posed ready to attack if needed. The hallway ends in an archway leading into the bright fire-lit room beyond. Keeping my back to the wall, I edge towards the opening. Movement catches my eyes, as a shadow moves slowly across the room.

Pressing myself against the wall I hold my breath. My heart is still hammering against my ribs and my magic threads itself through them trying to slow the beats. I can't afford to be caught now; this is my only chance.

Slowly, trying to move without making a noise, I peer around the corner. The room is furnished in warm upholstery, with a large sofa taking up most of the space. Further in, just out of my view is a grand fireplace. Before it stands a woman, warming her hands. Long blonde and neatly coiled curls fall down her back. As I take her in, my heart relaxes, and my magic pulls me to her, as if it knows her somehow.

She turns slowly, as if to leave but pauses as our eyes collide.

"Ceira?" I whisper, it comes out chocked through surprise and confusion. Walking into the room Ceira remains frozen by the fire, as if in shock, her eyes darting between me and the door.

"Éabha, thank the stars you're alive! I came to find you. We need to get out of here," she says, as her expression softens. I reach for her, reach for her shoulders to pull her into a hug. Relief floods my body as I take in my friend. My friend who has travelled all this way, through forest and wilderness to get to me. She pulls back from me, her eyes fixed on the door across the room, it is sitting ajar.

"How did you get in?" I ask following her gaze, her silent comments confirmed as we hear footsteps just outside the door.

She doesn't answer right away, still glancing around nervously, as if fearful we will be found. "It's a long story. We need to move, before they..."

Guards storm the room, coming through both entrances. Their heavy cumbersome footsteps echo through the stone passage I escaped through. I turn to Ceira but she's already making her way towards the door, pushing her way through the wall of armed men blocking our exit. I follow behind her, ducking out of the way as the first guard swings his sword at me. I slash through his arm with my dagger, causing him to fall back. Only for him to be replaced by another.

Lunging forward I aim for the man's chest, but his chain mail blocks my dagger's entry. I lose sight of Ceira as I am backed into a corner, "Ceira, run!" I scream at her. Again, I lunge with my dagger this time aiming for skin, wrist, neck or face, but each guard ducks out of my way each time. The guards around me follow this dance routine as they get closer and closer.

My magic untethers itself from my ribs. Like a whip, I unleash sparks of fire in their faces. My eyes glaze over, blinding me from the bright white light of my fire. But I can hear their screaming. And I know my fire is melting away their armour, roasting their skin.

Something collides with my head as I jump on the sofa for better aim. I sway slightly, trying to remain upright. My magic starts to come out in drips. Sparks fall to the floor, not even strong enough to singe the carpet. My head begins to throb as blood blurs my vision. Shaking my head I try to recover and take aim at the nearest guard.

Sparks leap from my hands, but they have little impact as he brushes them off. All six guards move closer to me, closing me in again. I can't quite make out the door, but I turn to jump in its direction. My balance is off from the blow to my head, and I fall from the back of the sofa onto the stone floor. I try to get up and run but I am not fast enough. Hands are on me as guards pull both my arms behind my back.

Screaming I try to twist out of their hold. Throwing my arms and legs in any direction trying to kick and hit my way out of their hold. But they are strong. My magic doesn't work as I need it to, and my head is still fuzzy. They drag me onto my feet, holding me with my arms tightly behind my back. I can't see

Ceira anywhere; she must have managed to escape as they were distracted by me.

As my relief for Ceira washes over me something slams into my side causing me to double over in pain. As I bend over my ribs puncture my lungs, their broken sharp spikes stick into the soft flesh, preventing me from breathing. I gasp and cough as the guards pull me back up. One guard on each side of me drags me through the castle.

# Chapter Twenty-Seven

## Eabha

My body slams on the stone floor in front of the King.

"I should have killed you on the spot. Maybe I will this time!" The king's shoes come into my line of sight. Slowly my eyes travel up his immense body. His decorative armour has been removed leaving him in black trousers and shirt, now slightly open exposing the bird whose wings decorate his neck. A sparrow, surprising I muse.

"Killing you will break whatever hold you have on my Commander." Falling back onto my heels with my knees firmly planted on the stone, I search the throne room for Cian. A dark chuckle comes from the King as he senses my need. He bends down on his hunches, grabbing my chin, caked with blood, and forcing me to meet his eye.

"Is it a spell?" he whispers so only I can hear. "Do you know who he is, is this why you have enchanted him?" My skin cracks as a smile escapes, if I could breathe without pain I would laugh. This further confirms how stupid the King is; to believe I have put some kind of spell on his commander and not that he is simply wrong about the prophecy. Or maybe he knows something I do not? What if Cian shares these confusing feelings, and is equally riddled with thoughts and lust and desire? This makes me smile wider, infuriating the King, he pushes me away and stands. I fall onto my back, the impact causing the sharp pain in my ribs to increase.

Instinctively, I reach for my side. Expanding my fingers across my rip cage I breathe in, hold and blow out slowly. Breathing only intensifies the pain further and I squeeze my eyes shut. Breathing in and out again I focus on the location of the pain, the broken rib. Images of ivy growing up walls and across plants, tangling itself together flood my vision as my ribs are slowly sown back together. The pain vanishes as the last fragment of bone is stitched together. Now healed, I sit up smoothly, taking in the King before me.

King Conor is red with anger, his eye bore into mine and he reaches for the nearest guard's sword, pulling it quickly and smoothly from its holster and pointing it directly at me.

"You dare," he spits stepping closer, so the point of the sword is under my chin, "Use magic in my court!" the room shakes in fear from his shout, and I suddenly get a sense of the danger this King poses. His chest rises and falls quickly as the sword moves slowly into my throat, I don't flinch or push back, caught in a trance from the anger running through the King's eyes.

Suddenly the sword is removed leaving a sliver of a mark where my jaw meets my neck. "Someone find my brother," he demands to anyone, "I want him to watch whilst we cut her in four and burn her body." A brutal death I know I will not recover from. Not be able to heal myself from. "Cian shall watch, and I shall watch my brother as your spell on him is broken."

Brother? Cian is his brother? Some movement signals guards leaving to find Cian, the King's brother.

King Connor turns, "You," he points with his sword into a dark corner. Ceira saunters out. Her clothes are untattered from our attack and she seems uninjured. "My little spy" the King smiles at my friend as he passes the sword off to a guard.

"Perhaps I should have instructed you to bring me the witch, as my brother shows his weaknesses, and my guards cannot seem to keep her locked up." Ceira walks into the light, her usual confidence radiating off her. I look between Ceira and King Connor for answers. Ceira is the King's spy?

"Tonight, Éabha, the scales will fall from your eyes, and you will see the truth of your existence. Your precious friend, Ceira, whom you believed to be your confidante and ally, is nothing more than a carefully placed pawn in my grand design." He moves back to his throne, "Knowing not to trust my guards to bring you to me, I sent Ceira to break you down and rip you apart."

"She interpreted this in a different way" He looked at her scoldingly, "She took her time, I see."

"I needed to confirm she is the powerful Witch you wanted," Ceira sits down on the steps, shrugging, "She didn't know how to use her power, so I had to push her." I stand, taking an unconscious step towards her. Confusion paints my face, as I look at Ceira. She no longer looks pretty. She is dressed and made up as she always is, but her face appears contorted, and her eyes are dark. "But Cian and his band of merry men, got there before I could push her too far."

"All those fights you found yourself in? The rumours about the *monster* in the water?" King Connor laughs again staring down at Ceira with pride in his eyes. "Your grandfather?" She smiles, as the memory of my beaten grandfather fills my vision, my heart aching for the pain I caused him, both of them. "All me."

"The bond you made with her," The King draws my attention away from my friend, as he slumps down on his throne, seeming bored now from this interaction. "The bond you believed was unbreakable. Is nothing but an illusion," He laughs, it booms through the hall, bouncing off the walls and landing before me.

"This is the power I wield, Éabha." He leans forward, resting tattooed-covered arms on his thick thighs, "To create, and to destroy, to shatter. Your fate was sealed the day Ceira entered your life. Now you stand alone, and I get to watch you break."

"What?" I whisper. Confusion takes over my face as I frown and shake my head, staring between the King and Ceira. Ceira, my friend, was the source of all the misery that not only I but my whole family faced. We were starving, scraping together pennies because of those rumours. My grandfather was nearly beaten to death. If I couldn't heal his wounds, he would have died. "I don't understand".

"Please, do you really think I could be friends with you?" her face turns to disgust as she looks at me. "Your mother was a whore, and you are a byproduct of disgusting cross-species engagements," she spits.

The pain starts in my chest, right over my heart. White scorching pain strikes across my chest ripping my heart in two. I clenched a fist to my chest, digging into my rips hoping to alleviate the extreme discomfort.

Ceira continues as I sway on my feet, "Éabha, you are worthless. You had no one before I came along. And you would have no one again."

Tears spill over my eyelids and stream down my face. She is right, she's always right. I am worthless. Useless. Insignificant.

"If you mattered to anyone, they would have fought to keep you when the guards came to get you, but they all stood around and watched. Everyone carried on with their day after."

Ceira and the King snicker whilst the pain ripping through my chest explodes through my body. Falling to my knees I scream. My hands reach out to stop myself from crashing face-

254

first onto the stone floor, but I am weak and my face smashes into the rock.

"No one cares about you."

Those were her last words to me as the ripping, through my chest, becomes too much to bear. All the truths laid out in front of me. All my insecure thoughts coming true. And my only friend in the world breaking my heart.

I shriek, the noise echoing throughout the great hall. The agony splitting through my body is too unbearable. Everything feels hot, like a fire was set alight within me and it is spreading, destroying everything in its wake. Suddenly a gush bursts out of me. My arms are thrown out and my back arches, with the impact. My eyes are sealed shut but I can still see the bright orange light exploding from my body. A surge of power follows it. Running after it like it's worried it will be left behind because being left alone with me is the last thing anyone or anything wants. It runs like a stream until it turns into a trickle then a dribble. And I collapse onto my front. The pain radiating through me slowing down to a simmer. Only then, the pain begins to feel like pins and needles, do I realise it was my magic that ran away from me.

Now that the truth about myself has been spoken aloud, even my magic, my whole being, doesn't want me.

The room is still. Not even the walls dear to breathe.

I lay on the floor. Resting my face against the cool stone floor, which offers little comfort to my aching hot body.

A slight breeze blows through the room. It's cold. And brings in a sharp smell of dampness.

Still, no one speaks.

I am unsure how long I lay on the floor. How long my audience remains non-moving. How long the silence lasts.

The sound of the hinges of the door creaking open echoes through the room, and footsteps come running into the front room towards me.

"My King," a voice says.

"Your Highness," another says, both breathless.

I move my head until my chin is resting on the ground and look up at the King. His eyes are on me. He cannot hide his fear as the temperature in his castle gets cooler, not look up at the new arrivals.

"Outside," the first voice gasps.

"The trees," the second stammers.

"The air," someone else breathes.

King Connor looks up now. Waiting for more information that does not come.

I try to get up. Pushing my hands into the stone floor only to rise a little and slump back down. My body is empty, my energy and magic are gone. I barely have the strength to stay awake. But I force my eyes open. I can feel in my bones, my magic has done something as it broke from me. I know, whatever it is, will have consequences. More severe consequences than being weakened. Whatever I did, whatever changes are occurring outside, the King will have me tortured and killed for them.

I can hear talking. Some muttering. Some loud commanding voices. All scared. It is hard to focus on what they are saying as all I can make out is colours, orange, yellow, brown and red. Either I am delusional, or my magic is running amuck outside.

Suddenly a hand is in my hair, dragging me to my knees. The King wrenches my head back, "What have you done?!" I look back blinking, unable to form words or process his questions.

He fists my hair, turning and dragging me through the hall. I scream, a weak cry, grabbing at his hands trying to pull them free as my hair begins to snap off from their roots. Through the large doors and across out into the outside air. The chill hits me first, settling into my damp clothes, and making me shiver.

He tosses me onto the gravel with such power I skid across the stones on my landing. Climbing to my feet, I am wobbly slightly on my assent. I notice my breath turning to steam in the air, like a kettle. My hot breath mixes with the cooling air and swirls out before me before disappearing into nothing. Groups of guards are scattered around me, their breaths coming out like steam also. The hairs on my arms stand on end, creating little bumps along my skin.

Looking out across the lawn, to the trees which decorate the gardens, once vibrant greens are now turning shades of orange and gold. Their colour is a bright contrast to the night sky. The wind begins to blow sending a chill, making some people retreat inside and others huddle closer together. It takes with it some of the leaves, and then more and more begin to fall, dancing through the breeze as they flutter to the ground. Soon the garden becomes a mosaic of fallen leaves.

The moon appears through the clouds. A silvery glow washes over the castle, as we all watch on in awe. The moon seems larger, closer to us somehow, framed by the inky blue of the night sky.

A swarm of birds fly overhead, all travelling in the same direction, away from here, towards the south. They fly with purpose as opposed to their usual playful laps, like they can feel something has changed in the air and are seeking refuge.

We all stand in silence, captivated by it all, the cold, the moon, the leaves, the birds.

"Put her somewhere until I find Cian," King Connor commands turning back to the warmth of the castle. Stopping he turns to me, he knows by the look on my face, I won't fight this time. I just hope what I have done is contained to the castle grounds. "Somewhere secure," he adds.

# Chapter Twenty-Eight

## Éabha

Guards roughly grab an arm each. I slump between them unable to keep my body up. Nausea erupts in my stomach, spewing into my throat. How could my magic do this, the rot. The trees were rotting, weren't they? Their leaves fall dead to the ground. The air freezing over with decay. My magic has destroyed. Just as Cain predicted. It is destruction I brought, not glory.

My heart beats slowly, through exhaustion. But each beat echoes through my body. A cold sweat drips down my forehead and into my eyes, the salt making them sting a little. I begin to tremble as they lift me up the steps into the castle. It's not from the cold though. Adrenaline courses through my veins, I can almost hear it as it charges from my heart, with nowhere to go, no release.

A knot forms in my stomach, twisting with each breath I take.

Unlike the drenching, I hope this is contained to Duiblinn. And doesn't seep out across Éire or across the water.

My body feels strange. Completely without energy or magic.

The castle is warmer than the outside. People run around with wood logs, lighting each fire as we pass. Others run around simply just in a state of panic. More and more people have appeared than previously, coming out of their hiding places to panic together.

I am dragged through the foyer towards the throne room, but we verge off and down a flight of stairs. The two guards huff with the weight of me. But I don't care, I let my feet drag behind us, letting them slap down each step of the long staircase. It becomes narrower the deeper into the castle we go. Soon it is only wide enough for one man to fit, and so they begin to slide me sideways down a now twisting set of stairs.

They readjust their hold on me at the bottom, I allow my body to slump further down so they are holding my full weight. They grunt and heave me up so my toes barely touch the ground. Letting my head fall back, I note another corridor leading in a different direction than us, we turn left.

Once at the bottom, we find ourselves in a dark corridor. Chills run through all three of us as our eyes adjust. They both light torches, allowing me a moment of reprieve to slump down the wall. My body feels limp, unable to hold itself up anymore. Drained my eyes begin to close, I want to let the darkness of unconsciousness take me. My mind screams at me to stand up and run, to stay away and fight them. But exhaustion takes hold of me in its warm embrace.

They both give up holding me up as we turn down the dark hallway which looks ever ending in the dim light. Silently agreeing between them to drag me along. The toes of my boots catch on every stone which rests out of place, the scraping sound of leather against the hard surface echoes down the hallway, chasing us.

Without warning my back is slammed against the brick wall, and my head follows, smacking against the hard surface. Too weak to scream, I grunt with the impact. Shockwaves flow over my head as I try to release my arms to hold it. But they are pinned to my sides. My eyes water, making it difficult to focus on what's in front of me.

I hear muttering in my ears. Or maybe they are talking normally, but the ringing from the blow drowns them out.

Calloused rough hands are all over me. Pulling at my shirt, and my hair, running their hands over my breasts and gradually squeezing harder and harder. Their hands become more determined as I begin to squirm and wriggle in their hold. My vision clears as the initial shock of the wall and the ringing in my ears fade. The two guards who brought me down here, have me wedged between them, their thighs pressed between mine and their bodies holding my arms to my sides.

"No, please stop," I plead as they laugh and pull, nausea gurgles in my stomach as their faces push against my neck. Their stubbled chins scraping against my skin.

Ripping sounds are followed by hands on skin. I try to push myself out of their hold, but their hold is like a clamp, pushing me further and further into the wall.

"Come on pretty girl, show us a magic trick," He runs his nose along my jaw down my neck whilst another's hands gather my hair together, yanking my head back. Everything feels slow and bumpy as I try to will my body to move, to fight back to scream. But I can't muster enough energy.

"What's wrong witchy?" A whisper comes to my ear, and I squeeze my eyes shut, willing myself to disappear, hoping my magic will return and help me vanish. "You seemed to like the Commander, why not us?"

The nausea slowly growing inside me threatening to burst out, turns to rage. My heart burns as the words echo in my ears. The mention of Cian, the presumption I had welcomed it, any of this, including Cian into my life. All these thoughts drove the rage. My body awakens, burning hotter than any flame, igniting a wrath that surged through my veins like wildfire.

They saw me as nothing more than a plaything to be used and discarded. Like the men in the bar, the men in the village. I don't need magic to help me here. I draw back and spit right in his face as he tries to pull my face to his.

"You fucking bitch," He steps away wiping the saliva from his eyes.

His friend to my right pushes my shoulder against the wall with one arm to restrain me. "Now sweetie, don't be mean," He smiles down at me. Until he sees something in my eyes. Something like power and loathing. Before he can let go, I rear my head forward colliding with his. A crack confirms I've broken his nose, his scream proves it. Blood trickles down between my eyes, and I smile at him, almost laugh at him, as he holds his nose screaming.

His friend joins me, laughing at the attack, "You like it rough eh?" he grabs me, pulling me towards him. I don't answer him, as I kick my leg out, sweeping it under his and knocking him to the ground. The heavy load of his body makes the corridor shake. And I run.

I run about three paces, until a bloody-faced guard is in my way, grabbing my waist and pulling me back. His hold is like a clamp as I try to claw my way out of it. Suddenly I am thrown in a cell. I skid across the small space until my back collides with the back wall. I try to roll onto my knees, to push myself up. But a boot connects with my stomach. Then another. I can feel bile being pushed out as more blood rushes to the internal wounds. They are screaming at me, laughing at me, all while boot after boot smacks into my body.

Each blow pushes air from my lungs, as I gasp to replace it. My entire body is in pain. Sharp tight pain throbs through my body. The cell walls around me become hazy, as my eyes stream with water blurring my vision. With one last grunting kick, they leave. I hear the cell door lock and footsteps slowly disappearing.

Rolling onto my back, I welcome the cold wet floor, as it soothes the aches radiating from my abdomen. The pain throbs with every uneven breath I take. My muscles clench trying to protect themselves, trying to stitch themselves back together. The air is wet, making me cough when I breathe. With each breath my mouth fills with coppery wetness, making me cough again. My stomach clenches in agony each time.

Slowly, my breathing returns to normal, my tears dry and my vision returns also. Looking around there is nothing in this cell but a bucket in the corner. Black metal rails keep me in the cage, locked together with a large padlock. But I remain on the floor, exhausted.

*

I hadn't realised I had passed out, until I wake to dripping sounds. My head bangs to the beat of my heart as I roll over onto my side. I can't make out what's around me, my eyes adjusting too slowly. The floor is caked in wet mud, it squelches under my hands as I try to sit up.

The cell is smaller than I imagined, stretching my legs out my feet touch the bars in front. My muscles strain at the movement. Almost creaking like they haven't moved in years. I sigh into the stretch, as they slowly release into a brief reprieve from the numb pain across my head and abdomen.

Now fully adjusted to the darkness, I can make out the space around me. Small shadows scuttle back and forth, some coming close and then running away. Little mice come over to investigate, but I don't cringe away. It's comforting to have another living thing down here with me.

I stretch my arms out, causing the mice to run away again. My shirt is torn from the collar down, one sleeve attached to the shoulder only by a few stitches. Splashes of blood decorate my once beige shirt, and I am not sure what is mine and what belongs to the guards, or what is simply just mud.

Trying to focus on my body, I try not to move and try to work out what hurts. Hoping my magic has returned so I can heal myself. I follow a rough trace of mud and blood along my cheek, between my eyes towards my forehead, but my arm pulls back. Pain shoots through my shoulder and down my right side preventing me from reaching up.

Trying a different approach, I relax each part of my body, starting with my jaw I wiggle it from left to right, the movement causes shooting pain from the back of my head down my neck. I remember hitting my head against the brick wall, my neck being pulled back with force and later headbutting one of the assaulting guards. Slowly and gently, I ease my head back to rest on the wall behind me. I groan at the soft impact, a tender wound appears, unnoticed until now.

The guards, their laughter and shouting, being dragged down the stairs into the darkness, is all I can piece together. Slowly images return to my memory, and I cringe away from them. They held me up, two on each side, pulling my hair, asking me to show them a magic trick, they talked of their Commander, Cian. I smile as I remember the look on the guard's face as I spat at him. And at the laughter that followed when I headbutted the other.

*They'll come back*. For more fun and to get revenge. I need to get out of the cell, hide somewhere safe, store some energy and try to heal myself.

The King has guards all over the castle, and escaping the grounds is nearly impossible. I need to find a corner, or a storage room, a cupboard to hide in. Just for a bit. Just long enough to muster up some more energy.

Reaching forward I use the bars to pull myself to standing. I rattle it just to make sure it is not accidentally open. The sound causes my headache to worsen and the mice to run off, squeaking as they go, jumping over each other. The throbbing through my body, makes it feel heavy, it is begging me to sit back down and stop moving. Resting for a moment, with my head against the cold bars of the cell, is all I can give myself.

My head and stomach ache as I try to pull on my magic to heal myself. It sparks in my chest a little, just enough to tickle me slightly.

The gate to the cell is closed with a chain and a padlock. Taking a few deep breaths, I reached for the lock. Groaning as the stretch tears at my wounds. But I keep going, I hold the padlock in both hands, closing my eyes whilst resting my head against the bars again. I need to draw on my magic, fuel it somehow, to get out of here. I think about the King, his guards, Ceira and this castle. I let myself feel the anger and rage and sorrow. I let it flow through my veins towards my heart. I let my magic dance with it like a storm.

The metal melts like it was made of ice, parts of the chain and cage door melting with it, dripping down my hands and landing on the floor in a puddle. Before cooling back to silver metal on the wet stone.

It feels like I am drawing magic from the well of my soul. That final spark of magic, my last surge of energy trickles out of my hands, dripping to the ground along with the melted metal. Leaving a tingling sensation, like pins and needles in my palms. My hands are still cupping the air as my body begins to tremble. My last flicker of magic is gone, leaving me weaker than before. A hollow ache forms in my chest, where she should be resting.

I need to get out of here.

Pushing the cell door open, I stumble out, using the wall for stability. The walls are wet in this part of the dungeon. Leaning against the wall, I clutch my right side. The pain intensifies there when it should be healing. I try to hold it together and think of mending a hole in a dress or filling in a hold with soil, trying to focus on healing the wound, even a little. Nothing happens. Slowly my breaths begin to get haggard as it gets harder to breathe.

Using the walls to navigate I shuffle forward in the direction the guards had dragged me from. My feet trailing behind me slightly. I have to continuously pull one leg forward each time I need to take a step. My eyes focus on my goal, the end of the hall, where the darkness consumes the light and I can't see any further. But I only make it a few meters before tripping on the uneven stone floor and falling.

I screech as pain on my side, stabs through me, sending a shock wave across my chest. Gasping, I am unable to take in air. I try to roll onto my back, away from the pain of the broken rib. I try to remember to breathe. I picture Cian, as he breathes in, holds, breathes out. Tears fill my eyes falling down my face into my ears.

*Breathe in, hold, breathe out.*

Each breath strains my lungs, which push against the broken rib. But slowly I am no longer gasping for air.

I lay on the wet, cold, stone floor for longer than I want to. Listening. I can't hear any movement on this level, besides the trickle of water running down the walls and the mice scuttling around, the castle feels eerily still. Like everyone has gone to bed. I feel disoriented, unable to discern the passage of time.

Determined to find a place to hide, I use the uneven stones in the wall as a leaver to pull myself up. The movement tears through my skin, as the bones puncher through. I scream trying to hold everything in place. Looking down, dark red blood spills out between my fingers. I try to ebb the flow and hold the wound tighter. I can feel the lift flow out of me along with the blood, as I begin to get dizzy.

I have to keep moving, to find any space to stop and heal where the guards cannot get me.

I crawl. On my knees, with one hand holding my side, I crawl until I can see the stairs.

Just as I make it to the first step, just as I think I have a chance of escape, I hear footsteps coming towards me, down the stairs, bouncing off the stone walls.

"Nope," I mutter as I use the first step to help me get onto my feet. I sway slightly as the blood drains from my head and rushes out of my wound and down my destroyed shirt. The footsteps get louder and closer. I will my feet to move, to turn and take me behind the stairs where I can hide.

I only make it one step into the shadow when two large hands land on my shoulders pulling me back into a hard chest. If it hadn't before, my heart sank. My last hope is snapped away from me.

The hands hold me and turn me around. There's a familiar fragrance in the air as he draws near, the crisp scent of rain mingling with the deep warmth of oakwood. It's a grounding sensation as if the forest after a storm has come to life in him. It wraps around me, a quiet reminder of safety, of something solid and unwavering.

Cian," I breathe in shock. His eyes, dancing with fiery flecks of gold as they travel from my pale and bloody face to my ripped clothing, my hand still clutching the wound to my side, blood smeared up my arms and across my stomach. His gaze feels like it burns with every movement up and down my body. I hold my breath so I wouldn't cry or scream.

"Who did this to you?" he asks then pulls me into his arms. My face presses snugly against his chest as his hand holds me there. The comfort fades quickly as my lungs ached for air. He releases me from his embrace. Holding my head in his hands, he searches my eyes, their brightness gone. His hands trail over my body; my face, my neck, my shoulders, before finally resting on my arms. He stands there, observing, taking in every little detail of me.

I don't know how long we stood like this, but my knees begin to give way as I sag to the ground, unable to hold myself upright. My focus on Cian was weaning, my vision blurring over again as I begin to loose sight of him. I hope he knows what I am thinking, how grateful I am at this moment for him.

"I can help you," He whispers, as he follows me to the floor, trying to hold me up, to stop me from crashing onto the stone, "You just have to say yes. Eve, I can save you."

I know exactly what he means. We had never spoken of this. Of the act of vampires. Never needed to as my fate was set. Yet here I lay, in his arms, bleeding out and magicless.

I can't form the words to explain. I can't find the energy required for it. I hold his eyes and hope that he understands. I may be injured, with no magic to help me heal, but I cannot risk taking his blood. I cannot risk the possibility I might die before it works. Not when I need my magic, I need my magic to be me. As a vampire, I would have to live without it. I could not risk that.

His frown lines between his perfect shimmering eyes deepened. "Please Eve, you're hurt, badly," he shakes his head, unwilling to understand

"I can't," I manage knowing he needs to hear it. After a moment Cian nods, but he doesn't agree, I know he wants it, he wants to open his wrists and bring it to my mouth. But he won't.

Finally, relief washes over me. With a sigh I close my eyes, trusting Cian will keep me safe.

# Chapter Twenty-Nine

## Cian

Éabha collapses. I scoop her up, carrying her like a baby. I don't know where I am going, but I know we need to get out of the dungeon. This part of the castle is strange to me, I can picture its layout in my head and follow the hallway past the stairs. There should be an exit down here.

Éabha moans in my arms. The wound has stopped bleeding, for now, but I can feel the rib sticking out from her side. My hands are covered in her blood. The familiar metallic smell surrounds me. However, it is not overwhelming. As this is Éabha's blood, not a random human, not a girl who has thrown herself at me, not a willing offering. This was Éabha. My Goddess, whom I have claimed as my own, and I will not let her die.

The hallway rounds to the left, growing darker and darker with each frantic step I take. Suddenly it ends with a door. Kicking it open I had hoped to be greeted by the refreshing air from outside and the relief of our escape. I curse as I find a room lit only by two lamps on a low desk in the centre. It's littered with jars full of browning fluids and papers crumpled into balls thrown around.

Carefully I pay Éabha on the floor. Cupping her face, I try to wipe away some of the blood and mud from around her eyes. Her eyes flicker beneath her lids in response to my touch. "It's ok, I've got you now, it'll be ok," I try to reassure her, mostly for my own benefit.

The back wall of the room was taken up with shelves, filled with the same jars, yet these jars glowed and swirled with some sort of white fluid. A row of wicker baskets lined the wall behind the door. Pulling them towards me, I begin to rummage through them, they are only filled with rags, boots and old guard uniforms. Pulling out a thick blazer, I ball it up and place it under Éabha's head. Followed by another, I rest it along her side, angling her wound off the floor.

Kneeling beside her I hold my breath, trying not to make a sound. I can't hear anything, not a breath, or a beat of her heart. Slowly I rest my ear on her chest and wait. It felt like I was waiting for hours, laying there trying not to crush her with my weight. Finally, a faint little boom echoed through her chest. Just one beat then nothing. It was longer before the next beat.

She is dying.

She didn't want me to save her, she made that clear. But I could. I could save her now and have the rest of time seeking forgiveness. One drop of my blood is all it will take; I think as I bring my wrist to my mouth. My fangs are ready for impact, ready to puncture my skin and draw blood.

I had been quiet for so long that I did not hear the approaching steps until they were right outside the door. It clicks open as I jump to my feet.

Long, grey, skeleton-like fingers creep around the door as they push it open. A frail figure follows, stepping silently into the room, his pale, nearly translucent skin catching the dim light. His unblinking, grey eyes sweep the space, cold and detached as if searching for something only he could see.

"You!" I growl as I grab him by the throat, bringing him to my eye level. He claws at my hand, gasping for air, sputtering words I cannot make out. I hold him there, tightening my grip around his frail neck as he starts to turn purple. Then his eyes land on Éabha, lying on the ground, battered, and covered in blood.

"I can help," He gurgles as he pushes himself up slightly for some air.

At his statement, I throw him with as much force as I can across the room. The open door breaks his fall. He lands in a heap, but quickly gets to his feet rubbing his red throat. He keeps his eyes on me as he steps closer to Éabha. I can hear his heart rate quicken, fear making him more cautious, as he stands over her.

I am desperate. For anyone or anything to bring her back, to stop her from dying. So, I let him get closer. He stares down at her limp body, a small pool of blood has formed on her right side, her once golden and sun-kissed face now so pale she is starting to look grey. A skin shade I know too well. "Her magic is fading," he whispered.

A primal growl escapes me at his obvious statement. But he doesn't react, merely smiles at me, "Sunlight! She needs sunlight!"

He jumps, rushing around the table towards the shelves. As I kneel to scoop Éabha up and take her outside. I curse myself again for not going straight out of the castle before now.

"No, sunlight!" He shouts as he opens jars on the shelves and sniffs the contents, "It's nighttime now, how do you not know?"

I turn to growl at him some more, to throw him around a bit and make myself feel better. That's when I notice the jars. The jars of glistening fluid have solidified into orbs, floating in the middle. They glow bright white, yellow, gold and orange.

"See, sunlight," he smiles, gesturing to the jars which line the shelves. I move to hold one of the jars nearest me. It's warm and I can feel the pulsing glow of the light within it. The orbs press against the jar, where my hand holds it, as it recognises me. I recognise it. This is actual sunlight in these jars. I can feel their call, their recognition of their creator holding them.

"How did you?" I ask opening the jar, "Did you capture..." I can't seem to get my words together as I look up at this frail old Fairy rushing around opening every jar. "How the fuck did you do that?"

I am in awe at this man, able to defy all known Fae abilities and steal a creation made by a God. He shrugs as if it is nothing, carefully taking one of the jars in his hands and gesturing for me to take it. I hold out my hand as he tips the jar over, the orb of Sun falling into my palm.

The orb relaxes into my hand. Warming it slightly, I imagined it to be hot, like holding fire. It doesn't burn, only leaving a slight tingle which runs up my arm. Once the orb is relaxed, it begins to shake and shoots off sparks, going in every direction.

"It likes you!" the Fairy beams as he spills out more and more balls of sunlight. They all bounce around the room, off the walls and furniture, hitting off me, I can feel their joy and relief from their release.

Slowly this joy turns to determination as some sparks land on Éabha. Eventually, all the sparks and orbs direct their energy towards her, as she lies motionless on the floor. I rush to shield her, to stop them from touching her, causing her pain. But the Fairy pulls me back with the same strength as in the library earlier. He gives me a reassuring smile and shakes his head. "She needs sunlight," is all he says in way of explanation.

Together, we quickly open all the jars, pouring the contents out and letting them bounce and dance around the room. The light becomes so intense it is difficult to see. Suddenly turning impossibly white, I can only make out my hands in front of me and the blurry dark outline of Éabha on the floor almost engulfed by the shooting, dancing beams of sunlight. I open the last jar, letting it smash on the floor.

Standing at Éabha's feet, I squint and strain to see her face, ensuring she is not in pain whilst the sunlight swarms her. Slowly the beams disappear, and I begin to see her more clearly. The beams are slithering all over her body, wiggling their way inside her somehow. Her skin glows a brilliant yellow. The room begins to dull as the last few beams jump around and eventually landing on Éabha.

The last beam of yellow light remains dancing over her skin before slowly squirming its way to her heart.

The room is still. Both myself and the old Fairy beside me holding our breaths, waiting for Éabha to wake. I don't know what we just did, if it will work, but I need it to. Need it more than anything.

"It's taking too long," I mutter to myself. Kneeling beside her, I push the hair out of her face, trying to wipe away mud and blood again. She isn't breathing, I cannot remember the last time she took a breath. She looks grey, her eyelids purple and her lips blue. Placing a hand over her heart, it feels cold. I try to find some movement of her heart beating even a little, but everything remains still.

We sit like this, in the silent and stillness for some time. Or perhaps no time, perhaps we were frozen in time.

Suddenly Éabha's eyes shoot open, she gasps for a breath sitting up at the same time. She reaches out grabbing a hold of my shirt, trying to grab anything to anchor her to this world. She gasps one more time before slowly becoming aware of her surroundings. Searching around the room taking in everything from the Fairy to the empty jars and then turning to face me.

Slowly she lets go of my shirt, leaning away from me, her face still pale but slowly turning pink. I reach out for her, to pull her back to me, to keep her safe by my chest. But her eyes stop me. Beams of light are dancing just behind her eyes as they had on her body. Slowly the white turned to yellow, then green then finally their beautiful sapphire blue. I sigh, wonderful sapphire.

Her hand instinctively falls to her side, where her broken rib had punctured her skin. But there was nothing there, only the trace of blood. I sit silent allowing her time to process her healed injuries, amazed myself at the power of the sunlight.

She takes in the room, looking around her at the jars scattered around us, some intact and some smashed. She stares for a long time at the Fairy, whose name I never got, standing behind me. I can feel his smug smile, almost hear him saying, *I told you.*

I can hear the airflow into Éahba's mouth and out again as her chest rises and falls at a steady rate. The matching *lub dub* of her heart echoes inside her chest. Of course, I am staring at her chest rising and falling, through her bloodied and almost non-existent shirt, as her eyes return to me. And she smiles. I think my heart stops then.

"Dia dhuit," she whispers softly, pulling me into a hug. I try not to laugh as I cradle her head in my hand.

"Hello, to you too," I whisper in her ear. Her hold on me tightens.

I can feel her head turn towards the figure behind me, I reluctantly let her go.

"Míle buíochas," she smiles up at him.

"Fáilte, Bandia," he turns to me, "I must return to the library Commander." Bowing at us, he leaves, closing the door behind him, our almost silent savour.

"What's with all the Gaeilge?" She's never spoken the ancient language before, never told me she had learnt it or understood it. Yet she speaks it so gracefully now.

"Since the mountain I…" she doesn't finish her sentence as she uses my shoulders to stand. I follow her, leaning against the large desk behind me I take her in, she has changed somehow. Not in her makeup, or her physical features.

Éabha cracks her neck from side to side and rolls her shoulders, her spine clicking in the process. Anger floods off her, she throws it into the air and wears it like a shroud around her. She stands tall, taking me in from head to toe. I don't know what she sees, or what she's thinking but I know from the look in the eyes she wants blood. I've seen the look of vengeance, worn it many times myself. It looks good on her.

"Take me to the King," she says with a smile. I return it, taking her hands and leading her out, to Connor.

# Chapter Thirty

## Éabha

Cian held my hand tight like he was worried I would vanish. He walks me through the castle, not quite in silence, but we don't talk. I can sense he has questions; they are ringing loudly around us. Especially when we arrived in the foyer, freezing cold, as the main doors were left open, letting the freezing air blow inside. Particularly when we pass groups of maids, whispering in hushed tones about the changes outside and the witch in the dungeon. And even more when we stop at the top of the grand stairs, where a window looks over the decorated gardens, now dark and covered in decay.

Cian believes the King to be in his quarters, however, he makes a detour to his rooms.

Warmth hits us as he opens the door. His fire has been lit, warming the room. He drops my hand as we enter. I remain near the door, allowing it to close behind me. The room is made up of a grand fireplace, desk and soft chairs. Cian walks through into an adjoining room, which I assume must be his bedroom. I don't follow, wanting to get to the King as soon as I can.

I still plan to kill him. He tortured me, emotionally, when he sent Ceira for Cill O'Laoch. It split my soul in two, broke my heart, draining me of all my magic. Then his guards assaulted me and left me to rot in a wet cell.

For this- this King will die.

Cian returns, holding a bowl with a towel draped over his arm.

"Sit," he instructs, indicating to a chair closest to the fire. I let out a sigh as I sink into the soft cushions of the chair. My body may have healed itself but it still aches. The fire roars beside us, warming my face and arms. Cian dunks the towel into the soapy water and dabs it across my forehead, into my hair, and down my cheeks and neck. Soon the water has turned dark brown from the mixture of dirt and dried blood. He doesn't speak, as he rings out the towel bringing it to my abdomen, where my open wound used to be. Now the only evidence is the amount of blood stuck to my skin. I watch as he peels back the remainder of my shirt, very gently, perhaps expecting me to gasp in pain. But I don't move, I don't say a word, as he washes away the evidence of the abuse.

Once satisfied I am as clean as he can get me, he rests his hands on my thighs. His large hands just cover my thighs. His nails are neatly cut. Veins protrude from the skin on his hands, twisting up his forearms. He flexes slightly as he runs his hands up and down me, causing the veins to move a little. We both watch his hands as he squeezes me slightly. My magic, now cuddled deep inside me, sparks a little with each squeeze.

We watch his hands as they leave my legs and start to unbutton my shirt. Three buttons are all that remain. The only thing that is holding the shirt together. He reaches up to push it off my shoulder, but I stop him, holding his hands together in mine.

"Cian," I warn as I let go of him, wrapping my arms across my chest, shielding everything from him. Although, embarrassingly, the shirt was so torn I am sure he has already seen everything I try to hide. He smirks, a silly lopsided smile, as he holds up a new shirt.

Letting go of everything, dignity included, I pull the clean shirt close to my chest, breathing in the scent of him. His scent washes over me—fresh rain on leaves, soft and inviting. It's more than a smell; it's a feeling, an embrace from the earth itself. Every breath I take draws me closer to him, to that sense of being home, even when the world around me feels distant and cold.

My stomach flutters with the comforting smell, warming my heart as my magic uncoils itself to join in the embrace.

"You want to kill him, don't you?"

I don't respond. When he asks, my heart aches. It's not my magic causing this ache. This ache is for Cian, because deep down inside I think he knows I have to kill the King. If he gets in my way, I think I will have to kill him too.

Cian's hands remain on my thighs. Their warmth spread all over me. The fire crackles beside us, casting him in a warm orange glow. Flecks of gold float through his eyes, they remind me of the sun. Like the sun resides in his eyes.

I am not sure what is going through his mind, or what he wants to hear from me.

After our moment of silence, sharing the warm closeness, Cian reaches up, combing his fingers through my hair. Parts are matted with dried blood. He reaches for the towel again, trying to clean my hair. Bringing my hair to one side, he splits it into three and braids it in place.

Cian's strong, calloused hands, delicately plat my hair together. Carrying an air of tenderness that magnifies his power and strength. As he works, his fingers deftly separate the strands, precise and controlled like in combat.

Each braid is a promise of protection, his touch lingering in the space between them. Four days ago, Cian was a brute, a vampire sent to capture me and bring me to the King for execution. The contrast between his usual role as a warrior and

281

this gesture of care shows his real strength lies in control and in the gentleness beneath the battle-hardened exterior.

My heart swells as I follow his eyes moving from one strand of hair to the next, as I feel his hands along my hair on my shoulder and down my chest. My magic flickers in response to each touch.

This moment becomes a silent conversation between us, where each twist and pull of my hair feels like an unspoken vow. A vow to each other. A vow of protection.

Once finished, he ties the end with some string. He holds out his hand, I take it, and we start the short walk to the King's rooms.

Our footsteps echo along the corridor as we silently walk to the King. Cian has one hand in mine and another on his sword. His reluctance hangs in the air between us, alongside my determination. It pulses through me with unyielding force. My magic gathers itself around me, trying to prevent my anxiety from getting in the way of our goal.

Images and memories float through my mind, each causing my chest to tighten. Guards touching me in the dungeon, Ceira confronting me at the lough, my grandfather's beaten face, Ceira's other friends whispering, the King dragging me outside to see when I had done. Every bit of heartache or hurt has been caused by the King and his drunkenness of power.

The warmth of Cian's hand anchors me. Acting like a tether and keeping me grounded in the here and now. Yet I don't have a plan for what happens next. Each step we take is driven by resolve, yet with every breath, the shadows of the unknown whisper louder. Twisting my determination into something fragile. My magic hums in my ears as it tries harder to fight back the anxiety.

As we approach King Connor's door, it looms large and imposing, the heavy wood darkened by centuries of age, etched with intricate carvings that tell of past conquests and ancient power. The iron hinges gleam dully in the low light as if bearing the weight of countless secrets hidden behind them. My breath catches, and my heart is pounding in her chest. Suddenly it feels like there is a pressure pushing down on my shoulders. I squeeze Cian's hand trying to ground myself again, trying to remember what I have learned, how to breathe.

A tiny little beat pulses from his hand through to mine. His heartbeat. I had never noticed it before, never thought about it. But Cian's heartbeats again sending its little pulse through his hand to mine. Smiling, as if he knows, he brings my hand to his lips, pressing a soft kiss along my knuckles.

Like a spell, the pressure releases from my shoulders and around my heart.

Dropping my hand Cian steps forward. His fingers curl around the cold iron handle. With a sharp tug, the door groans open, revealing the dimly lit chamber of the King. Soft murmuring we could barely hear stops abruptly as Cian enters, pulling me behind him.

The King's private quarters are lavishly adorned, reeking of power and corruption. Beautiful tapestries hang from the stone walls, depicting mythical creatures and ancient battles. A large, roaring fire crackles in the open hearth, casting a flickering golden light across the room, illuminating the deep reds and golds that decorate every corner. The furniture is massive and ornate, polished wood with velvet cushions, creating an almost suffocating sense of luxury. The air is thick with the scent of burning wood and rich incense. Despite the opulence, there is tension in the room, a sense that danger lingered just beneath the surface.

Connor sits casually beside the fire in a high-backed chair, his posture relaxed but his eyes sharp, flickering between me and Cian as he takes us in. A decanter of dark wine sat on a low table beside him, its crystal facets catching the firelight. He is surrounded by men, wearing the same casual guard uniform as Cian. Their faces are sharp with suspicion. At his side, Ceira stands, our eyes clash together, and her lips twist into a smirk.

I trusted Ceira more than anyone. She was the one who knew my truth, my fears, my dreams. She was my anchor, my ally. I thought she was the one person who would never turn on me.

But here she stands, the very embodiment of betrayal. Now, all I see is a shadow of that person, standing there among those who wish me dead. My chest tightens as her eyes, once so familiar and comforting, sparking venom which curdles with the magic inside my chest. A hollow ache opens in me, filled with disbelief and deep, gnawing sorrow. This new wound festers inside me.

"Ah, Cian!" Connor drawls, "And you brought your little *Pet*." He reaches to fill his wine glass, "I thought I put you in the cellar?" He lifts his goblet, taking a slow sip as if our arrival is of no consequence.

I can feel Cian tense beside me. "Connor, this stops now. Éabha is not dangerous."

Connor snorts, finally turning his cold eyes toward me. "Not dangerous?" He stands and waves toward the window. "Brother, look at what she's done. Look outside."

Cian moves across the room, past the grand desk, and pulls aside the thick drapes. His face twists as he gazes out, but he says nothing. My heart sinks. As images of the rotting decay, I left outside fill the space around us. The guards around the room, shift from foot to foot anxiously, knowing my power.

284

Understanding my strength, even from their friends who groped me in the dungeons.

Draining his goblet, Connor turns to the nearest guard, "Take her back downstairs. We'll execute her at sunrise."

Before I can react, the guards move in. Their rough hands reach for me, but Cian is faster. In one swift motion, he grabs the arm of the nearest guard, twisting with such force that the man's hand rips clean off. Blood splatters on the floor as the severed limb is tossed into the fire.

The guard clutches his stump, screaming in agony, and the room falls into stunned silence. I stare, my breath caught in my throat. Even Connor's smug grin falters, his eyes locked on Cian's.

"This has to be part of the plan, brother." Cian's voice is low, trembling with anger, "Éabha is one of us. She is part of me."

I blink, confused by his words. Part of him? I try to understand, but there's no time.

Connor's advisor steps forward. His face is a mask of disgust, eyes narrowed as he spits, "She's a witch, cursed and foul. All magic is a blight upon this land! Kill her now, before she poisons the earth any further! M*allacht an domhain*!"

Cian growls, a deep, animalistic sound that vibrates through the room. "You'd do well to hold your tongue. Do you even know who you are talking to?"

But the advisor doesn't listen. He presses on, frantically trying to convince Connor to act. "She'll destroy us all! Magic must be purged—kill her!"

My magic slithers off of my body and crawls the short distance between me and this man. I can see her working her way through the thick lush carpet, creeping closer and closer. Aiming to attack.

Cian attacks first. In one fluid movement, he grabs the advisor by the throat, lifting him off the ground, just as my magic reaches the man's toes. It reaches up off the floor after him, wanting to join in.

"Éabha can defend herself," Cian says through gritted teeth, his eyes burning with fury. "She's stronger than you'll ever know. But tonight, I'll take the honor of defending her."

The man gasps, his face turning purple as he struggles for breath. Cian holds him there, eyes locked in a cold, dangerous stare. For a moment, it seems he might let go. But just as the advisor's eyes show a flicker of relief, Cian tightens his grip, and with a swift motion, tears the man in half. Blood and entrails flood the floor, pooling around my feet.

I should be horrified, but instead, I feel an overwhelming awe. I watch the man I love defend me, and something inside me deepens and solidifies. I am falling in love with him all over again.

From the corner of the room, I hear her voice. Ceira steps over the remains, her expression unreadable. "Éabha is a danger to every living creature. Our laws are clear. She must die."

Cian growls, his eyes narrowing. "Who the fuck are you?"

Ceira's face remains calm as she lists the crimes I've supposedly committed. "She has disturbed the natural order. She's—"

Cian interrupts, his voice cutting through the room. "And what if Éabha is a God? Do these laws still apply?"

The room shifts. Tension hangs like a blade over all of us. Ceira's mouth opens to respond, but Connor cuts her off. "Enough!" His voice booms through the room. "The law has been weighed, and Éabha will be executed at dawn."

But Cian's had enough. He moves faster than I can comprehend, grabbing Ceira by her hair and lifting her off the ground. She screams, her feet dangling as she struggles.

"Éabha is Mother Nature," Cian growls, his voice low and dangerous. "She's here to restore this land, to save Éire from itself. It's a shame you won't be here to see it."

Slowly, deliberately, he moves with grim prevision as he begins to scalp her. Using his fingernail and in sift, practised motions, he cuts through her hairline, digging into her scalp. Her screams fill the room as Cian tugs firmly until the skin gives way, peeling back with a sickening rip. Blood wells and drips down in dark, thick rivulets as Cian continues, his expression cold and focused as hears the scalp free, leaving behind a slick, exposed patch of raw flesh.

Before Ceira can collapse to the floor, Connor moves, turning to me, his face twisted with hatred. His hand finds Cian's sword, and in one violent motion, he thrusts it toward my heart.

Pain explodes in my chest as the blade presses into me, but something inside me shifts. My magic surges forward, melting the blade in Connor's hands before it can pierce me any further. The heat of the magic burns through me, making me smile.

Cian grabs Connor and hurls him across the room, the two of them vanishing in a blur of speed. I can't see them, but I hear the sounds of their struggle, the clash of bodies and snarls filling the room.

With a scream thud, Cian stands with Connor in his hands. He throws him onto the ground, causing the entire castle to quake. Connor doesn't move as Cian looks down at him steadying his breath.

"Let's go," Cian growls, grabbing my hand.

Running through the castle, we rush out the doors into the grounds. Cian pulls me as I try to keep up with him running across the grass. Finally, we enter the security of the forest. I can feel it's cold, stillness. Like the trees don't know how to react to these new changes.

"When I say jump, just jump, don't ask why." Cian instructs as we run further into the forest. I squeeze his hand tighter in agreement, unable to speak through our breathless run.

"Jump!" he shouts, and I do.

We land in the forest. The same forest. Nothing has changed. I keep running, but Cian stops, letting go of my hand. Skidding to a stop I find him looking around us, like he is admiring the trees. Turning to me he smiles, his eyes sparkling.

# Chapter Thirty-One

## Three days later
## Éabha

I do not feel betrayed. Although I feel surprised, I do not feel betrayed. I do not feel scorn, raged or hurt. I feel the sorrow of grief and the heaviness of loss.

I had a friend. She was wonderful. She was a best friend.

She betrayed me. She didn't care for me, want to protect me, want to show me how to fit in. She confirmed everything, all of the bad thoughts I held for myself; she proved me right. I am the mallacht an domhain, I should have disappeared, hidden away, and removed myself from everyone's life so they would not have to feel the effects of me. She made me believe I was the problem, I needed to change to be accepted. She convinced me to change my beliefs and reinforced those feelings that those who should love me wanted me dead.

And now I fear I have lost myself. I fear I do not know who I am as I changed so much to please her. I adapted so I would fit into her world, and she allowed me to. I needed friendship more than I needed myself. I needed to feed the hole that the loneliness craved. And she was the plug.

I am embarrassed it took me so long to work it out. Someone wanted to be my friend, spend time with me, and seem happy with me. And now my soul is split in two. It released a huge amount of power, it reshaped the world. I can feel it as I sit here. The cool air, the crunch to the ground, the vivid shades of red.

Laying back I land on hard ground and look up at the trees. the world above me has transformed. Golden yellows, burnt oranges, and deep reds create a patchwork in the canopy, as sunlight filters through the thinning leaves. Some leaves flutter down, spiralling softly to the ground, like delicate whispers. The branches appear skeletal, swaying gently in the cool autumn breeze. I miss the green.

A dark shadow creeps into my beautiful picture. He stands staring down at me. Broad shoulders and tall frame. I frown, shielding my eyes from the stark contrast of dark and light. I can make out Cian's face, it looks perfect like someone has sculpted it, and his curls fall forward, reaching out to me.

For three days we have camped out in the forest. Surrounded by my magic. Surrounded by this new world I have created. And Cian has sat by my side.

He made the camp, kept the fire going, and tried to talk to me. Well, tried to talk me into returning to the King. But I refuse.

What he has done, by accident I am sure, is create peace. Peace for me, right here, in the forest, away from everyone. It's more peaceful when he is near. When he is close, I can feel him. I feel the connection that confuses us both; a tug on my heart or a squeeze to my chest. The comfort of him is warming and, well, peaceful.

"Let's go for a walk," he holds out his hand for me to take. I stare up at him, not moving. "Come with me," he urges, looking over his shoulder, "I want to show you something."

I take his hand and he effortlessly pulls me to standing. He holds my hand for a moment, our eyes meeting which makes him smile. A cloak is arranged over my shoulders, and he fastens the buckle. He talks, but I don't listen, my ears travel to something slightly further away. Through the forest, I can hear drums.

Leaving our place of hiding, I follow Cian through the forest. The floor is blanketed with dried leaves of yellow and red. They crunch under our feet as we move around them. The scent of damp earth fills the air, mingling with the fading sweetness of decaying foliage, as the quiet forest seems to hold its breath, watching our every step.

Soon we come out of our hiding place in the trees and a small settlement emerges. The village is alive with energy, the air is thick with the smell from the fires which are scattered around to keep the workers warm. The ground beneath my feet is soft, trampled by the many villagers who are rushing around us. Baskets, overflowing with apples, squash, and bundles of wheat, are carried from field to home by men with broad smiles, their sleeves rolled up after a day's work. Wheelbarrows piled high with pumpkins and barley, creak as they're pushed toward the gathering.

Women and children dance in a circle, their feet stamping against the earth in rhythm with the fiddles and pipes that play. Laughter echoes through the streets, and children dart between stalls, chasing each other with handfuls of harvested nuts and berries.

In the centre of the village, beneath towering oak trees shedding their golden leaves, stands a temple. Its structure is circular, fashioned from weathered stone and draped with ivy. The thatched roof, adorned with vibrant autumn leaves, blends seamlessly with the surrounding foliage.

The warmth of the bonfire crackles, its flames stretching toward the sky, while women lay out freshly baked bread and roasted meats, their scents mingling in the cool breeze.

"They are calling it Autumn," turning, I find him smiling at me.

"Calling what Autumn?" he doesn't answer, simply gestures around him, toward the forest which is dying, the people dancing, the temple, all of it. Dropping my hand he starts to walk towards the temple. "Humans are funny. When something happens that they cannot explain, they create a God or Goddess to own it"

"This place is beautiful, but I don't understand,"

"They are also celebrating the Goddess Banbha. They call her the Earth Mother. They are thanking her for the harvest. Sorry, you didn't get the credit for it." He laughs, it sounds like gold. I don't think I have heard him laugh before.

"A Goddess? For what just happened?" Cian avoids my eye, moving closer to the temple, and greeting people as he goes.

"It didn't just happen for them." He finally declares. Before I can reach him, to ask what he is going on about, baskets of food are thrust in our arms. My basket contains carrots, all the colours of carrots imaginable, still with their fluffy green leaves attached. I look towards Cain as he gestures for me to lead the way into the temple, his is full of huge red apples, almost spilling over.

We walk through the grand archway, intricately carved with swirling vines and symbols, which frame the entrance. Above it, a mosaic of amber and gold depicts the Goddess crowned with a wreath of leaves.

Inside, the temple exudes warmth and tranquillity. I hadn't noticed my racing heart until it began to slow. The floor is a mosaic of earthy tones, leading to a polished oak altar surrounded by a stone ring inscribed with runes. Tapestries on the walls showcase harvest scenes—golden fields, ripe apples, and winding forest paths.

Soft, warm light filtering through stained glass windows casts a golden hue, making the space feel warm. Without a fire, I did not think it possible. Wooden benches line our walk to the altar, each carved with swirls and knots. Symbols of the Old Gods, their surfaces gleaming in the temple's serene light.

"It's the first day of autumn, so they bring harvest foods to the Goddess," Cian explains as he finds a place for his apples by the altar.

"Cian, it's only been three days max since I...." I can't finish my sentence, unable to find the words to explain what I did. Cian takes my basket from my hands and places it beside his own. Above us is a statue of who I believe is Banbha. The detail in the carving is spectacular. A tall woman whose dress is made of leaves, with each cut, curve and vein of the leaf evident down to the bottom of her gown. Her hair curls down over her shoulders, resting by her elbows which are decorated in bangles. Her face, the image of perfection, I think to myself as she smiles down at me.

My magic pulses inside me, reaching out to the statue. But I turn to leave. Following the flow of the crowd back outside.

"Why autumn?" I whisper as we make our way back outside.

"It means fall or harvest. The leaves fall from the trees, the food needs to be harvested and the land is laid to rest." Cain explains, taking my hand and leading me towards the music. But I pull back, coming to a stop.

"Laid to rest until when?"

"Until autumn ends, I guess?" He shrugs, pulling me forward again, but I don't move. They are celebrating what I created. My magic released death and decay, coldness and frost, yet they celebrate it.

293

I stand there, watching the joyous festivities unfold. The earth, though it changes, is not dying but transforming into something new and wondrous. The people gather to give thanks for the harvest, to revel in the warmth of their shared celebration. They find joy in the very thing I had thought to be a curse, the end of the earth. The warmth of realization washes over me like a gentle breeze. In their eyes, I see that what I created is cherished, a moment of beauty in the endless dance of time.

Yet it has only been three days since it felt like my soul split in two and my magic broke free. How can these people celebrate this change and harvest, like an annual ritual?

"Where are we?"

"Éire," Cian says as if I should know, as if it should be obvious.

"We cannot be," I look around. When we left the castle, we did not go far. Yet there is no sign of the castle nearby. And this town was not here before, was it? I notice the people around me. What I thought were costumes on the performers is the style. The women, wearing trousers and blazers. Men wearing bright colours, usually reserved for the King himself.

"Think about it, Eve," Cain lifts both my hands holding them tight in his, "You know what question you want to ask me," I look up at him, his gold eyes shimmering in the dull light. I don't need to think about it because I know. I know we are not here now.

"When are we?"

"At least a hundred years in the future."

In a flash, I see Cian for the God he is. It bursts across my vision like it was happening in front of me, yet not happening at the same time. Cian looms taller, like an ancient God crawling out of a child's nightmare. His chiselled features and body were shrouded in the armour of the primal Gods. The air around him clogs with the unyielding authority of his power. His eyes, once glistening with light, now cold and piercing, glow with an eerie light, bearing the burden of countless ages and the promise of impending doom.

He is not like other vampires. He is the first vampire. He is so much more.

I take a few steps away from him, his hold on our hands is tight but he eventually releases me. Backing further away I bump into someone, without turning to see who, I apologise and run.

Cian calls after me, "Eve," I hear him in the distance, but it feels like my ears are full of water, "Éabha wait please."

I whirl around to face him. My hair following wildly with a slight delay. I expect to see the giant God of Gods before me, in his armour, but all I see is Cian. His loose hair, and gold eyes. Wearing the same dark trousers and shirt he wore when we left the King.

"Chronos," is all I am able to say as I try to catch my breath.

"Just as you are the Witch of the Earth, I am the creator of time," he explains, walking slowly towards me, "We are one and the same."

"The same?! Cian, if what you say is true, you are older than time." He stands before me, the threatening vision of Chronos, the nightmare we all have of him, seems silly as I take in his handsome features and soft eyes. "You are older than the Gods who rest in their planets, you are older than Night and Day."

Cian shrugs, looking at his feet with his hands in his pockets. "I did not ask for it as much as you asked for your role," he murmurs.

"Role?! What role?" He doesn't answer me. My heart beats hard with anger and frustration at this ridiculous man. He can hear it, he hears everything. But he also knows how to help me.

He holds me, one hand on each shoulder and waits for my heart rate to reduce.

"The Father of Time, the God of the sun and the moon, needs to set the Earth into motion and create stability before he can meet Mother Nature, the Goddess of the Earth. Together they will restore the world to glory." I know the prophecy off by heart as well. He has said it thousands of times since we arrived here. Used it to convince me to fight with him.

"Cian ..." I pull away from him, turning towards our little home in the forest.

"You cannot deny it now Eve!" he calls after me as I return to our campsite.

Returning to my spot on the ground, I shake off the browning leaves which have fallen on the rug, and lay down. The sky begins to turn colour, with deep shades of blue, turning turquoise, to yellow to pink to orange. All while the sun sets. The harvest sun, I decide, was the prettiest thing I had ever seen. The lighter shades turn deeper as the sun creeps towards the horizon. The trees around me turn into black shadows. Painting the picture before me with tall, long twisting branches, and leaves falling to the floor occasionally in the breeze.

Soon glistening white gold dots, appear in the sky and the sunset's yellow, pink and orange glow drifts down, leaving a navy-blue night sky. My magic throbs through me as I attempt to warm the freezing air around my new sanctuary. Magic comes more naturally now. I can do more than grow and heal. More than creating fire and water. I can change the earth around me, the temperature of the air, the weather in the sky. All these things impact the people and the animals of the earth. When Cian first brought me here, I felt the call of the birds as they flew overhead. Calling for their kin to fly with them to warmer weather.

I see him returning in my periphery. Gently, he lays beside me. My world has changed so dramatically. Once I dreamed of living alone by the lough, living off the land and thriving in the peace and tranquillity I created. Now, the God of Time, Chronos himself; The father of not just time but of night and day, has stolen my dreams. Forced me into a world where I do not belong. Into a battle I have no business being part of. And now hides us away in time, where I cannot return to my home.

The King believes I have put a spell on his brother but in truth, it feels like he has bewitched me. When I first saw him in the town square, his gold eyes glittering in the sunlight, I felt it. When he saved me from the mountain people, I felt it. When he brought me to sunlight and allowed me to heal, I felt it. A warm fluttering in my stomach. It almost feels like comfort or what home would feel like. It feels familiar, which is the most annoying part of it as I do not know this man, this God who lays on the cold solid ground beside me.

"I can't read your mind, but I can feel you," he whispers, his breath creating puffs of smoke rising above us.

"If you feel what I feel, you do not need to read my mind to understand what I am thinking." Tears well in my eyes, not for the first time since arriving here. I don't care if he sees them now. I can't stop them when they do come, they slip out and stain my face with grief and sadness.

"Can you take me back?" I ask rolling over to look at him.

"Do you wish to fight with me?" He has asked me this before, he knows the answer.

"No."

"Eve," he reaches for my face.

"Please do not," I sit up and look down at him. His dark curls flop down around his face as he moves to sit. This autumn

297

sunshine highlights the various colours of browns and reds hiding in his hair.

"I've been fighting for a long time and I'm tired. Tired of never feeling good enough. Tired of never being anyone's first choice. I wish to find a place, where I will live out the rest of my life, in peace and solitude." My tears fall onto the rug by his hand. He brushes them away, sitting up to face me. He looks as sad as I feel, his eyes glowing in their own tears.

"I don't know who I am anymore. I have lost myself." I stand, his eyes becoming too much, his pittiness for me I do not need to witness. "I used to know myself, for a brief moment in my life, I liked myself. But can't you see? Have I truly put a spell on you, that you cannot see who I really am?" I sigh, turning to face him again. Hoping in my heart he tells me I am wrong and proves it to me somehow, but he doesn't. "I am no one Cian, I do not and should not belong, so please let me go back."

He doesn't say anything.

"I have created," I can't find the words as I look around us, at the fallen leaves and naked trees, "Autumn. And in the process, I have lost everything."

"You haven't lost everything," Cian reaches for my hands but I move away.

"I have lost my family."

"What family? Grandparents who kept you for the money you brought in? Aunts and uncles who denied your existence?"

He is right. I throw myself back onto the rug, exhausted. Looking up at the stars which poke through the dark trees above me. I didn't have a family to begin with. I didn't have a home. I had food and shelter, but I did not feel like I belonged, like I was part of the family. I fitted in yes but didn't belong there.

"I am lost," I whisper realising that true belonging should never ask us to change, to fit in. A sharp cut strikes across my heart, leaving a lingering ache which clogs my throat. I have betrayed myself. Who I am, who my ancestors were and what I have been created to do. I have betrayed myself for not living up to this, for changing myself, for suppressing myself, just so I had a space in the world.

"You have been mourning the loss of a friend you never even had! When I have been right here. Right here waiting to fill in that hole. Waiting for you. For all of you."

"You can ignore these feelings we have for each other. You can call it magic. You can turn your back on me. On all this. But I will wait for you Éabha. We were born to be together. We were made to be great. You were created to be so much more. And together. Together, we can be spectacular. And we can destroy those who took the most from us."

It is maddening, my inability to understand why he loves me. He's never said the words. But I can feel it in the air between us. It's thick, it clings to me. I can't fathom the thought that someone, anyone, could love me this much. So much so that he is willing to start a war and finish it.

*Anamchara.* The ancient word floats into my head and lingers there smiling at me. I don't think I have a choice anymore. I reach up for his hand, he pulls me close to his chest.

In this autumn air, his scent has not changed. His presence fills the space between us, and with it, that intoxicating scent— rain-drenched oakwood, raw and untamed, like the forest after a storm. It clings to him, pulling me closer, until I'm surrounded by it, by him. Every inhale feels like a promise, soft and unspoken, but they are all the same, lingering on the air between us, drawing me into him like gravity. I meet his gaze, and for a heartbeat, time seems to still. Then, slowly, tentatively, his lips brush against mine. The world around us fades as I surrender to the kiss, to the warmth of him, to the scent of rain and oakwood that now belongs to us both.

# Chapter Thirty-Two

## Éabha

Walking through time is like walking through a forest. It doesn't feel like magic, there is no wind no unusual happenings, not even a lurch in my stomach. We walk through the forest until we see the castle.

This is the first time I have seen Mullach Íde castle, properly from the outside. It's beautiful with a warm yellow glow from each little window. We walk hand in hand across the lawn, leading to the main entrance. Shrubs, unaffected by the autumn skirt around the castle. Two large towers, flank the front door, as if they grow out of the shrubs and foliage on the ground. The ivy-clad front softens the austere stone, leading up to large arched windows. Windows that Cian looked out of, at the decay, I created, taking hold of the grounds around us.

Cian pushes the navy wood door open, and a breeze hurries us inside. The stone floor of the foyer clicks as we hurry across. The castle is silent. It's nearing dusk, yet it feels like everyone is asleep.

The last time I was in the castle I couldn't take in the expansiveness of the entrance hall. The stone walls are adorned with rich tapestries depicting scenes from ancient history, their deep colours a striking contrast to the cool, grey stone. High above, a beamed ceiling with ornate wooden carvings, I can't quite make out as they are covered in a thick layer of dust.

The door to the throne room leads us forward down the short hallway. The walls here are lined with portraits of past inhabitants, their stern faces watching silently as you make your way.

The throne room, I had not noticed its grandeur before. Dark wood beams support the tall ceiling which is lit with chandeliers hanging from them. A fireplace arches over one wall. The blaze sits and crackles as we walk past. The flames licking out to greet us.  The heat follows us as we make our way towards Connor.

He sits alone on his throne, with the stone bear and lion at his feet. Connor doesn't look up at our approach.

"Where is everyone?" Cian asks, dropping my hand to reach for some of the empty bottles littering the floor.

"Run scared," the King Connor takes a swig, before turning to me, "because of that Witch," he spits, pointing at me with the neck of the bottle. Standing he marches towards me, taking another drink. "You little Witch, have caused quite the stir around here," he stops when our toes touch, "Undo it," he spits.

"Connor," Cian warns, placing a hand on his brother's shoulder.

"And you ran off to hide again brother?" taking the last drink from his bottle he tosses it in the fire. Missing, it smashes against the stone wall, sending glass in all directions, "Very noble."

"He does this a lot you know," Connor addresses me, looking around at the mess of bottles, "Runs off to hide within time. Hopes no one will notice whilst the mess he creates is resolved without him." He moves away kicking the empties as he goes, "Not this time brother. You befriended the Witch, you could have killed her a week ago, years ago even. But you waited until it was too late to turn back." Connor laughs. It's humourless, echoing around us, like a threat.

Finding another bottle half filled with whisky he takes a long swig.

Pointing his bottle at Cian he says; "Cillian was right to leave when he did. You are not a God. You are not a King. You just about fit the role of brother."

"Connor," Cian starts but the king throws his bottle at his brother. Cian shields his face with his arm as the glass shatters around him.

"Do not address me so casually! I am your King!" He roars.

"King of what Connor!?" Cian roars back. "You've been King for almost thirty years and where has it got you? No kingdom, fickle friends, and alone." Cian gets closer to him, "But you have me." Grabbing his brother by the shoulders he gives him a reassuring squeeze, smiling as he says, "And now we have Éabha."

They both turn to look at me now. *I trust Cian, I trust Cian, I trust Cian,* I repeat in my head. Yet my trust in him quivers a little as they step closer to me.

They both turn to look at me and a trickle of fear runs through my blood. Cian looks just as menacing as Connor. I naturally take a step back

"We have to find Morrigan and kill her."

"Kill them," Connor corrects

"And then we can return to our lives."

"To our families."

Connor saunters towards me, with a drunk swagger. I cringe away as he closes in, bringing his face to mine. The overpowering stench of alcohol clings to him, mingling with his slurred, unsteady words as he leans in too close, his breath hot and acrid against my skin.

"Well little Witch?" he strokes my hair, the same way Cian does but it feels off, and a heavy sickening feeling falls into my stomach. Connor leans closer again, bringing his face to my hair and sniffing.

I can hear Cian move behind him, to pull his brother back, I see his hand reach over his brother's shoulder pulling him off me. But I am quicker. Dagger in hand, I scrape it up his chest and right into his neck. I hold it there, threatening to push further if needed. Connor's eyes darken, he growls from his chest as he steps closer, but I move with him, taking a step back. Keeping us at arm's distance.

"You have spent twenty-eight years being King? Well, I have spent twenty-eight years keeping myself safe whilst being used by others. You will not be one of those people, *My King*." I spit at him, plunging the knife in further, just a little bit. But enough to cut through his crucial vein. Blood runs out around the dagger's edge as Connor groans in pain. We both stand there in a silent standoff, waiting for the other to retreat.

Cian places a gentle hand on my wrist. He doesn't pull me away, he puts no pressure on the touch. It's a reassuring gesture, it says if you wish to act, I will be with you. But I pull the dagger out, slowly with a slight twist.

Connor remains silent as I drop the dagger to my side. His eyes bore into mine, as the hole in his neck slowly seals over. Cian's eyes remain on Connor, sending a warning to his brother. The tension loosens as Connor's eyes follow my hand down to my dagger.

"That's a pretty dagger," He reaches for it as I step away pulling it to my chest. "Where did you get that from?"

"It was my mother's," I whisper, a memory of a dream floats into my mind; *Standing the young man holds up the dagger, presenting it to the wailing woman. "He would want you to have this. He would want his baby to know he loved you."*

"We've seen that before Cian." Connor reaches for it, but I pull away.

"It's Lugh's dagger," Cian explains to his brother. I lift the dagger letting the light from the fire shine off the jewels.

"It's my mothers," I whisper again, as the dagger tingles in my grasp, a recognition of its owner.

Cian moves his hand up my arm and across my shoulders, pulling me into his side. "Lugh was a God," He explained, "before I was a God. His father is my namesake," he smiles at Connor then, both sharing a moment in remembering their shared past life together.

"Lugh was once thought to be a God of Justice. But we know him for his craftsmanship, in sword making," he turns me to face him, his eyes are gentle as they follow the dagger I roll in between my fingers. Mesmerised by the colours shining in the glow of the fire and candlelight. "When he died, he left behind his spear and his sword," Cain reaches for my hands, holding them as I display the dagger, "but, he once made a dagger encrusted with jewels and dedicated to a nameless woman he loved."

*A nameless woman he loved*. I smile up at Cian, wondering why he had never shared this story with me before. Never helped me understand where my mother got the artefact from.

"How did you come by this dagger?" Connor asks.

"It's my mothers," I explain, again. The brothers look at each other.

"Do you trust me now brother?" Cian asks after the silent communication

"Daughter of Lugh," Connor doesn't finish as shouting outside draws our attention. We hear footsteps in the hall before the door to the great hall opens. Guards come rushing in, bearing swords and shields.

I grab my dagger and instinctually take a step beside Cian. He in turn moves to shield me from the possible attack.

"Commander," the guard leading the parade greets Cian, "Your Highness, apologies I did not see you there," they bow for their King. All the guards, possibly twelve in total, stand straight with the swords at their sides. "The castle has been surrounded, my Lord," Their leader continues, "By Fae."

Cian and Connor, leave with the guards following closely behind. Taking the stairs two at a time the brothers reach the landing, leaving me to push my way through the mass of large men trying to get to the window looking over the gardens below.

Below us stands an army of Fae. Unlike the King's army, with his guards standing like tall replicas of each other, the Fae present themselves as individuals.

More species of Fae begin to emerge. Some I do not recognise, others I have only seen drawings of in books.

The Sidhe, like the Fae of the Danu Tribe, are tall and slender, their eyes glowing like stars against their pale smooth skin. They stand in a crowd near the front of the castle. Men and women alike, their chests dressed in gold, moulded to their forms, with ribbons tied around their arms, waists and thighs. They've come with weapons. Swords, shields and spears. All adorned with jewels that sparkled like dew in the morning sun.

Scattered around I can pick out Pookas, jumping from shadowy smoke to a horse-like creature, grinning up at us from below. Their shadows move with grace around their Fae kin whilst their solid forms, march and prance with precision.

I could see light within the tree line, like a fire had been lit. I take a step back, holding my breath in shock as a Fir Bolg steps out into the garden. I could feel the heavy steps quake the ground beneath us, its stone skin cracked and emitting embers from within. Cian reaches for my hand, holding me in place,

306

pulling me closer to stand beside him. His face is stoic, like he has practised and perfected this indifferent stance, giving nothing away, being on no one's side. Yet I can feel his concern. We both know why the Fae have come, why they have banded together and marched on the Vampire King.

Something else catches my eye, across the gardens by the water stands a band of elegant women and gentlemen, naked, looking up at us with blank stares. Their skin glistening in the dark like the moonlight bouncing off the water. They seemed both regal and wild. Around their necks and wrists, they wore intricate chains of silver and gold, set with gemstones that glowed softly with an unearthly light.

It wasn't until I spied the seals in the water beyond, that I realised who they were, Selkies. Another long-forgotten creature thought to have disappeared long ago.

Other creatures I could not name were scattered around, headless beings walking back and forth. Small grey-skinned beasts with sharp teeth and sharper eyes, crawled around the ground. Small firefly-like pixies fluttered around. Wearing garments of fine string, like they have been woven by spiders.

The air grew cooler, and the scent of wildflowers and earth filled the air, mingling with an undertone of something ancient and powerful. My magic stirred trying to get out, reaching to greet those who have joined us.

A tall slender man, one of the Sidhe, steps forward. His presence brings with him silence, not just to the outside but within the castle as well. He holds a commanding spirit, and even the bravest of the king's guards felt a shiver of fear as they gazed upon the Fae.

"We demand the head of the Witch who caused this rot," His voice booms, yet he does not appear to shout. The guards behind us murmur, whispering that the King should send me outside for my long-awaited execution. Connor turns to them, I imagine his face dripping with rage and anger as it silences them. Cian squeezes my hand, as he pulls me closer to him, trapping me under his arm, like this was enough to prevent them from taking me.

"We are not known for our patience," The Sidhe draws a spear from his back, "You will send her out so we can return Éire to her natural state." Instinctively I pull away from Cian, my first thought is to go out and do as they request. My magic sings inside my ears, a reminder that Autumn is not rot, it is not decay, it is not a slow death, like I once thought. Like everything here believes. Autumn is rest, it is abundance and it is warm. It is a time for the earth to rejuvenate. To restore her energy only for her to give it back to all creatures, humans and Fae alike, when she awakens. I picture the celebration and the offerings to the Banbha. In time mortals, Fae and all living creatures will celebrate Banbha for giving them Autumn.

Connor pushes away from the window and makes his way downstairs, "I will resolve this diplomatically." He shouts up to us as we watch him disappear.

Outside the Fae gesture together and in silent communication, all draw their weapons. Spears are directed towards the window, all aiming for me. As I stand there like a beacon welcoming them all. They pull back and release them with great force. I watch them spin through the air growing bigger the closer they get.

Cian is faster, pushing me out of the way just as they crash through the window.

I can hear Connor shout as he arrives at the bottom of the stairs and the Fae surge forward, breaking their way through the walls, windows and doors, storming the castle.

Cian pulls a sword from a guard's holster and trusts it into my hand. But I push it back to him, lifting my dagger in one hand and forming a ball of fire in the other. He smiles cupping my cheeks and pulling me in for a kiss. It is brief but leaves a burning on my lips and in my heart. We stand together, resting our foreheads against each other, whilst the guards move down the stairs and into battle. It feels like time slows around us, just enough for us to have this brief moment together.

Over the banister, a war unfolds. Spears, shields, clubs, arrows, fists and swords clang together as the king's men and Fae dart around, smacking, puncturing and slicing at each other. Blasts of colourful power bounce off the walls, waves of water run through the windows, and mist creeps into the forest. All with one target, mortal, vampire or me. Above it all, the air shimmers with the fluttering wings of miniature, glowing sprites, their high-pitched cries adding to the cacophony.

Cian runs past me down the stairs to join his brothers, the guards he trains and commands, and his kin whom he would follow into any battle. His blade swinging through the air, with a blur of deadly precision as he cut down an advancing Fir Bolg. The stone body falls to the floor, cracking the ground beneath it and crushing a floating soul on its descent. Cian's movements are almost too fast to follow, as I stand at the top of the stairs, unnoticed, following him, waiting for the right moment to join him in the fight. The weight of his countless ages bore down with every strike he takes. Turning, our eyes meet, his glow and sparkle with gold, as I make my descent. Making my way to his side. The battle parts to let me through, the king's guards taking down any creature who dare to near me.

Once I reach Cian, his eyes darken. Turning he resumes the fight with me by his side. I try to match his style or his rhythm of attack, stabbing out with my dagger and blocking blows with my arms. But I can't keep up.

My magic flares around me, and effortlessly I throw bolts of green energy knocking back the Sidhe, who dared to approach. The energy turns to thick vines, which spread around his body, constricting his chest. He gasps for breath as it squeezes tighter, bringing him to the floor. Around us a deathly melody of bells and screeches, as more and more Fae became victims to my vines. I let my magic reach out around me. I give it free will to protect me and Cian.

Another Fae steps forward, as if to prove himself. I send more balls of light towards him. They bounce off his stone-clad skin and fall to the ground before fizzing out. Again, I send the balls of energy, concentrating on their impact, wishing them to melt through his stone casement and rip him apart. But again, they fall to the ground.

He charges towards me, pushing me out the door. I faulter, taking a few steps back and slipping down the steps onto the gravel outside. He roars with success as he pounces, sharp teeth exposed, and eyes hungry for blood.

Time slows again. Looking around I see Cian in the distance, taking advantage of the extra time he has given himself to slice through the Fae he has locked in battle. The stone Fae is in midair as I turn back. I scream, forcing all the air from my lungs as my magic pours out of me, colliding with the beast. The burst of fire and air hits him in the chest and he explodes. Flesh and blood and bone scatter around me. Staining the tan gravel and splattering on my face.

Time resumes, along with the sound of clashing swords. The cold night and autumn air bites at my exposed skin. Around me, the courtyard and gardens are a battleground, strewn with fallen guards and Fae alike. The clang of metal on metal, the cries of the wounded and the roars of the defence echo around us all.

The moonlight casts everyone in shadows and highlights the fallen. I follow the path of light as I catch my breath. Along the river at the edge of the battlefield stands three dark silhouettes. They appear dark against the navy moonlit sky. Their eyes gleam with malevolence, their hair flowing in the wind along with their skirts, still decorated with the stars from the sky.

A mocking smile appears on their lips, as they catch me watching, sending a fresh wave of rage through me. I can feel the earth move. It starts with a rumble, and then begins to shift beneath me. My rage pours out of my feet and into the earth, which she answers with a quake. It rises up where the Phantom Queen's stand, forming an edge of a cliff. Morrigan turns back towards me, laughing. The sound mingles with the howling wind.

Power tickles my fingertips, and sparks appear. This Queen destroyed Cian's life, his brothers and his families. And me, she wrote a prophecy which blanketed me and my family with dark sorrow. My magic mixed with the rage and the vengeance inside me. Together we formed another ball of energy, its target, the queen. With my magic ready in my hands I run towards them, not wanting to miss the look on their faces as I end them.

# Chapter Thirty-Three

## Cian

The earth begins to move around us. Slowly we all stop, trying to steady our footing. It comes in a ripple, like a wave moving towards the water's edge. I look around to find the source of the disturbance, knowing who I would find.

Éabha, covered in blood which sparkles in the moonlight, stands by the castle entrance. Her eyes are trained on the river. The earth begins to crack as the waves become too much for the solid ground to handle. I scream for her to stop, but my voice is lost as the ground splits, sending the ground by the edge of the water up into the sky.

There in the moonlight, along the newly formed cliff face stands The Phantom Queen. Red hair from Fate, whips in the wind, Life reaches up to tame her golden blond hair, whilst Death manoeuvres hers out of the weather so it sits neatly.

They draw their swords, as from the air, and wait for Éabha to race to them. Fire erupts from the soil within the cracks. Bursting up through the air, catching men, Fae and vampires in its wake. I turn to move towards Éabha, to hold her and get her to stop. But her rage pushes me back.

"Éabha, it's ok. Please stop!" I scream. Connor hears my cries and runs towards her. But has to fall back as fire appears in front of him from the cracks.

I had not noticed we had stopped fighting until the clang of swords clashing together fills the air once more.

Éabha takes up a sword fallen on the ground, holding it in one hand and a fireball in the other, she fights her way towards

Morrigan. Fires erupt and spew around the Queen, which casts a yellow glow to their otherwise pale complexion. I follow Éabha on her advance towards them. I need to stop her before her rage gets her injured.

To my left, Connor takes down a Fae, slicing his sword and cutting his head clean off. His roar of celebration distracts me from Éabha.

Something collides with my side and I fall. Rolling back onto my feet, I find myself advanced on by three tall Sidhe. Their hair has fallen loose from their braids, blood is smeared across their chest and arms as they smile at me.

I spy Connor taking off towards Éabha and Morrigan. Readying himself to protect Éabha. He screams as he nears them, drawing the Queen's attention away from Éabha. Ignoring the Sidhe, I run, joining Connor in less than a second. The demon of Morrigan will not make it through the night, I promise myself. For the curses she has placed on me, my brothers and now my heart.

Thunder blows through the air as our swords clash together. The fighting behind us continues, as wild grunts and screams follow us with every blow we attempt to make.

Éabha screams in frustration as her magic bounces off Fate, like they have a shield around them. The scream distracts me causing Death, with her brunette hair dancing around her, to overpower me, pushing me back to the ground. I push her back with my sword. Coming back to my feet I can feel her strength pulsing through her sword. I try to get a better advantage, bringing my sword down across her as I turn to face her. But she follows my movements as if we have rehearsed this dance a million times.

Her sword comes down on my wrist, the impact causing me to let go of my own. Instinctively I reach to catch it, but she is faster. I stand, the point of her sword resting just below my chin.

I hear Éabha scream again, but do not turn to look. In my periphery, I see a wave of her power washing over us. Connor and Life fall staggering back, but Death and me remain in place. I hear Fate scream as she falls, the blow from Éabha sending her further away from her sisters.

I can feel myself flickering. My rage bubbles to uncontrollable levels like a primal force crawling at my insides. My heart races as I stand eye to eye with Death. Her face is a picture of joy as the battle around us continues.

I need to stead my heart. I need to remain calm. I need to slow my thoughts. Pulling on the primal God within me, time slows. I make it slow. Everything around me blurs, Connor runs towards Lifes appears like jittery steps, like I can only see one image at a time and not a full sequence. Éabha whirls towards me so fast all her colours blend together.

I close my eyes and steady my breathing. Breathe in, hold, and breathe out.

The sound of the battle around me becomes more intense, now I have closed my eyes. But it begins to become foggy, more distant. As I breathe in, hold and breathe out. I begin to feel the pull. A little tug in the direction I wish to move to, like a child pulling on my shirt sleeve. Only I am not simply being pulled to a different location. I am being pulled through time.

Although the sound of battle sounds far away, miles away. A sound near me starts to get clearer. And I feel a pull in a different direction. Not the same type or pull. Not a pull to get me to move. But a pull to get me to notice- Éabha. The pull I get around my heart when I am near her or need to be near her. I feel that tugging at my chest now. Her scream is getting louder and louder.

I snap my eyes open just in time to see Fate grab her from behind. And time speed up.

Fate has Éabha with one arm around her middle and another around her neck. Éabha screams "NO!"

The scream distracts Death long enough for me to push past to get to Éabha. But she is quicker. As her sister adjusts her hold on Éabha, Death pulls out a dagger and holds it to her throat. Éabha's eyes scream out to me for help.  The blade pushes deep into her neck and a trickle of blood falls. I stop, motioning for Connor to do the same.

"Please, you don't need to do this," He begs them, "You need her alive." Tears fall from Éabha's eyes as my heart breaks.

I step closer raising my hands in surrender, "Take me, Éabha's journey has just begun you don't need me."

Death ignores me as Fate pulls Éabha closer to her chest. Life appears behind her sisters and laughs at the scene playing out in front of her. "Two of the Conlon Brothers, one a God and another a King, begging for the life of a Witch. All we are missing is the smart one."

"We have waited long enough sisters." Using her free hand Death pulls Éabha's head back using her hair as a leaver. "We must see if we have success with this one." Death turns to look at her sister Fate, all three sharing a look of joy and laughter as she takes the dagger to Éabha's ear and quickly slices right across to the next.

I scream.

I fall forward, or backwards. Not physically, but I try to fall through time. Try to get there before it happens. Try to reach Éabha before the knife cuts through her, before the knife even appears. But I can't.

I hear Éabha take in a breath. But it doesn't make it to her lungs, as the air gurgles out of the wound on her neck. Her eyes are locked on mine, pleading for help, tears staining her cheeks as the colour drains from them.

Fate drops her. Letting Éabha fall to the ground. She lands on her knees, briefly trying to stop herself from falling. But already her wound has drained her of life, she falls to the side onto the wet grass. Blood staining the green.

And I understand. Understand what Éabha meant when she said her soul split in two when she realised her friend betrayed her. When she realised, she was alone. The one she loved. The only one she loved was taken from her.

I hear the last beat of her heart, the last flutter of her lashes and the last tear that spills over her lids and down her cheek.

Morrigan join together and laugh at Éabha, cheering their victory. Life, Fate and Death hold hands and rejoice in the death of the Witch of the Earth. "It is done, sisters."

Connor is the first to move. Diving for the dark queen, Death, who cut Éabha's throat. But in a puff, she's gone. The others are not as fast. He roars and grabs them both by their hair pulling them to the ground. They screech in pain but continue to laugh. "Silly boy King Connor," and they disappear into nothing but mist. Leaving Connor looking at his empty hands. He screams in frustration and drops to his knees.

I still haven't moved. Eyes focused on Éabha. Who's staring at me unblinking in her dead state.

Connor roars again. I don't know why, or what it means, or if his roar was a command. But the fighting behind us slowly stops. Vampire and Fae drop their weapons. I sense movement towards us, to gaze upon the Witch of the Earth they were all fighting for or against. To see her defeated body lay helpless on the ground.

A large hand grabs my shoulder and turns me away from Éabha. Connor says something, but I cannot hear the words. I continue to search for her heartbeat. Continue to reach further and further for that little tug I get around my heart when she's near. That feeling in my stomach when she's using her magic. The sound of her breathing, the way she sighs when she sits down. There is nothing there.

Connor's hold on me loosens a bit. He is still talking but I can't hear him, I feel like my ears are full of water. But I do not care what he has to say.

I turn back to her. She hasn't blinked, her eyes remain open, and she hasn't moved. She hasn't moved her wavy hair off her face. Or dusted the dirt off her clothes. She is not muttering to herself. Or smiling up at me.

She's not doing any of those things because she's gone.

"I never told her I love her," I whisper, "My anamchara." Connor says something as he tries to turn me away from her. More people have gathered around us. Some have even dared to get close to Éabha's body. I wave them away. Stepping closer, I kneel in front of her. Placing a hand over her face I close her eyes. Her hair is still soft like silk, I feel it as I push it off her face and pull it out of the pool of blood. Gathering her up into my arms her head falls back revealing the slice through her throat.

Someone gasps behind me. I cuddle her closer. Just like I had planned to do under the stars when I told her I loved her.

Bringing my lips to her forehead I smell her earth and floral scent for the last time.

I don't know how long we stayed like this. The air begins to chill my arms, as the fires around us shrink back into the earth. I stand with a sigh, cradling her body in my arms and move towards the last remaining fire.

Walking into the flames with her lifeless body I feel tears run down my face. They make no difference to the flames that lick the sides of my legs, biting at my hands, burning my clothes away as I place Éabha on the ground. Stepping back the flames engulf her.

I weep silently and proudly. It chills those around me, as my scream continues to echo in their ears.

The remaining Fae retreat into the forest or the waters below the cliff. Vampires return to the castle. Those who understand the impact of such a death remain behind to witness the loss of the Witch of the Earth. The death of Mother Nature. Whilst I, Father Time, step back from the flames, leaving my heart behind. We watch silently and wait for the flames to burn themselves out.

It feels like my heart is bleeding. I had found happiness within her. Comfort and love and home within her. The fire, relentless and unforgiving, looks like it was blanketing her, protecting her from the world, warming her before her descent to the afterlife, leaving only embers of a love that once burned brightly.

The embers flicker and pulse glowing hot as the sun begins to rise. Turning the sky pink. A pink sky in the morning of the death of a soulmate. I will make it so, every time one passes. I will make that for Éabha. A pink morning sky, my tribute to my *Anamchara*, a marker of our undying bond and the profound void I have in my soul.

The flames begin to smoulder and die away. Nothing of Éabha remains. The fire taking all of her, leaving nothing left. I move to poke the embers, not quite ready for the fire to die. Not ready for the loss of life within my heart. Not ready to move on, as moving on means being without her.

I could not offer her a life of sunshine, I could not promise her the comfort she seeks, I could not promise her an easy life with no danger where we could grow old together. But I could promise her my heart. "I never told you, I love you," I whisper to the embers. A pulse in recognition of my devotion, tugs against my heart.

Moving ash around a line of silver reveals itself. Crouching down I lift Éabha's dagger. Holding the emerald handle I feel a pulse of power. The last ember of my love's magic channelling to find me. And she is truly gone.

Holding the dagger I stand. The gems sparkle in the pink morning light, untouched by the flames. If it is possible, they appear to gleam brighter now, than when I first saw Éabha pull it nearly a week ago. The handle made of solid emerald stone is cool and heavy in my hand. The cross guard displays the vivid array of gems forming a resplendent rainbow. Each gemstone, Lugh once said, represented a facet of his love, from fiery passion to serene tranquillity.

I smile at the sheer injustice of our evening. As I hold the dagger made by Lugh, the God of Justice. A dagger given to a woman he loved, and passed onto his daughter, forever unknown to him.

A faint trace of magic, almost like the comfort I have grown to hold when Éabha is near, runs over my shoulder and down my arm. Following it with my eyes, ink seeps out of my skin like sweat and an intricate tattoo begins to form.

Holding my arm out I twist from side to side as a vibrant tapestry of ivy leaves and vines of flowers intertwine growing up towards my shoulder. As the black ink begins to dark, within the tapestry of vines the leaves take the shape of delicate letters forming an 'E', appearing as if written in an ancient language. It stays almost hidden amongst the pattern of vines and flowers.

Their elegant curves resemble the sinuous patterns of sea creatures.

A silver dagger emerges on my upper arm, its blade adorned with intricate knots of symbols identical to Éabha's dagger I hold in my other hand. I try to interpret the symbols. Symbols used to communicate love, devotion and connection, their ages radiated power intertwining of two worlds, mortal and divine.

A final burn radiates across my chest. Looking down an hourglass gracefully rests near my shoulder. Its delicate curves and fine grains of sand. Marking me as the God of Time, a title I have avoided since creation. This branding of passing time, together with my reminder of my soul mate, Éabha, symbolises the inevitability of change, the newly formed nature of life and death within the Earth.

"What now brother?" Connor asks as I place the dagger through my belt. Looking up I see my brother in a new light. Like a weight has been lifted off him. He is no longer King, now the people of Éire must find a new ruler. The Conlon brothers must move on.

"Morrigan dies." I respond.

# An Deireadh

The end, for now…

Printed in Great Britain
by Amazon